David Burnell was born and bred in York. He studied mathematics at Cambridge University, taught the subject in West Africa where he came across Operational Research. His professional career was spent applying the subject to management problems in the Health Service, coal mining and latterly the water industry. On "retiring" he completed a PhD at Lancaster University on the deeper meaning of data from London's water meters.

He and his wife live in Berkshire and also in North Cornwall. They have four grown-up children.

David is now starting to plan the eighth "Cornish Conundrum".

Earlier Cornish Conundrums

Doom Watch: *"Cornwall and its richly storied coast has a new writer to celebrate in David Burnell. His crafty plotting and engaging characters are sure to please crime fiction fans."* Peter Lovesey

Slate Expectations: *". . . combines an interesting view of an often over-looked side of Cornish history with an engaging pair of sleuths who follow the trail from past misdeeds to present murder."* Carola Dunn

Looe's Connections: *"A super holiday read set in a super holiday location!"* Judith Cutler

Tunnel Vision: *"Enjoyable reading for all who love Cornwall and its dramatic history."* Ann Granger

Twisted limelight: *"The plot twists will keep you guessing up to the last page. This is a thrilling Cornish mystery."* Kim Fleet

Forever Mine: *"An intriguing mystery set against the backdrop of a wedding in sleepy Cornwall, where all is not as it appears."* Sarah Flint

Peter Lovesey *is winner of the Crime Writers Cartier Diamond Dagger.*
Carola Dunn *writes Daisy Dalrymple and Cornish Mysteries.*
Rebecca Tope *writes Cotswold and West Country Mysteries.*
Judith Cutler *writes, among others, the DS Fran Harman crime series.*
Ann Granger *writes, among others, the Campbell and Carter Mysteries.*
Kim Fleet *writes the Eden Grey Mysteries.*
Sarah Flint *authors the DC Charlotte Stafford series.*
Richard Drysdale *writes political thrillers around Scottish Independence*
Malcolm Summers *writes broadly-true stories with a historical basis*

CROWN DUAL

David Burnell

Skein Books

A Cornish Conundrum

CROWN DUAL

Published by Skein Books, 88, Woodcote Rd, Caversham, Reading, UK

First edition: May 2019.

This book, although set in real locations, is entirely a work of fiction. Goonhilly Earth Station, the Trengilly Wartha Inn and Trelowarren Estate do exist and space flights from Newquay Airport are being considered. There is a Pepys Library in Magdalene College, Cambridge. But none of my characters are based on any real person, living or dead and any resemblance is purely coincidental.

ISBN: **978-1091993457**

The front cover shows Mullion Cove harbour on the Lizard Peninsula, with Mullion Island behind. A faint picture of Porthoustock cottages provides the backdrop. Other photographs appear inside. I am grateful to Dr Chris Scruby for taking and fine-tuning the main photographs; and to my wife, Marion, for the photo of me outside Goonhilly Earth Station shown on the back cover.

THE LIZARD

EARLY JANUARY 2019

Kynance Cove on a summer's day

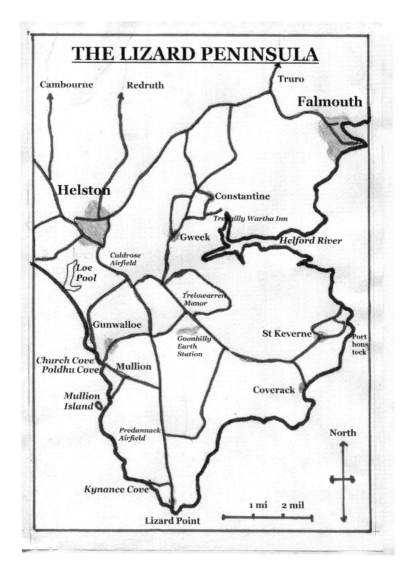

PROLOGUE

A buzz of excitement had gone round the port when the news leaked out. At first no-one believed it but gradually it was accepted. The King was about to give up this part of his kingdom.

Even so, facts were few and far between. No-one knew why, or precisely when; or even whether the step was forever. But the harbourmaster confirmed that more than one vessel had been booked for the departure. Everyone knew there were plenty of items linked to the kingdom that could be taken away. One or two were valuable but plenty more were merely whims of careless indulgence or the sprawls of excess wealth.

Of course, the King himself wasn't here at this moment. It was said, with an arch smile hinting at impropriety, that he had plenty to do back in England. The King had paid one or two visits over the years but everyone could see that North Africa was never really his domain. A thick coat and an elaborate wig might be fashionable in Whitehall but either was far too hot for summer-time in Tangiers. And this King was old, far too intransigent to change his ways.

But as the boats started to be loaded, the mood in the port changed. The British troops sensed that the locals, once enjoying their patronage, were now eager to witness their departure. And keen to make sure that not too much of the King's wealth leached away with them.

3

Initially they had been willing to offer their carts to help carry the King's possessions from the Palace to the port. It earned but a pittance; but for many a pittance was better than nothing. Then, suddenly, like a tsunami of insight, there came a collective realisation: there was no real need to help the evacuation at all.

Regal bundles started to disappear into the narrow side passages that led off the main road on the way down to the harbour. Once off the master thoroughfare the items quickly vanished altogether, into any one of a hundred dark doorways.

Of course, the British soldiers saw what was happening. They rebuked the porters and complained at their diversions but in truth the garrison was hugely outnumbered and they couldn't watch everywhere. If it came to a straight fight between Moroccans and British, the British, despite their muskets, would be heavily defeated. The loss would be humiliating and ricochet around the world. As one of the senior soldiers observed sadly to his colleague, 'Once the façade of power is gone, it cannot easily be restored.'

Among the locals were just a few that had been brought into British ways, had regular access to the Palace and felt some vestigial loyalty to the colonial power. One of these was Hassan; he spoke a form of English and had been the King's personal servant on his last two visits. In truth, his way had been helped by the willingness of his wife to entertain the King in ways that, mercifully, he couldn't fully imagine.

Overall Hassan had been treated well, was saddened by the news and wanted to send a token of friendship to the English court.

He recalled, as he pondered, the King's love of dates. He had been told that the fruit was not available in England. But they were in season now, here in the bazaar. A small chest full of the delicacy would not cost him much and would be highly welcomed. And who knew where that might lead in the future?

Yes, it was definitely a plan to be pursued. But he would need to keep the dates protected for the whole voyage. Hassan had never been outside Morocco, had only the faintest idea how long a ship would take to reach England and what storms it might hit on the way. But he had friends who were sailors. They told him that, once he had collected his dates, covering the containing box in a layer of pitch was the best way to help ensure its contents stayed safe from the contaminating salt water.

Another problem, Hassan reflected, was that the dates were so moist that they might all stick together. But that, too, was soluble. From his work in the Palace, Hassan knew that many papers were left in desk drawers. The inner rooms of the Palace had been occupied by a myriad of senior visitors over the years. Drafts of documents they had worked on were often left behind. Carefully he unlocked the desk, then interleaved the layers of dates with sheets of paper. He had no idea what the papers proclaimed. But he was sure they'd be adequate for his purpose.

Once the chest was full and the lid closed, the faithful servant took it to the bazaar and arranged for it to be coated in hot pitch. After this had been done and the chest allowed to cool, Hassan himself carried it down to the harbour. His precious treasure hung on his arm. It was getting late in the day now; he sensed the mood among his compatriots had changed further and now was turning ugly.

Once at the port he made sure his treasure was safely housed in the master cabin of one of the ships that would shortly be heading for England. There were plenty of chests there already, though the rest had not been water-proofed. Maybe he had been over cautious? He tried to see what else was being sent back, but was thwarted: all the others were locked.

While on board Hassan took the chance to explore the vessel. He had seen it from afar but never before been on board. The Schiedam was a three-masted sailing ship, originally Dutch and now used for trading round the world. It was clearly going to sail soon: he found half a dozen of the King's horses stabled in a hold near the bow. Cannon were mounted on the front deck but Hassan thought they would be little protection against a predatory warship. The ship's sides were merely a single layer of planks. If it was spotted a turn of speed was their only hope of escape.

It was dark now and time to return home. But as he looked down the gangplank Hassan could see that the mood in Tangiers was now one of open revolt. Across the town fires had been started in many places. Raucous Arab shouts filled the air and these were not celebrations of joy. Occasionally, around the barracks, he could hear the sound of musket fire. But they were not being fired in the systematic manner needed to guarantee control, they were tokens of fear and panic.

Then he saw men in British Naval uniform heading for the Schiedam, some jogging along the jetty. Hassan had never intended to go to England; but he didn't know how he would be treated by his compatriots in Tangiers, especially once the British had left. They might be hostile to a collaborator like himself. Violence could not be ruled out and a painful death was a strong possibility. Perhaps England would be the safer place to be?

Quickly he turned back and found his way once more to the

master cabin. *Then slipped inside and locked the door behind him.*

It was the next morning before Hassan emerged. The Schiedam was out of sight of land, rolling in the stormy seas off the coast of Spain.

He had expected trouble as a stowaway but the crew had bigger problems. Only two thirds were on board before the decision had been made to slip anchor. These included several Moroccan crewmen so Hassan was able to put himself among their number. After a short struggle he mastered the basics of rigging the sails.

An uncomfortable ten days went by. The British sailors had no reason to suspect that Hassan had a grasp of English. What he picked up from the British sailors and then passed on turned out to be a useful way of building rapport with his fellow Moroccans.

'They are intending to land at Falmouth,' he told them. 'But they fear the currents and gales around the Lizard on their way.'

His companions had heard of the Lizard. 'It's a monster peninsula, Hassan, stretches out like a sore thumb into the English Channel. Many ships have been wrecked there over the years.'

'But why?' asked Hassan. 'The Captain must know its position.'

'It's suspected that many of these disasters were the result of wreckers, operating from the home shore,' replied one of his companions.

'They light misleading lamps on key headlands,' said another, 'so as to lure boats like ours onto the rocks.'

There were plenty of things wrong with Tangiers but Hassan found it hard to credit anyone could be that evil. But he knew that at that time – 1684 - there was no reliable time keeper that ships could use, to make sense of the stars and identify their position. As his sailor friend had explained, 'On the rugged Cornish coast, with one headland after another, a small navigational miscalculation could be very costly.'

And so it proved. A raging storm had built up as the Schiedam closed on the English coast. No stars were visible through the clouds, even if they had been able to interpret them. The Captain had intended to stay out in mid Channel until the following morning but he was nowhere near as far offshore as he imagined.

Then, in the distance, the Captain could see lights: surely that must be land?

Now the storm gave them no choice. Quickly, unavoidably, the Schiedam was blown in towards the shore. In the blackness the crew could see very little, could only guess where they might be about to hit land. There was just a chance, the faintest of hope, that it would be on the long beach that was reputed to stretch south down the Lizard from Porthleven.

But in fact they were a few miles further down. And the reality was that they could not see the sharp-edged rocks stretching out just below the surface, were unaware of their presence until the agonising scrape and tearing of nails, as the planks of the hull were pulled off and torn away, reached their ears.

And by then it was too late to do anything at all. In a few minutes the Schiedam had disappeared below the waves without trace.

Hassan had just got to the master cabin to check on his treasure as *the final disaster began. He was determined to protect all his personal valuables for as long as he was able. He knew exactly where the chest had lain for the last ten days, had checked it on a daily basis.*

He had just gathered his most precious treasure and emerged from the cabin when the Schiedam hit the rocks. There was a tremendous shudder. Without warning Hassan was swept off the top deck and out into the boiling sea.

What saved him, when the rest of the crew all drowned, was that the chest which he hung onto so desperately contained enough air to act as a primitive life belt. As the winds roared and sheered, the Moroccan was pushed and pummelled away from the ship and towards the rocky shore.

Hassan himself had long given up all hope of survival when a monster wave seized him and flung him onto land.

EXHIBIT X

The following handwritten article was in a collection under the overall title, "Secrets of the Lizard" in Constantine Village hall. Its sub-title was "Python's Pad" and the author was not named.

The lad had tramped across the heath and climbed almost to the top of the old windmill. He had binoculars round his neck and a packed lunch in his backpack. It was the summer holidays, 1968; he would be here for some time.

Elsewhere in the country, youngsters went train spotting. There were a few steam engines left in Cornwall but none on the Lizard. This was an outlying area: it didn't lead anywhere.

There was, though, a remote airfield. The nature of the terrain, a flat piece of land beside the English Channel, had made the option inevitable. The place had flown Spitfires throughout the Second World War, helping to protect the southwest from enemy bombers. It had almost been closed in 1945, but now had a new role, supporting the nearby major English base for military helicopters.

The lad had become an expert on helicopters. His sharp eyesight supplemented the high-powered binoculars. From his eyrie he could now identify all the types of craft in regular use. It was quite a cycle ride so he wasn't here every day, but he would check the place every few weeks.

Over time there had been a number of changes. The Military was here regularly. There were also helicopters on Air-Sea rescue missions. He didn't expect any of these in good weather like today.

Over recent months the airborne activity had been supplemented by building work on the airfield itself. The lad hadn't a clue what this was about. But he had seen scaffolding and a big screen erected, behind which, he assumed, something was being built.

The youngster quizzed everyone he knew with any connection to the airfield but without success. It might be a special hanger for a new helicopter. But if so the craft would be seen once it began to fly. Why hide its home from view for months on end?

Might the secrecy hide a new military gadget? His dad said relations with the Russians were still tense. Was this a new form of radar, to give early warning of missile attacks? It was a regular topic of discussion at school.

Right now nothing was happening. No signs of activity around the screen either. Maybe whatever was being built was now finished?

After a while the lad decided it was time for lunch. Then he heard the thudding beat of a helicopter. It was coming from the Truro direction and heading for the airfield - but it sounded faster than he was used to.

He reached for his glasses and examined the craft carefully. He couldn't recognise it - was it a later model? No camouflage, it was all gleaming silver and looked highly impressive. Was this a visit by someone who mattered? Even an overseas visitor?

The site had received visitors when the lad had been "on duty". They'd always landed close to the airfield buildings.

This time was different. The helicopter was heading for the development work on the far side. So was this the official opening?

No, that couldn't be. There were no other cars in sight: if it was going to be declared open, senior staff would be present, surely?

Without fuss the helicopter put down close to

the building area and the rotors came to a halt. The watcher focussed his glasses on the craft.

He could just make out where the visitor would emerge. He kept the spot in focus and waited to see what would happen.

The newcomer was in no hurry. Maybe he was being briefed on the whole development?

Suddenly, a set of stairs dropped down. At the same time a man in uniform emerged from the development. After which a middle-aged man appeared in the helicopter doorway, looking around him before coming down the stairs.

The new arrival was in a grey suit - maybe not a military man at all? The lad squinted through his glasses but he was too far away to be recognised. His profile did, though, look faintly familiar. He wasn't tall and he wasn't exactly slim. Not that young, either; his wavy hair was starting to turn white.

The two men shook hands and disappeared inside the new development. They were gone for some time.   The lad had just decided that he might as well start his lunch when the two emerged.

It was a high-level inspection. The two were chatting cheerfully; the visit must have gone well.

The only change he could detect was that the civilian was now carrying a salmon pink folder.

But the visit was over. The civilian shook hands with the military man and turned back to the helicopter. He climbed the steps, gave a brief wave and then stepped inside.

A minute later the rotors started to turn. Then the helicopter was in the air and on its way.

That was that. The lad had just one further question as he started on his sandwiches.

The helicopter had flown in from the east. Why then did it disappear out to sea and off to the west? Where else could the mysterious civilian be heading?

CHAPTER 1

I'd been caught off guard in that start-of-year interview. It was awesome – by which I mean awesomely bad. Not a single redeeming feature.

I recalled the points Professor Townsend had made. First of all, he'd asserted, the History Department at Exeter University was in a financial black hole. 'Brexit might be good for the country in the long run, Harry,' he told me, 'but it certainly won't make things better in the near future.'

Evidently my own view of Brexit, which was more nuanced, wasn't even worth discussing.

The professor went on, 'We've got joint history projects with countries across Europe. Every one of these now hangs in the balance. When we leave, which for heaven's sake is less than three months away, then funding from the European Union for these projects will stop – and I can tell you, that will be sorely missed.'

There was a long rant about contemporary events from his perspective then the talk became more threatening. The latest student response to my previous term's lectures on "Life under the Stuarts", collected just before Christmas, was now in.

'Findings for all our staff are here, Harry. I'm afraid that for you it's very disappointing.'

There was a moment's silence. What was I supposed to say?

For now I wasn't given much chance.

'The thing is, Harry, we know you've a fertile imagination and you're good at problem-solving. That's why we hired you. Trouble is, your students say, it "keeps interfering with the flow of the lecture".'

'What the hell does that mean?' I interposed.

He looked down at the form for an example.

'You start a discourse, say, on the causes of the English Civil War. Then you get distracted. You ask a question that could launch a PhD thesis, but is way over the heads of a second year student – or at least, the ones we've got here. That leaves 'em baffled and confused. Sometimes angry.'

Townsend went on in this vein. I tried to make the counter case – surely it was better to be stimulating than boring – but apparently that wasn't open for debate.

Finally it was all over. 'In short, Harry, there are two ways you can make things better. First, you can stop all this free thinking in your own lectures – you're not at Cambridge now. Stick to your prepared script; keep the asides for postgraduates. Remember, clarity is the goal.'

Apparently this was not a conclusion I was meant to argue with.

The professor ended, 'Second, you can find us ways to win the Department extra funding, something that doesn't depend on the EU.' He concluded, 'Maybe, with all your free thinking, you can spot something that the rest of us have missed?'

Outwardly chastened though inwardly boiling, I closed the door gently and then stomped back to my room. I was a self-aware forty seven year old, I'd known that I was struggling but hadn't realised things were this bad.

It was four o'clock on the first Friday afternoon in January. There was no-one about. It was in the foyer outside my office that I ran into my visitor.

'Dr Jennings, I presume?' he began. 'Glad to meet you. Don't worry, I haven't been waiting long.'

I was six feet tall but my visitor was even taller. I sensed an air of authority alongside his Cornish lilt. The man was probably in his fifties but it was hard to be sure: he was wearing thick glasses and a magnificent beard that would have done credit to Methuselah.

I remembered now, my secretary had told me before she'd gone home, someone I'd never met had booked to see me later. With a burst of concentration I even remembered the name.

'Ah yes, Mr Stewart. Sorry I wasn't here. My Head of Department kept me longer than I'd expected. Do come in.'

I pointed him to an easy chair. 'Which would you prefer, Mr Stewart, coffee or tea?' On my own I'd have had a large whisky but I didn't want to start on the wrong foot. You never could tell, Mr Beardy might have access to finance.

Stewart said he'd prefer tea. A few minutes later I'd sat down opposite him for my second chat of the afternoon. I could only hope this one would go a little better.

'Now, what can I do for you?' I began.

'I looked up your record, Dr Jennings, on the University website. I must say, it's very impressive: a first class degree in

history at Cambridge, then a PhD on the life of Samuel Pepys.'
He smiled, 'I suppose he could claim to be the Ian Hislop of his
day. Then you had a variety of jobs, here and abroad. You wound
up in Exeter as a full-time lecturer five years ago.'

I nodded. 'Sounds about right. I could have gone straight into
academic life after my PhD but that seemed very narrow: I feared
being bored by learning more and more about less and less.'

Stewart chuckled sympathetically. 'The thing that intrigued
me, Dr Jennings, was this period between Cambridge and Exeter.
I couldn't find any details on the official record, not even where it
happened.'

I didn't show it but I was pleased: one of my secrets was safe
anyway. 'No, there wouldn't be. I decided it was more exciting to
delve into the raw facts of history on the ground. Of course,
there's a mass of data in the official records but that's been
trawled for decades. The most intriguing facts are those that lie
beyond. Sometimes you can find someone willing to pay for
them to be dug up. For years that was a good place to be.'

A pause as I reflected on glory days in the past. Then my
visitor dragged me back to the present.

'So what brought you home?'

'Oh, lots of reasons. Too many to go over right now. Anyway,
that's me.' I shrugged, doing my best to appear unfazed and
decisive at the same time. I wasn't going to give more away to this
stranger, anyway.

'So to repeat, Mr Stewart, how might I be able to help?'

He took stock. 'Well, I might be one of those people you just
mentioned. Someone willing to pay for help in finding some-

thing of historic value.'

I felt a twitch of interest but knew I mustn't sound keen. 'I'm afraid that sort of thing is in the past for me now.'

'The thing is,' he went on, 'I've been looking on my own, on and off, for several months but I've got nowhere. Then I thought, maybe a proper historian, one used to quizzing people and digging below the surface, might be more successful.'

I gave a sigh. 'I'm sorry, Mr Stewart, our university term starts in two weeks. I'm scheduled for another series of lectures about life in Hanoverian Britain. A dynasty of Georges. Maybe I could do something for you in the summer?'

Stewart looked dismayed. 'No, no, no. That'd be far too late. What about the next fortnight?'

It was impossible, of course. Then I recalled my earlier conversation with Professor Townsend; I'd been given two routes to reinstatement. Was this a new source of funding? I gave Stewart a fresh glance.

'That time isn't meant to be holiday,' I explained. 'We don't all go skiing: most of us can't afford it. But if it meant fresh funds for the University, I wouldn't need to stay here. I've given this course before, so it doesn't need much preparation. So to be blunt, my question is, "How much are you willing to pay?" '

Stewart considered. 'This is a personal matter so it'll come out of my savings. On the other hand the result might tell me a great deal.'

He mentioned an amount per day. It was below commercial rates but still worth having. It would be enough to show Professor Townsend that I'd got the message, anyway.

I smiled. 'We might be able to come to an arrangement. But to give this our best shot I need to know what I'm looking for, why you believe it exists, and finally, where you've looked already. I've only got a fortnight. As someone in Brussels might put it, "The clock is already ticking." '

An hour later Stewart left, both of us fairly satisfied. I hadn't learned as much as I'd hoped but I had picked up quite a lot.

By some means, which he had not been willing to disclose, Stewart had heard "rumours" of an old document which might affect him.

'I understand the thing came ashore from one of the shipwrecks around the Lizard.' My visitor had produced a list of wrecks from his inside pocket. It looked fairly substantial.

'Where on earth did you get that?' I asked.

'From the internet. I'm sure they'll have more details in the museums on the Lizard itself.'

My historical senses were aroused. 'So what period are we looking at? When did this document first appear?'

'I reckon the seventeenth century. It'll be handwritten.'

It sounded intriguing. 'Hm. A two week game of "hunt the slipper", set on the Lizard?'

For the first time in our conversation he looked alarmed. 'Please don't misunderstand me. This is not a game, Dr Jennings, it's much more serious than that. It's important that in this work you don't mention my name at all. And now I think of it, I'd much prefer you to use a false name for yourself as well.'

Weird, but I was desperate and willing to humour him if it

meant funds changing hands. 'OK. What name d'you suggest?'

He mused for a moment. 'Well, I'm a Stewart. Maybe you could be a Tudor?'

'I suppose there's been at least one Henry Tudor before,' I laughed. 'The last one caused plenty of waves. Alright, you're the client. If that's a condition of the project I suppose I'd better comply.'

Coverack Harbour, Eastern Lizard

CHAPTER 2

The phone conversation between two Cornish police officers had no operational significance. For the time being, anyway.

The first speaker, Peter Travers, was a rugged man in charge of Bude Police Station. 'Frances, I've just had supper with an old friend. She's a widowed lady in her forties called George Gilbert. She's coming down your way, got a business project at Goonhilly. But she tells me she doesn't know anyone on the Lizard.'

The second speaker, Frances Cober, the Police Sergeant at Helston, was tall, willowy and bursting with energy. She was the sort of woman who preferred to take action rather than instruction. But Peter was a colleague she respected and she sensed the unspoken question. 'I'd be glad to make her feel welcome, Peter. She can muse over our latest drowning if she likes.'

Peter laughed. 'George will have enough work to keep her busy. It's the evenings that might be a problem. If you could meet up for a meal or two that'd be great. Thank you very much.'

George Gilbert, industrial mathematician and sporadic solver of mysteries, had arrived on the Lizard in early January. Saturday morning had been spent in her newly-rented cottage. After lunch she'd driven across the Lizard to the coastal village of Coverack. A local lifeguard was giving a talk on the geology of the Lizard.

George had been invited here to meet Frances Cober, a police officer who was also off-duty for the weekend. Coverack wasn't far from Helston, but far enough, the officer hoped, that she would not be recognised. The previous day had given her a nasty shock.

The women emerged from the car park and met as each studied the geological display at the end. They were of contrasting appearance. George was short with a mass of dark curls; Frances was tall with hair flowing and golden. Little and large, they walked amicably into the village hall.

The talk began a few minutes later. The speaker, Richard Marshall, was a grizzled man in his forties. 'I'll talk for an hour,' Richard began, 'then we'll have a discussion at the end.

'We'll start three hundred and seventy five million years ago,' he said. 'I hope you're sitting comfortably. In those days the land on our planet was very different. The main land-masses were what we now call Gondwana and Euramerica, with an ocean between the two.

'At that point the Lizard was deep below the ocean in the southern hemisphere. It was pushed up by intense pressure from the molten rocks below in a layer we call the "mantle". It came through the surface layer – the "crust" – and became attached to the edge of Europa.

'As a result, the Lizard possesses a complete sequence of rocks from the earth's mantle to the crust. Does anyone know the name of the junction between the two?'

Silence and then Frances tried. 'Is it the "Moho line"?'

Marshall looked pleased. 'That's right. After a chap called

Mohorovičic. It shows how international geology is. Though, given its role is to make sense of the whole planet, that's not really surprising.

'I mention this,' he went on, 'as Coverack has a special secret. It's the only place in England where you can see the Moho line, laid out between rocks from the mantle and others from the earth's crust. If you walk along the shore near the car park you'll find rocks from each layer, close to one another. And a rock from the Moho line itself. That's called "troutstone".'

The speaker produced a rounded stone. He handed it to a couple in the front row and urged them to pass it on.

Richard talked lyrically about Kynance Cove with its caves, outcrops and islands and the serpentine rock beneath them. Then he showed maps of the boundary fault between the Devonian slates of Cornwall and the serpentine of the Lizard. 'The fault runs right across the Lizard,' he reported, 'from Polurrian Cove near Mullion to Porthallow, near St Keverne, on the east.'

The hour went by in a flash. Richard was just drawing to a close when a newcomer rushed in. 'You're needed, Richard. A board's capsized offshore near the Moho. The passenger's still in the water.'

Richard turned to the audience. 'I'm sorry about this. But my wife knows as much about this as I do.' He gestured to a woman on the back row. 'Mary, please can you take over.'

George would have been happy to stay but Frances wanted to go with the lifeguard. Was that a more interesting option? A moment later she had followed her companion outside and they were trailing the lifeguard down the road.

'Unless he's got someone else I'd better stick with Richard,' explained Frances. 'I may be off-duty but I'm still a police officer.'

'I've had dealings with the police too,' replied George. 'What can I do?'

'Call the ambulance service in Helston. It'll take 'em half an hour to reach us, they might as well start now. Then go on the beach, please, and watch us. That'll mean you can direct them when they get here.'

It was almost dark. George crossed the road but the waves were choppy and she couldn't see much. Richard and Frances headed for the tiny harbour, where the lifeguard grabbed a small inflatable with an outboard motor. A few minutes later, lifejackets on, the pair were bouncing over the waves.

George saw the man who had raised the alarm standing uncertainly outside the hall. She beckoned him over. 'I've called the ambulance. Can you show me where it happened, please? I'm George, by the way.'

'I'm Jeremy.' They started walking back towards the car park. 'It happened further along here.'

'Tell me in a minute. We need to get onto the beach. Are there steps somewhere?'

Jeremy pointed to a staircase halfway towards the car park and they hastened to use it. George kept an eye on the lifeguard's boat. Its speed through the choppy water was making the waves worse and both passengers were already drenched. But that didn't matter; their immediate challenge was to find the swimmer in the

25

gloom.

She could see now what Frances had seen at once, that the lifeguard couldn't do it all on his own. The boat had reached the area opposite the Moho and was circling round. Richard was in the stern, keeping the boat as steady as possible amidst the buffeting of the waves. Frances was in the bow, soaked as she desperately scanned the waves. Darkness was coming and back on the beach George and Jeremy could do nothing at all.

Suddenly there was a breakthrough. Frances pointed to the left and Richard eased the boat starboard. A minute later they were alongside.

As Frances reached out from one side the lifeguard leaned over to the other so they wouldn't flip over. Cautiously two arms came up. Frances grabbed one hand and then another. Slowly, inch by inch, a figure was hauled up and into the inflatable.

The first stage of rescue had been achieved. A little more slowly now, the craft headed inshore.

CHAPTER 3

An hour later George was back in her rented cottage, heating up two large portions of oven-ready fish and chips. Frances was thawing out in the bath along the corridor. George mused on an eventful afternoon.

The ambulance had come down the hill into Coverack, just as the inflatable was about to land. Jeremy knew there was no way the vehicle could get onto the beach. He'd rushed back to guide the crew, plus their stretcher, down the nearest steps.

George, meanwhile, had run to the edge of the water to make sure the craft came in to beach rather than rock. Then she took a grip of the mooring rope and helped to pull it ashore.

Between them Richard and Frances lifted the rescued swimmer gently onto dry land and laid them on the sand.

It was a woman and she was barely conscious. Frances immediately checked her throat was clear and then started on treatment. But she'd hardly begun before the ambulance crew arrived and took over the operation.

Five minutes later the woman's breathing had been restored. The crew decided it would be better to continue treatment in the ambulance. 'It's cold out here: we need to get her to hospital.'

George gleaned there was a Minor Injuries Unit in Helston.

Richard had set out to take the inflatable back to the harbour.

'In fact,' he admitted, 'it's not mine at all. But I can do that on my own.' He shook Frances' hand firmly and departed.

George had seen Frances was soaking wet. The improvised rescue had obviously taken a lot out of her, mentally as well as physically. George, cold and wet from the knees down, felt a wave of sympathy and companionship.

'Frances, look, my cottage is only just up the road. What you need is a hot bath. Would you like to come to my place for an early supper?'

Frances had hardly hesitated. 'You'll bring me back for my car later?' Without more ado she'd extracted a bag of spare clothes from her own car, prised herself into George's mini-Cooper, the heating had been turned to maximum and the pair set off back up the hill.

'Fish and chips ready,' George called.

Five minutes later Frances appeared, looking more composed than she had on arrival.

'That's better. With a bit of luck that'll keep me from a cold. Wow; that looks good.'

George was already dishing out the meal. 'It's hot anyway. Do sit down.'

They both sat and started to eat. For a few moments there was a contented silence.

'I'd been going to suggest we had a meal together somewhere, after the geology talk,' said George. 'I only got here last night. I don't know anyone on the Lizard at all.'

'How long are you down for?'

'Not long. I'm a business analyst. I've got a short project at Goonhilly Earth Station. You live in Helston?'

'In Gweek, actually. It's four miles out of town. I'm the Police Sergeant in Helston, in charge of the Station, so I prefer to keep my private life away from the town itself. That's why I suggested we met in Coverack.'

George picked up a key word. 'Ah, that's how you know Peter Travers. He's in charge of Bude, lives in Delabole for similar reasons.'

'Yes. We were on a training course together a year or two back, down in Plymouth. He's a very wholehearted policeman.'

George smiled. 'Not the only one, Frances. You could have left the lifeguard to it. You didn't need to get so cold and wet.'

'Police are like doctors, George: always on call. It's a good job I was there, actually. That sea was rough. Richard might not have found the woman if he was searching on his own.'

George reflected for a moment. 'The whole thing was odd, wasn't it? While we were waiting for you I talked to Jeremy.'

'Who the heck is Jeremy?'

'He's the guy that raised the alarm.'

'Oh right. I meant to talk to him but he disappeared.'

'He told me he'd just happened to look along the coast when he saw someone windsurfing towards Coverack.'

'Windsurfing: in January?' Frances sounded sceptical.

'As they got closer he saw it was a woman. But she hadn't got a wetsuit.'

Frances was astounded. 'George, I was pretty cold and I was fully clothed. Standing up unprotected on a board in that wind

29

she must have been absolutely freezing. Did he say how she'd ended up in the water?'

'As she got closer to Coverack, he said, she started to dodge about. Then she fell off and the whole thing keeled over.'

'Poor kid. Maybe I need to talk to her. Did you get her name?'

George shook her head. 'But we know they were taking her to Helston. They'll keep her in for the night. She'll still be there in the morning.'

The afternoon had reminded Frances of her latest case and she frowned. 'There might be more to this than meets the eye. I'd rather talk to her tonight. I mean, it's not exactly late, is it?'

Frances' decisiveness reminded George of their mutual friend Peter. He too would rush off in mid-meal. So she was ready to slow things down. 'At least let's finish our fish and chips.'

But the delaying tactic didn't work for long. George offered to take Frances back to Coverack for her car but she didn't want to lose time. Twenty minutes later they were off. George reflected that the logistics of a shared vehicle would bind them together for the evening. It would also help build a friendship

In any case it was hardly a burden. 'I've got nothing else planned, Frances. It's good to be doing something useful. After all, I've as much interest in the victim's survival as you have.'

When they got to Helston the Minor Injuries Unit was not hard to find.

Once inside, Frances' status as a Helston police officer allowed her to brush aside data protection protocols at the reception desk.

'I'm a police officer. My colleague and I were involved in a woman's rescue from the sea at Coverack this afternoon. Your ambulance would have brought her in a couple of hours ago. We'd like to see her, please.'

Slowly the receptionist scanned down her record of recent arrivals. 'Ah yes. It was an emergency admission. She should be in Poldhu Ward.'

This was Frances' local hospital. The internal links were like a maze but the police officer knew her way round. Swiftly she led George along a series of corridors until they reached the ward.

It was there that their difficulties began.

'This hospital's busy tonight,' observed George.

'It's Saturday evening. Demand is always higher than supply.'

Eventually Frances cornered a nurse and explained their quest.

'Ah yes. The girl in the swimsuit. Only been one today.' She smiled: 'We don't get many swimmers in January. She was conscious when they brought her in but not really with it. While we thought about what to do with her we put her in that room over there.'

A moment later Frances and George were inside. There was just one bed, recently occupied but now empty. It looked as if the victim, whoever she was, had discharged herself through the ground floor window.

31

CHAPTER 4

Waking on Sunday morning, George Gilbert wondered for a second where she was. Sunlight was filtering through the curtains and there was no noise at all. Then she recalled: she was in her cottage on the Lizard. She had slept like the legendary log.

A moment later she remembered she had a visitor. Frances Cober was in the other bedroom. After a lot of commotion chasing after the rescued swimmer – without success – Frances had decided it would be less trouble to stay for the night before George took her back to Coverack.

Twenty minutes later the two women were having breakfast. They could now see out across the Estate. It was sunny but cold; the austere, leafless trees were covered in frost.

'A pleasant place you've got here, George.'

George laughed. 'It's not mine. Goonhilly Earth Station is a Business Park these days, it's always having visitors. They've got half a dozen cottages on the Trelowarren Estate booked out for short-term lets. It's only a mile from the Station so it's very convenient. It might be joggable once I've settled in.'

'Have you got access to Trelowarren Manor? That's very old, I understand.'

'No idea.' George considered. 'They do have concerts from

time to time. I'll let you know if there's anything interesting.'

'Thank you.' Frances gave her porridge a stir and took a mouthful. 'Have you had any more thoughts on our missing victim?'

'Well, it seems fairly clear it was an accident that the girl landed in the water. But what was she doing without a wetsuit? Trying to escape? If you and Richard hadn't got there when you did, she could easily have drowned.'

'And you think vanishing from the hospital was an extension of the same process?'

George mused for a moment. 'She wouldn't be too hard to track there, would she? The ambulance was distinctive enough. Anyone in Coverack could guess where it would be going. And as you showed, the hospital reception's security wasn't exactly watertight.'

Frances put her hand to her mouth. 'You mean . . . she might not have left on her own. You think she was abducted?'

George smiled. 'Calm down, Frances. She was conscious, they said, so presumably she'd have screamed. Plenty of people would have heard her. Whereas in fact the nurse we talked to hadn't even realised that she'd gone.'

There was a pause. Two slices of bread popped up in the toaster. George retrieved them and fetched out some jam and honey.

'Take your pick,' she invited. 'What I don't understand, though, is how she made her way through Helston on a Saturday evening, dressed in no more than a swimming costume?'

'Even if she did I can hardly log it as a crime. My boss says I'm

33

too pernickety. It'd be just one more instance on my file.'

George noted the hint of stress but decided it was none of her business.

'She might not have been that cold. She might have found a hospital gown of some sort in a cupboard. Trouble is, all the staff team were busy. It's frustrating, mind, that no-one found out her name.'

Glancing round, Frances saw a pile of maps on the sideboard. She reached over and seized the Explorer map of the Lizard.

'Suppose she was trying to escape, George, could we guess where she might have come from?'

George walked round and looked down. 'I don't know the Lizard at all. That's down to you.'

'Hm.' Frances had opened the map on Coverack and was studying it carefully. 'She was coming from the east. No villages for a bit, the next one's Porthoustock. Just a quarry and one or two isolated cottages.'

George considered. 'How far might she have come on her surf board?'

'Depends if she was any good. Experts can travel for miles.'

George was intrigued. 'How d'you mean?'

'Well, d'you remember that Concorde crash twenty years ago in Paris? The pilot killed there had once windsurfed solo right across the Atlantic.'

'Wow. Mind, it's unlikely our victim was that good.'

'No, but she could have come a few miles. It's an efficient form of transport when the wind's behind you.'

An hour later the pair set off for Coverack. As they drove George asked, 'By the way, when are you next on duty?'

'I'm off till tomorrow. How about you?'

'I've not started work yet. Once I begin it'll be heavy going but today's free. D'you fancy a walk? It's a shot in the dark, but we might see some sign of where our surfer started her journey.'

'I'd be interested in the exercise anyway. We could find somewhere for Sunday lunch – there's a good pub in St Keverne.'

Soon they had reached Coverack. Frances was relieved to see her car looked undisturbed. A few moments later, boots on, the pair set off eastwards along the Coast Path.

For a while they were high above the shoreline, their view blocked by trees. Then the path dropped down and they were just above the waves.

The sea was calmer today. Fishing boats plied their trade. Further out was a line of large vessels, a mile or two offshore. 'That's the queue for Falmouth,' said Frances.

George had been looking nearer. 'D'you remember the talk? The speaker mentioned a raised beach caused by the last ice age. Look at these round pebbles. I think this is it.'

'I wouldn't like to risk coming ashore on a surfboard here,' commented Frances. 'It's very rugged. You know, Coverack's probably the first place she could land.'

They continued until the coast turned sharply northwards. A little later they passed a quarry on their left.

'Do you reckon that's been abandoned?' asked George.

'That metal fence is modern. I'd not fancy climbing it – not just in a swimsuit, anyway. I'd say it's a working quarry.'

Some recently-dated notices confirmed her view. 'Even if it's not in full scale operation it's hard to see how you could keep someone captive in there,' mused George.

'And if they did manage to escape, it's not obvious where they'd find a surf board,' added Frances. 'You know, thinking about it, the best place for that would be a beach or harbour where people kept their own.'

George seized the map. 'The next place along here is Porthoustock. Trouble is, we've got to go inland to get there.'

'It'll give our lungs a good workout,' said Frances, as they climbed up to the hamlet of Rosenithon. 'Downhill from now on,' she added cheerfully.

Half an hour later they reached Porthoustock. There was a pebble beach and some windsurf boards among the armada of fishing boats along the shoreline.

'Trouble is, all boards look much the same. Unless we've got the one used yesterday to show people, I don't see how we can tell if this is where it came from,' observed Frances. 'It was a windy night, remember. Whatever's left of our victim's board will be miles away by now.'

'But at least we've got a theory,' argued George. 'This is the back of beyond but there are a few houses. It's not impossible one of them was holding our woman captive.'

Not impossible, thought Frances, but there was no way to take the idea any further without a great deal of extra evidence.

CHAPTER 5

To fulfil Stewart's remit there was no time to waste. I set out for the Lizard on the Sunday morning and booked in at the Inn he'd suggested.

Helston's only antiquarian bookshop came via the internet. "C.T.Wicks", it said. "Purveyor of historic documents".

It sounded a good place to begin. These places never open early and I'd timed my ride to reach there just after ten.

That's right, I was on a bike – I'd decided cycling was the best way to do this research. The exercise would do me good. I didn't know where my quest would take me but this way there'd be no problem with parking.

As I locked my bike I saw I'd judged it well. There was a light on inside the shop, anyway.

With a cheerful 'Good morning,' I stepped inside. There were no other customers and the shopkeeper was busy checking his records. He looked up, mildly surprised to see anyone this early on a Monday morning.

Wicks was a short man in his sixties, slightly plump, wearing a double-breasted suit. His sombre face was lit up by a neat moustache. I could see he'd struggle to retrieve a book from his top shelves.

'Good day to you, sir,' he said. 'Are you just after a look

round? We've plenty more upstairs. What kind of book might you be after?'

'We'll get to a book eventually,' I replied. 'What I want first is your expertise.'

The owner put down his records. 'That's free at least. Supply might be limited, mind. What's your problem?'

'I've been asked to look for some old documents. My client believes that these came ashore from one of the shipwrecks around the Lizard.'

'Ah. Well, there are plenty to choose from, anyway. With all the cliffs and the gales, and those winter fogs, it's the most deadly stretch of the English Channel. Least it was till they got instruments to navigate it properly.'

I eyed him quizzically. 'How long ago was that?'

'Now that's a good question. I'd say the crucial advance was a chronometer that you could take to sea, so you could accurately tell the time. That'd give you a chance of making sense of the stars.'

'Provided you could see them.'

Wicks nodded. 'That's true. Mind, you'd always be able to see the sunrise. That'd give you your longitude. They started using such gadgets, I believe, in the eighteenth century.'

'Right. And they probably didn't have written records at all before . . .?'

Wicks smiled. 'There's another good question. Depends on the type of document. Well, the first "passport", though they didn't call it that, was 1414. Those were signed by the King himself so they'd be rare. They moved to things issued by the Privy Council,

I believe, in 1540.'

'Henry the Eighth had too much else to do, I expect.' I found it odd to be referring to my supposed forerunner. For now I was happy to let the shop owner take the lead.

'So it's passports that you're interested in, sir?'

'To be honest I'm not sure. The person who asked me to search just talked about rumours from the older generation, on material that might be of interest. It's rather vague, I'm afraid.'

Actually it sounded worse than that – hopeless – now I said it out loud. I wasn't even sure, looking back, that "Stewart" was my client's real name. Come to that, was his beard any more than a theatrical prop?

On the other hand, the task I'd agreed to tackle was intriguing and had brought me to a new part of Cornwall.

'Could we start with a general history of this part of Cornwall?'

'Right, sir. In that case, why don't we both take a seat?' Wicks gestured to a pair of Georgian chairs towards the back of the shop. 'I'll have to break off, of course, if I get any more customers.'

C.T.Wicks spoke confidently for half an hour. He obviously enjoyed sharing local history.

'There's little that's unique to the Lizard itself,' he began. He pointed towards a seventeenth century map on the wall behind him. 'As you can see, it's not on the way to anywhere. But I can sketch out the history of Cornwall; that'll give you some context.'

'I don't know much history from a Cornish point of view,' I

39

replied. 'Anything you can tell me might be relevant.'

'Right. Well, let's start in pre-Roman times. The British Isles' main reputation was for Cornish tin. That gave Cornwall plenty of visitors, from Phoenicia and later the Roman Empire. In fact our links to Europe were closer than to the rest of England. The Cornish language was nearer to the speech of Brittany than to anywhere else in Britain.'

'How long did all that last?'

'Cornwall was distinct for centuries. It had its own laws, for example, to control the sale of tin. Cornish was all the locals spoke.'

I nodded. 'It's easy to forget how long it took for the English nation to be welded together.'

Wicks nodded. 'That's right. Henry the Eighth was the first strong centralising force. So after the Reformation, Henry wanted everyone to use the English Prayer Book. That was what caused our Rebellion in 1549.'

I smiled. 'Which of the Thirty Nine Articles didn't they like?'

'It wasn't theological, sir. They just didn't speak English.'

I could see a snag. 'But they wouldn't speak Latin either.'

'No, but they were used to the rhythm of Latin services. Trouble was, they paid a heavy price.' Wicks looked sad. 'A fifth of the Cornish population was killed in one year. It was the start of the end for the Cornish language.'

I knew most of this already but hearing it from a local made it far more intense. 'Was that the last rebellion here?'

'Oh no, sir. Cornwall had a distinct role during the English Civil War.'

'You mean down here was Parliamentarian?'

'No, no. Cornwall was the most Royalist part of the south-west.'

'Why ever was that?'

'Well, you see. A tradition had begun, centuries before, that the King's oldest son would become the Duke of Cornwall. As a result, they believed the King would protect the laws that gave them control over their tin.'

I recalled that my client had been interested in Stuart times. This might be important. 'So who was their leader?'

'A man called Sir Richard Grenville.'

'I think I've heard of him.'

'You're probably thinking of the friend of Walter Raleigh, he was this man's grandfather. My Richard put a plan to the Prince to create a semi-independent Cornwall, in exchange for his support. It would have made Cornwall a colony, a bit like Gibraltar.'

Wicks sighed. 'Trouble was, the King lost the War so the plan came to nothing.'

At this point another customer came in. I remained seated, pondering what I'd been told and how it could affect my project.

Twenty minutes later we started again. Wicks seemed to have exhausted his passion for Cornwall. Maybe not much had happened after the Civil War? But I still wanted to tap whatever expertise he had on old documents.

'So where did the shipwrecks happen?'

'Ah. You're not the first to ask that.' He turned to the old map

41

on the wall behind him. 'This was the perception of the place two hundred years ago. You'll see it's rather distorted. The Lizard was this massive piece of land here, jutting out into the English Channel. That's because most of the wrecks happened to the incoming boats on the western coast.'

I stood to see where he was pointing.

'Everywhere from Porthleven, here, down to Lizard Point had its share of disasters. These are rugged cliffs with not many places you can land safely. Then, if a ship managed to get past all those, there were the Manacle Rocks. It would be easy to hit one of those on the way into Falmouth.'

'Have you a list of the boats wrecked in these parts?'

Wicks shook his head. 'There are plenty listed on the internet but even that won't cover them all. If I was looking I'd start with the local museums. They might have some ideas on documents as well.'

CHAPTER 6

I felt I'd made a good start with C.T.Wicks. I left him the details of my local inn (he was tickled by the notion of asking for "Henry Tudor") and promised to keep him up to date on progress. The best fieldwork always had sympathetic local contacts.

As I came out I spotted Helston Museum just down the road. Might they have a better list of wrecks? I wandered in and put the question to a middle-aged Curator. He smiled, delved below the desk and produced a battered folder for me to browse.

I was amazed at how many there were. The list was in chronological order, starting from the St Bartholomew at Lizard Point in 1321. It gave the names of each vessel, their nationality, what they were carrying and in some cases their tonnage. There was also an indication of where the wreck had occurred, though no clue on whether any were still visible.

I decided to start with location. I got out my notebook and tallied the places mentioned. An hour later I had a result.

The most common resting places were The Manacles, Porthleven and the Loe – a sandbank just down the coast. After this were some down the western coast, near Gunwalloe, Mullion and Lizard Point. A few more had happened elsewhere.

I took a while to scrutinise these locations, imagining how the wrecks had occurred. The Manacles didn't look promising. They were off southeast Lizard; the chance of any documents (or anything else) making their way ashore must be remote.

I noticed some places were near to Porthleven and others in the middle of nowhere. The Museum was quiet; I turned once again to the Curator.

'I'm interested in items rescued from one of these wrecks. Would it be best to start with the ones near a town?'

'Well, if there's a town nearby, the wreck would be news the day after it happened. There'd be plenty of folk there to bring stuff ashore.'

I frowned. 'But if anything was found, wouldn't it be taken in by the authorities rather than being left in local hands?'

The Curator thought for a moment. 'You're probably right.'

The documents I was after had remained obscure, maybe for hundreds of years. The best chance for that, surely, would be if they had got as far as some remote village and then got no further?

I thanked the Curator and went back to my list. Was there anything else? Lots of nationalities of boat had floundered on the Lizard. Should I concentrate on British vessels or ones from abroad? Should I care about naval vessels? There had been several battles off the Lizard over the years.

Without more clues it was hard to tell. I wished I'd grilled Stewart harder. Did his "rumours" show the type of document he was after?

The Curator was still pottering about. I turned to him again. 'I've been asked to look for documents from shipwrecks. Do you know what kinds of papers these boats might have carried?'

'Well, they'd all carry documents showing where they'd been registered.'

The trouble was, I couldn't believe that would interest Stewart. I tried again. 'What about papers relating to their cargo?'

He thought for a moment. 'All sorts of things were reported as lost over the years, sir. Gold sovereigns, silver bars, spices, drugs and diamonds. And works of art, like paintings.' He shrugged. 'I guess there could have been details relating to origin or provenance.'

I pondered. If I'd been asked to look for any of these cargoes themselves it might have made some sense, although they'd need a maritime recovery expert rather than a historian. But documentation wouldn't be of much use if the cargo itself had been lost.

Or for that matter, if it had survived.

I sighed. This was going to be harder than I'd first realised. All I could do for now was to push one or two doors and see if they opened. Starting, perhaps, with other museums which my map showed were scattered down the coast.

I calculated that I could cycle to the nearest museum at Poldhu Cove, close to Mullion, and also obtain a late lunch.

The journey was hard work. Maybe the bike had been a bad idea. I'd been told the Lizard was "relatively flat", but that didn't seem to apply to roads down to the coast.

I pedalled past a huge airfield just outside Helston and turned off two miles further on; a road that led, eventually, to Poldhu Cove. It was quiet enough, the beach was approached through a sandy marsh. The museum was up a hill to one side. I pedalled slowly up there, past a stylish stone building that looked like a hotel. The museum was tucked away behind.

I felt disappointed. It was just a wooden hut. But at least it was open. The focus was Marconi's work on telecommunication at the start of the previous century. I joined the other visitors as the introductory film began. When Marconi started his research, the commentator explained, it was believed radio waves could not be detected beyond the visible horizon. Marconi disproved that in 1900 with links to another radio station on the Lizard.

Then, in December 1901, he made a transmission that was picked up 2000 miles away in Newfoundland. A magnificent breakthrough; and it took place from this unassuming hut.

When the film ended I quizzed a guide about data on ship-wrecks. 'Hm. The Museum did pick up the first radio distress signal from a boat in distress. That was out on the Scilly Isles.'

Obviously local shipwrecks were not their sphere of expertise.

I came out. Interesting but not exactly what I was after. I was about to cycle into Mullion for lunch when the thought came, could I get anything in the local hotel? The place stood on top of the Poldhu Point, with a magnificent view up the coast.

I wandered in. The reception desk was unmanned. As I waited I glanced round. On the far side of the reception was a notice board inside a glass case, containing items of local interest.

Still no-one came. I moved over for a closer look but I could see nothing on shipwrecks. I was about to turn back when I saw a name I recognised. Someone who had stayed in this hotel, for a whole month, a hundred years ago. A man that I knew had outstanding detection instincts.

'Can I help you?' asked a piercing voice behind me. Turning back, I saw the receptionist had now returned. She looked rather severe.

'Is this place a hotel?' I asked.

'Not for many years, sir. It's a private Care Home. Is that what you're after?'

A few minutes later I'd beaten an apologetic retreat. It was going to be Mullion for lunch after all. But the visit here had not been entirely in vain. Maybe not in vain at all.

The former hotel above Poldhu Cove

CHAPTER 7

Police Sergeant Frances Cober had gone back to work on Monday feeling that, even if she had acquired a new friend and had had a decent walk on the cliffs, she hadn't really had a weekend off.

Her biggest case was a body that had been discovered early on Friday morning in the Loe – a deep pool of fresh water which ran from close to Helston down towards the coast near Porthleven.

Since this had also been a young woman in a swimming costume, it wasn't a surprise that the events on Saturday afternoon had given her a feeling of déjà vu. Of course, as it was a police matter, she'd not felt free to share any details with George Gilbert.

Frances' boss, Inspector Kevin Marsh, was based in Truro. He had overall responsibility for police stations in the west of Cornwall. He was an old-school policeman, who assigned resources as problems presented. He wasn't minded to look for trouble before it was shown to exist.

As she drove in to work, Frances thought back to the events of the previous Friday.

The body in the Loe had been discovered at eight am. Frances had taken her new recruit, Tim Barwell, down to the coast in response.

The place hadn't been that easy to find. There was currently work under way at the point where the Loe Pool came to the massive sandbar that separated the fresh water from the English Channel. The only road in, on her map, was a single track leading through the Penrose Estate.

'I'm Sergeant Cober. What's the problem?' she'd greeted the manager, once they'd finally got to the specified location.

She remembered that he'd looked slightly sick. 'It's the body of a woman. Looks like she got caught in the drainage channel we were installing, to help water in the Loe Pool escape to the sea. My men came across her as they started work this morning.'

'Let me see, please.'

The man had led her down a steep footpath from the road to the beach and through a temporary fence of six-foot high wire netting. 'This is where we've been working.'

He'd pointed into a culvert being dug through the sand, a metre wide, two metres deep and twenty metres long. One end started at the Pool. It was filled with water and had hydraulic equipment part way along.

Frances had walked along and peered down. At the bottom, visible through the water, was the body of a woman. She was still, clearly dead.

Immediately the officer had called up an ambulance and the police doctor. There was no evidence that this was anything other than an accident so she didn't call out Scene of Crime. But as a precaution she'd set Constable Barwell to put police tape round the whole area, after which she'd interviewed the man who had found the body.

There had been nothing on Friday morning to suggest it was any more than a nasty accident, although the incident raised many questions. When she had reported the case to Inspector Marsh he had been dismissive. 'Folk have been drowning on that beach for years, Frances. Perhaps she'd gone into the water the evening before to settle a bet. Or had too much to drink? She swam out of sight of her boyfriend and then got cramp, say, or was overcome by the cold. I mean, it's hardly midsummer.'

He paused for a moment and then concluded, 'Don't put any more resources into it for now. Give the post mortem a chance to raise issues if there are any.'

Since there was no way the post mortem would happen before Monday, Frances had felt it was safe to take her scheduled weekend off. It was overdue and followed several weekends on duty. The trouble was, the events in Coverack on Saturday had raised fresh concerns and made her less willing to put the case aside.

Once at the Station the initiative was taken out of her hands. 'We had a call from Truro General,' one of her colleagues, Dennis Penhaligon, reported, as she got to her desk. 'The post mortem on that woman from the Loe will take place at eleven. D'you want to go yourself or shall we send the barn owl?'

'I'll go myself,' she replied. 'I can think of other things Barwell could start on. For one thing I need a summary of the accidents around the Loe over the past few years.'

The youngster wasn't in yet. He was more owl than lark. Punctuality was one issue needing action if her boss would ever lend his support. In the meanwhile Frances got her various other cases in order.

When she got to Truro, Frances learned that the post mortem would be taken by Emily, a doctor with whom she had some rapport. She felt a sense of relief. She didn't like post mortems at the best of times. And there were things about the swimmer in the Loe that it would be good to bounce off a sympathetic professional.

'Another drowning on the beach near Porthleven, Frances?' asked Emily, as she carefully arranged the swimmer's body on the mortuary table, now covered by a green sheet.

'It looked that way. But this was inland, not out to sea. It's an odd time of year to go swimming,' Frances replied. 'At this stage I've an open mind but I'm keen to know whatever you can tell me.'

'Right.' Emily began with the doctor's report that had come with the body.

'Dr Smith says there were no signs of rigor mortis when he got there,' she observed. 'So she probably died a few days ago. Mind, with the effect of the cold water on her organs it's hard to be precise.'

'So it's not just a swim that started the evening before?'

'Not a recent swim, anyway. But she presumably wasn't in the channel for long?'

'I'll have to check where the maintenance men were working. I don't know if they were dealing with the channel every day. But there is a steady flow down the Pool. She probably drifted into the channel the night before she was found.'

There was silence as Emily carefully removed the swimming costume, put it to one side and then inspected the cadaver inch by inch.

'No obvious bruises; and no marks of injection,' she concluded. 'And no signs of sexual interference. We'll have to wait to see what she'd just eaten and if it had been doctored. Or if she'd had too much to drink.'

The pathologist turned to Frances. 'The lab will be able to tell us more about what she'd been taking, if anything, from the blood tests. I won't have the results back, mind, for a day or two.'

The autopsy continued.

'It looks like death by drowning,' the doctor concluded. 'There's fresh water in her lungs. She wasn't dead when she entered the water, anyway.'

'So, overall, no evidence of foul play?'

'There's nothing I could point to in court.'

As the post mortem was drawing to a close, Frances raised another issue. 'Even if it was just an accident, Emily, we need to know who she was. Her next of kin needs to be informed. Have you got her DNA sample and fingerprints?'

'I was working on those before you got here. But there are no signs of either on the national database. She wasn't a convicted criminal, anyway. And there was nothing distinctive about her swimming costume.'

Emily frowned. 'You know, identifying this woman might not be that easy.'

' I'll use anything I can, Emily. Could you contrive a photograph of her face for the media?'

'I'll try.' Emily picked up the unit camera and took a series of shots. 'I'll email these through when we've finished. They're not brilliant but they're better than nothing. Be thankful nothing had happened to her face.'

As Emily began to tidy up Frances started examining the victim's swimming costume more carefully.

'I may be whistling in the dark,' she began. 'But I reckon this costume is "bottom of the range". It's plain black, no decorations. And feel the material; it's thin. The sort of thing they sell in Tesco's.'

Emily sensed that her colleague had a question. 'Yes?'

'But the woman's well groomed. Her hair's a mess 'cos of the water but it's been well looked after: plenty of curls. And she's got painted nails.'

Emily put her head on one side and studied the victim again. 'I see what you mean. And on the same lines, I'd say the costume wasn't a perfect fit. I mean, she was a generously-built woman. Now I think about, the thing was one or two sizes too small.'

Frances had no idea where this was taking them but it left her with a feeling that the death was peculiar, if not downright suspicious.

She would need to persuade Inspector Marsh of that, however, before she could give it much more attention.

CHAPTER 8

It was mid-afternoon by the time Frances started her journey back to Helston. She was not a happy bunny.

She had caught Inspector Marsh on a bad day. That was the most charitable explanation, anyway. The same thing might have happened to a male colleague with the same data. Her suspicion that it wouldn't, though, was almost as bad as certainty.

She had seen Marsh's secretary and booked half an hour just after lunch. She'd remembered too late that, following in the steps of Inspector Morse, he often had a liquid lunch and was not at his sharpest straight afterwards. Marsh, who had a ruddy face and a brooding presence, was never enthusiastic. But whatever the reason, he had been dismissive of the need to do much more about the body in the Loe, except to use the media to seek information on the woman's identity.

'You've no medical evidence it was anything more than a nasty accident,' he averred, once Frances had given her account of the post mortem. 'It's not clear what on earth she was doing there. But there are Brexit demonstrations every week. We're fully stretched, Frances. I haven't the resources to make sense of every oddity we come across.'

In desperation Frances had mentioned the under-sized swimming costume. In retrospect she could see that that had been a mistake.

'We can't start treating the wrong size of swimwear as evidence of criminal activity,' he'd barked.

Given his reaction, Frances didn't dare tell him about the other swimmer from Coverack who'd disappeared from the local hospital.

In the end Frances had been grateful to slip away without a categoric closure. She still had a few ideas which wouldn't make much of a dent in her Station's resources.

What about the second woman whom she'd rescued and then lost? There were similarities. She knew Marsh would be scathing about the idea – it couldn't fairly be labelled any stronger – that the two cases were linked at all.

Fresh-faced Tim Barwell had something positive for her on her return to Helston. He might be a late starter but he was certainly energetic.

'I've got the list of recent accidents on the Loe that you asked for, boss,' he began. He handed her an A4 sheet.

'Six drownings on the seaward side,' he continued. 'The Coroner rated them all as accidental. It's the effect of the rip tide, you see, makes a calm sea look so harmless.'

Frances looked down the list. 'Were these tourists who ignored the warning notices?'

'That's right. And there are two fatalities related to boats on the Loe itself. Both due to excess drinking at late night parties – works events that went wrong. Still, it makes for a lot of deaths in a small area.'

Frances turned over the page but there were no more names.

'I phoned that works manager,' Barwell continued. 'He insists they'd been digging the fatal channel all week. The woman must have drifted into it on the Thursday evening. His men would have seen her if she'd been in there any earlier. He asked me when they could start work again, by the way.'

'Mm. Well, Tim, the post mortem didn't identify anything suspicious. The pathologist said she'd died a few days earlier – and almost certainly out in the Pool. I'd say there's no need for them to stay clear any longer. I'll give them a ring once we've finished talking.'

Frances gave him a careful glance. He might be a late starter but his eyes were alert now. He was certainly inquisitive, it would be worth stretching him further. Time for a challenge. 'What should we do next?'

'I was wondering how the girl got to the Loe, boss. If it was an accident as a result of a swim on her own, there's probably an abandoned car on one of the car parks nearby. There are only three places shown on the map. I mean, if you were coming from Helston or Porthleven you'd get as close as you could before you stripped off – at this time of year, anyway. If you like I could go round them all late this evening and note the numbers of the cars still parked.'

'Yes. That's a good idea, Tim. Then we could get in touch with all their owners and check it's not any relative of theirs that we've found. With a bit of luck there might not be many vehicles out there at this time of year.'

Timothy looked enthused. 'And if that doesn't go anywhere, I could cycle the whole path round the Loe – it's only six miles or so – and see if I can see a pile of clothes anywhere. She might have been a fitness fanatic – even if not that successful. It's just possible that she walked or ran in.'

'Right. And meanwhile, tomorrow, I'll call a press conference. Show the picture of the woman's face to the media and get them to circulate it. Someone around here must know who she is – the question will be, are they willing to tell us?'

Frances could see no other obvious line of enquiry. 'Mind, if none of these things lead anywhere, we'll need to ask ourselves whether it was an accident at all.' She might be back to Inspector Marsh once again.

The Loe Bar on the west Lizard coast

CHAPTER 9

George Gilbert had enjoyed her first day at Goonhilly Earth Station. There was plenty of security. A tall, barbed-wire topped fence surrounded the site, which stood on a large stretch of heath in mid Lizard.

Its most striking feature was its satellite dishes. The largest, "Arthur", was ninety feet high and built in the 1960s. It was an icon. George was told it had handled the pictures to the nation of the first moon landing in 1969.

In recent times the site had been privatised. It was now an Enterprise Zone for small businesses needing high-tech communications.

The project which had brought George to the site might turn into one of these. For plans were afoot to develop a Space Station at Newquay airport. This was a government initiative to show forward thinking, despite the controversies of Brexit.

Newquay's long runway pointed straight out to sea. That would allow an aircraft to launch with a rocket-powered load that could be sent into space. It was also close to Goonhilly, with its history of space communications.

George's remit was an independent assessment of this proposal, to ask awkward questions. What would be required, was it sufficiently reliable?

George's security clearance allowed her to probe the site and talk to staff. Her immediate task was to find how the place ran and to assess how robust would be the links to Newquay.

It had been a busy day, meeting a series of managers and analysts. It turned out there was no on-site catering so George hadn't had much lunch. She was ready for her supper by the time she returned to Trelowarren. But she was scarcely back when her phone rang.

To her surprise it was Frances.

'George, could I come and see you? I've a problem. Is there any time this week when you're around?'

George didn't need to think for long. 'Come this evening if you like, Frances. I'd be glad to see you. I've got more convenience meals in the cupboard; would you like to come for supper? Say, in about an hour?'

An hour later the policewoman had appeared. She wasn't in uniform; her hair was down, so not on duty. That lowered the pressure anyway.

Frances held out a box as she came in. 'I called at Sainsbury's: it's a lemon cheesecake.'

George thrust the gift into the fridge. 'That's very kind, thank you. Right, shall we start with whatever's bothering you? We'll eat afterwards.'

The two women eased themselves into the easy chairs. The cottage was geared up for visitors. George looked at her new friend curiously: what was coming? Frances paused for a moment, working out how best to begin. Then she leant forward.

'I need to talk to someone outside the Station to make sense of my latest case. It's just possible it's connected, you see, to the woman you and I rescued in Coverack.'

George smiled. 'I'm happy to help if I can.'

'I should confess, George, that I've had another phone conversation this afternoon with Peter Travers. He spoke highly of you, very highly indeed. He sends you his love. He said you had a rare gift of asking deeper questions about complex issues.'

'That's very kind of him. I've always liked solving problems.'

'That's what made me feel I could come and bounce ideas off you in this irregular way. I don't normally talk police business to outsiders. Plus, of course, you're the only person who knows about our rescued swimmer.'

George sensed some reassurance was needed. 'Frances, I'm happy to listen. Take your time. I won't tell anyone, I'm used to keeping secrets. Tell me everything that you think might be relevant.'

For the next half hour Frances went through the case of the dead swimmer recently found in the Loe, her post mortem discussions with the Truro pathologist and finally the afternoon meeting with her boss.

Once the tale stopped, George wanted a few minutes to reflect. 'Before we talk more, can I make us some tea?'

Ten minutes later the discussion resumed.

'So let's get this straight, Frances. You've had two peculiar cases, both involving female swimmers, on two successive days?'

'That's right. Am I going crackers or is there some sort of

connection between the two?'

George frowned.

'At first sight it does seem a bit of a coincidence. It's a pity we've no hard evidence from our girl at Coverack. We don't even have a name.'

She frowned again. 'How certain are you that there's anything odd about the Loe girl? You say your boss wasn't convinced.'

'It's a series of oddities. For a start it's a dismal time of year to go swimming, especially at night. Also, I suppose, the undersized swimsuit. My boss didn't understand. But no woman would choose to wear one that didn't fit her, would they?'

George shook her head. 'I didn't notice anything like that with our Coverack girl. But she was slender anyway. A small costume would be fine on her.'

'Both costumes were unadorned black. Might they have come from the same place, d'you reckon?'

George puzzled for a moment. 'Well, the two incidents happened on the Lizard, but on opposite coasts. So not really the same place. The main thing that links them that we know about, actually, is you. It just happens that you're a conscientious police officer.'

'Plus timing: I came across them both at almost the same time.'

'Well, that's true, Frances, but I thought the pathologist told you that the Loe girl had died a few days earlier? So . . .'

'In the same week, anyway.'

'And both cases involved a girl in a black swimming costume . . .'

Silence for a moment; then George made another suggestion.

'If there is any similarity, is it possibly that both girls were trying to escape? Thanks to our efforts Ms Coverack made it, but poor Ms Loe didn't.'

Frances nodded. 'It's possible, I suppose. I haven't a clue, though, why they might both have been held captive in the first place.'

Another pause and then France mused. 'Do you think, George, that the two cases are more suspicious when viewed together than either on its own?'

George shrugged. 'I suppose that's true. I think we're running out of ideas. Let's leave it completely and have our supper.'

Over sweet and sour chicken, at Frances' request, George sketched out her forthcoming role at Goonhilly Earth Station.

'I'm no expert on space flight,' she admitted, 'though I have read quite a bit about it. It's one of those "frontiers of knowledge" ideas pushed by wealthy billionaires.'

'So how come you're involved?'

'I work for a consultancy in London that does all sorts of management projects. My boss is well connected and knows lots of influential people. That's how we got asked. And once that happened he handed the problem on to me. I've got a cottage near Tintagel, so they give me first claim on all our projects down in the southwest.'

'So your role here is to . . . think outside the box?'

'I'd like to think so. I assess what will be needed and ask awkward questions on whether it can be done. It's very easy for a high-profile project like this to be carried away by what you might call heroic rhetoric. Top people are easily taken in by big ideas. I like to challenge everything.'

Frances could see George wasn't holding back. In response, as confidence in her friend grew, the police officer sketched out some of her problems with her boss in Truro.

'He's probably juggling all sorts of issues,' responded George. 'Demand for resources is bound to be much bigger than supply. Your instinct has been aroused but there's no hard evidence to back it up. Maybe once you've probed a bit further you'll have more to say.'

Frances was far more enthusiastic about her new recruit, Timothy Barwell. 'He's only just started and he's not very organised but he's got plenty of energy.' She explained what he had done today and what he was hoping to do later this evening.

'So by tomorrow, George, we might have some progress on Ms Loe's identity. Either from my press conference, via the photos, or via the registrations on the vehicles left in the car parks.'

'If it really is just an accident, Frances, it shouldn't be too hard to find out the poor girl's identity. But if you can't then the case becomes a lot more interesting.'

Later, after enjoying slices of the lemon cheesecake, the women sat back once more in their easy chairs.

Frances felt relaxed. She had asked the questions that had brought her here, even if she hadn't got many answers. It had been good to share.

George, though, felt she hadn't done much thinking yet "outside the box". What else might she add?

'Have you had any other cases like these in recent months, Frances? Either here in Helston, or, maybe, at another Station?'

'Not as far as I know.'

'Presumably it'd be easy enough to check. Say by the energetic Barwell?'

'I guess so. Aren't two cases enough?'

George mused on. 'Another point. Ms Coverack has gone but you've still got Loe-girl's swimsuit. Why not take it along to the supermarkets in Helston, find out if it's one that they sell?'

'How might that help?'

'I bet they won't sell many in the depths of winter. If they do I'd ask them next when the last ones were sold.'

'Yes?'

'The key thing would be if the sale was recent – say, in the last week.'

Frances looked puzzled. 'What on earth are you driving at?'

'I don't know how tight security in supermarkets is down here. They must have CCTV cameras. If you were very lucky they might still have pictures of whoever made that purchase. If they'd paid by card they might even be able to tell you their identity.'

Frances nodded, though wondering how much work this would require. In summer it would have been a lost cause. It was the rare combination of swimsuits and depth of winter that might just make it feasible.

George continued. 'The other thing that we need to reflect on is the wrong-sized swimsuit. It doesn't make sense.'

'I agree. No woman would choose a swimsuit that doesn't fit.'

There was silence as the question was pondered.

George spoke. 'Well, one way it could happen – perhaps – is if the girl hadn't bought it for herself but someone else had bought it for her.'

'Hey, yes. Any man, even the most doting husband, could easily buy one that's the wrong size. A man would never know about cup size. Was it a Christmas present that went wrong?'

'Perhaps,' said George. 'Although it wasn't the sort of glamorous item a man might buy his partner as a present, was it? I was thinking of another sort of man. Could it be one who was holding the victim prisoner?'

'That's a wild idea but we shouldn't ignore it.'

George felt she'd made a contribution. The women kicked the ideas around without getting any further.

Frances left a short while later. She'd been given at least a few ideas to muse on.

Goonhilly Earth Station with "Arthur", the satellite dish

CHAPTER 10

It had been an intriguing afternoon. I'd secured lunch at a café in Mullion. While settling up I'd asked the owner for comment on my find in Poldhu.

'You know, Sir Arthur Conan Doyle did once come down. He stayed at the Poldhu Hotel: 1907 or thereabouts. He'd been prescribed a month's rest by his doctor. It was an event for folk here, of course. Doyle was the major celebrity of his day.'

'Did he travel as far as Mullion?'

'Oh yes. Plenty met him or knew someone who had. My grandfather helped to run this café in those days. He remembered him coming in here regularly.'

'Was he down here for research or something?'

'I think he was supposed to rest. His doctor in London thought nothing ever happened in Cornwall. But of course Doyle was a restless spirit. He'd find doing nothing almost impossible. I'm sure he'd have found a local mystery to delve into.'

'But your grandfather didn't remember what that was?'

'Well, if he did he didn't tell me. You've got to remember, Conan Doyle was a medical doctor. He was used to keeping secrets. Even if he'd found something exciting he wouldn't have wanted to tell everyone. He was in his fifties. His problem was avoiding the media, not winding them up.'

I pondered for a moment. Then I had an idea. If Conan Doyle had found something, he wouldn't turn it into an academic paper. That would just raise his stress level. But might he not have used it as a starting point for one of his fictional tales?

The owner was busy dealing with another customer but I was in no hurry; it was a long shot but these were my speciality. Eventually he was free and I could ask my question. 'Did the famous doctor write any Sherlock Holmes stories while he was in these parts?'

The owner considered. 'Just one, I think. It was called something like "The Adventure of the Devil's Foot". It was in his last book. It must have been one of the last Sherlock Holmes stories he ever wrote.'

Pursuing this was a shot in the dark but more interesting than anything I'd picked up in today's museums. And it was important I worked on ideas that Stewart hadn't tried. 'I don't suppose you've any idea where I might find a copy?'

Of course, the café owner didn't possess a copy of his own. 'I'm not into books,' he declared. 'But I know someone who might: there's a shop-keeper further down the village who deals in second hand books.'

I thanked him and headed down the street.

The bookshop was in need of fresh paint but it was out of season. At least the place was open. I locked my bike and stepped inside.

I wasn't the only customer. A garrulous lady was ahead of me. Her tangled request sounded like the script for "Only Connect".

But the commotion gave me a chance for a look round.

Most of the volumes on the ground floor were leather-bound books from long ago. Eventually I found a shelf of modern day classics. They weren't that modern, to be fair, but they were in alphabetic order. And there, to my joy, I spotted "The Penguin Complete Sherlock Holmes." If the story was anywhere it must be in here. I seized it and headed for the counter.

'I gather Conan Doyle once came here,' I said as I handed over the volume. 'I'm after the story he wrote while he was here.'

'Could be,' said the shopkeeper. Light fiction was not his speciality. He flipped through the book – yes, it was in fair condition – and handed it over. 'Six pounds for that, sir. It's had several previous owners. For a thousand pages of top class writing I'd say that's a bargain.'

I could have gone back to the café to study Doyle's writings but it was already mid-afternoon. I didn't fancy cycling home in the dark.

I was staying at an Inn well off the beaten track, ten miles away, near the village of Constantine: "Trengilly Wartha".

The Inn was remote but it was comfortable and the food was delicious. 'Mention my name,' Stewart had said, 'and they'll offer you a discount.' I'd been sceptical but they had. So far it was the best part of the project.

I'd go back there to grapple with any clues to be gleaned from Sherlock Holmes.

Over a pot of tea in the snug, I found the specified story and read it carefully. It was years since I'd read Sherlock Holmes. I was surprised at the clarity of the plot; it was easy to see why it prompted imitation. Some aspects of the style had dated, but for something written a hundred years ago it felt surprisingly modern.

Was there any evidence Conan Doyle had hinted at something important about life here within the tale?

It began with Sherlock Holmes dispatched to Cornwall by a doctor from Harley Street. He and Watson found themselves in a small cottage on a grassy headland overlooking Poldhu Bay. So Conan Doyle had used his own experience as a basis for the plot. Maybe the tale had other realistic elements as well?

Conan Doyle must have drawn on his own experience while at the Hotel. I remembered the view up the coast. Gunwalloe Cove, the next inlet, had featured in my record of shipwrecks. That was promising.

The action started in a small village surrounding an "ancient moss-grown church". The first person Holmes and Watson encountered was the local vicar, "something of an archaeologist, middle aged and affable, with a fund of local lore". Was there a present day equivalent?

The story trundled on. Among other characters was an explorer who had spent most of his life in Africa. Was this another clue? Was there a ship wrecked here on a voyage which had started in Africa?

A lot happened, including a family quarrel, and an unrequited love affair between the explorer and the sister of one of the other characters. This couldn't all be clues. But there were phrases that sounded evocative: "The vicar knew. He was in our confidence" and "He came down into my cottage and I showed him my African curiosities".

In the end Holmes applied his own version of justice. "Our investigation has been independent and our action shall be also."

Had Conan Doyle come across some skulduggery that was above or beyond the law of the land?

By the time I'd read the story a few more times and underlined the key phrases it was time for dinner. What would the master chef of Trengilly Wartha have on offer tonight?

I decided to dress for dinner; it was time to look smart. I put on my college cravat and slipped into my purple dinner jacket. I needed to eat well. I'd certainly be cycling back to Poldhu Cove tomorrow morning.

CHAPTER 11

In any project she worked on George Gilbert was conscious of the clock ticking. Someone was paying her firm a high price for her efforts and they would be expecting results.

A key question was how easy it would be for Goonhilly to track the space plane as it took off from Newquay and was flown high over the Atlantic. In principle such a process was easy but she soon saw that she needed to know a lot more about the issues raised.

Was coverage always possible? How often were the satellite dishes taken offline for maintenance and what might make them unavailable? For that matter, how reliable were power supplies and internet links? Were outages predictable and how long might they last? Was backup always available?

It was one thing for a client to expect monitoring capability; something else altogether when lives depended on it.

This was why she was down here: to talk to Goonhilly experts. A few minutes later George had arranged for a meeting later that Tuesday morning. Dr Jim Harvey, she was advised, was the key Station Manager to talk to.

The notice on the door said "Security Officer". Harvey was tall, well-groomed and darkly handsome. The trouble was, he was almost aggressive in his reaction to George's concerns.

After twenty minutes of polite chit chat the analyst decided to get serious.

'The thing is, Dr Harvey, this isn't just about maintaining data links. If this really happens, people on the Newquay space plane will depend on it working all the time. Or at least, all the time the plane is in the sky.'

'We have high standards, Mrs Gilbert. Internationally recognised. We're not just a software house, you know.'

'I know your reputation, Dr Harvey. I'm sure it's worked well over the years. But data flows can go wrong and be picked up later without lives being lost. This is different. If a plane's in the sky, travelling at the speed this one will be going, you can't afford to lose it.'

George could see he wasn't convinced. She would have to drill down further. 'For example, what about power supply?'

'That's easy. We have the National Grid.'

'And if that cuts out? There are blackouts – especially in a cold winter. Those might get worse. The nuclear power plants they're building today might not all be finished to schedule.'

'We have diesel generators on site. And – before you ask – we make sure their fuel tanks are topped up every month.'

He was sounding almost over confident. George frowned. 'Do these generators start up at once? How often are they checked?'

Harvey looked irritated. 'The engineers give them a full run-through every six months. They start up pretty well straight away.'

It sounded fine but George sensed an admission of weakness.

She wasn't an auditor but this was crucial to the Newquay project. 'Do you have records of these tests?'

He shrugged. 'They'll be filed away somewhere. It's all archived.'

'In that case, could I see them please?'

Harvey looked like he might blow but managed to swallow hard and contain his temper. 'I'll get one of my staff to show them to you afterwards, if you insist.'

George gave him her best smile. 'Thank you. OK, can we go on to the reliability of internet links?'

It was a tough session and didn't get any easier. George was glad when the time she'd booked was over. Harvey had another meeting, though she still had plenty more questions. She would need to come back.

At the end Harvey called up one of his team to guide George to the site archive. A slim, animated woman in her early thirties, Anna Campbell, arrived a few minutes later and introductions were made. The two left Harvey to his next meeting and made their way to the hut next door.

Once again George explained her role. Anna could see why reliability was so important. 'You're right, George. Human life is far more precious than data. Let's see if we can find the records.'

It turned out that Anna hadn't worked at Goonhilly for long. Her role so far had been more of a "gofer". But she'd acquired enough sense of how things were arranged to navigate her way through the archive. George guessed it would be much easier to work through her directly rather than having a series of tussles with Dr Harvey.

The generator test reports were finally unearthed. They didn't happen as frequently as Harvey had implied.

'Could I take these back to my office, Anna? I'd like to go through them this afternoon.'

'I don't see why not. No, why don't we go to my office, photocopy them and bring the originals back here. They're very strict on records at Goonhilly.'

'I'm pleased to hear it.' George was happy enough to see more of the site as they walked. Various other facilities were pointed out. The place was larger than she had expected.

'It's a pity they don't have catering on site,' observed George.

'It's 'cos it's a male-based organisation. I bring a couple of sandwiches and go off-site to eat them.'

'That's a good idea. I'll do that from now on.'

'You can share mine today if you like. I'm not that hungry.'

Ten minutes later George and Anna, warmly clad in hats and scarves, had shown their identity cards at the gate and wandered down the road.

'There's a Nature Reserve down here,' said Anna. 'It's quiet enough and got a couple of picnic tables we can use.'

There was a car park but today no-one was using it. The place was surrounded by heath and bushes. Anna divided her lunch in two and they each tucked in to a large cheese sandwich.

George was glad to have some lunch and the chance to know someone on the site a little better.

'So what do you do when you're not at work?'

'I've managed to find an amateur drama club near me in Constantine, even got a part in their latest production.'

'Is that local? I need something to do besides project work. I'd be happy to come along and see it.'

'We're not doing many performances, I'm afraid. We're not professionals, you see. Mind, the standard of acting isn't bad. We've got a script from the BBC and a good Director. He pushes us really hard.'

'OK then. You've convinced me. When's the next performance?'

'We're at Trelowarren Manor on Thursday evening. That's – '

George smiled. 'I know where Trelowarren Manor is. I'm staying in a cottage on the Estate. What a coincidence. I'd love to come. What's it called?'

'It's based on an Agatha Christie book. The original title was politically incorrect. Now it's called, "Then There Were None". It was a BBC Christmas Special three years ago. Do come, I'm sure you'll find it very entertaining.'

CHAPTER 12

Police Sergeant Frances Cober was at work early on Tuesday morning. Her consultation with George Gilbert had boosted her morale. It even allowed her to view her colleagues at the Station with a degree of empathy.

Timothy Barwell wasn't in yet but she could hardly complain. Frances recalled he'd spent the previous evening checking the car parks around the Loe. In the meantime she did her best to process her paperwork. If the Loe case turned out not to be an accident it would consume all her energy in the days ahead.

After dealing with the most pressing items Frances started to plan the press conference which she'd called for that afternoon. She chose the best of the images Emily had sent over. How should she present the problem to the media?

One risk was of making the drowning so routine that it would hardly make page ten in the Cornish Gazette. Conversely she could make it so frightening that readers might think the whole of the Lizard was under assault. Somehow or other middle ground was needed.

She was just double-checking background material about recent drownings when Barwell arrived. She let him take off his jacket and turn on his computer before she started to bombard him.

'So how were the car parks?'

'It took longer than I'd expected, boss. There might be only three official car parks around the Loe, but there are plenty of places where you could leave a car for an hour or two at night. I didn't get home till after midnight.'

'So how many vehicles have we to worry about?'

Barwell pulled out his notebook and counted. 'Fifteen. There are one or two large vehicles – one bus and two lorries – that I'm inclined to ignore.'

'Right. Ms Loe won't have come in those. Have you ever worked back from car numbers to their owners?'

Despite the late night Tim still had plenty of energy. Frances got him started and then left him to it. 'When you start doing the calls, Tim, even if they've got no link to our dead swimmer, ask 'em – gently – what their car's doing there. Then check: had they been there before? And if so, had they seen anything suspicious, in or around the Pool, on any recent visit?'

'Yes, boss.' He hadn't thought of the innocent car-owners as potential witnesses. This would all be good experience.

'Make sure you flag up anyone that's not there when you ring. They might just be out shopping, or that might be the vital clue. And for those you can get hold of, make sure you keep a record of exactly what's said,' she counselled, 'even if it seems like a dead end. You don't want to do fifteen calls and then be unsure of who said what.'

Frances had little hope that any of this would lead anywhere but it was important to instil good practice.

The talk of cars around the Loe had given Frances another idea. Was there any check on boats allowed to sail there? Was there any sort of registration scheme? A phone call to the Council showed that there was. Half an hour later, the current year's entries – which Frances was pleased to see included the owner's address and contact details as well as boat specifics – had been emailed through.

'Further work for Timothy Barwell,' she thought. By now it was almost time to head for the press conference.

Frances had made sure Inspector Marsh was aware of the time of the meeting but was relieved when he didn't show up. Was this confidence in her press-handling ability or simply lack of interest? Or was there a bigger case breaking elsewhere? Whatever the reason, it gave her freedom to pitch the appeal as she wanted.

There were no television cameras present, just half a dozen local reporters. Frances had met them all before and they all knew her. This would be a low-key meeting, which was fine by her.

Frances began by outlining the known facts. She showed them a large-scale map and the final location of the body. 'But she didn't die here. She died somewhere in the Loe Pool, probably a week ago,' the police officer estimated. 'We have no reason to think her death was anything other than an accident.'

Then she unfurled the picture of the dead woman taken at the post mortem. 'I'll send out a digital version when we've finished talking.'

'Our key problem is that we have no idea who this lady is. She doesn't match anyone on Missing Persons; nor is her DNA on the UK National Database. So we're appealing for anyone who thinks they might recognise her to come forward. And we're hoping that you, between you, can present the case in a way that will bring that about.'

There wasn't much else to say. Frances waited for questions.

'Can you give us the name of the person who found her?'

'There's no way that can be relevant. The post mortem showed she died two or three days before she was found. The maintenance gang had been working the channel for the previous week and she wasn't there then. The woman must have floated in, already dead, during Thursday night.'

'Walking round the Loe Pool is a popular Helston pastime. Have you asked if any of these walkers know anything?'

'It's also a popular jogging and cycling route,' added someone else.

'That's the sort of thing I need help with,' responded Frances. 'Also anyone sailing, swimming, fishing or jet-skiing. Whatever the activity, we need to hear from the participants.'

'Why d'you think she's local?'

'I don't. But it's the most likely guess. If today's meeting doesn't identify her then we may need to go for wider coverage.'

'Is there any chance that it wasn't an accident?'

Frances paused before she answered. It was crucial to get this right. She did her best to sound confident.

'There is no evidence at all that it wasn't an accident. The police always have to be led by the evidence, so that's where we've got to start.'

There was a moment's silence. Frances decided to take the chance to close the meeting.

'Thank you all very much. I'll make sure you're all kept in the loop as we learn more.'

Helford River and Scott's Quay, Constantine

CHAPTER 13

I was later than expected starting out on my research on Tuesday morning.

By chance I'd met someone I could relate to, over the Trengilly Wartha cooked breakfast. Someone else with a professional interest in the past and how it might apply to the present. She was called Sam. Only in her case it wasn't Tudor, Stuart or even Georgian history.

'That all just happened,' she laughed dismissively. 'The really interesting stuff started so much further back.'

It turned out there was an Old English Settlement not half a mile from the Inn. 'It's straight over the fields, down near Scott's Quay.' Sam had spotted a spark of interest in my eyes and shown me the Settlement Ring on her map before my interest faded.

'I'm camped there for the next fortnight,' she told me. 'I only came to the Inn to buy milk. Then I smelt the coffee and couldn't resist the cooked breakfast.'

She was on her own so I invited her to share my table. 'It's not that much fun eating on your own. My name's Harry, that's Harry . . . Tudor. I teach history at Exeter University. I'm doing some research too.'

A moment later she had joined me. Sam didn't look like she'd had a hot meal for some time. She was attacking the bacon, sausage and egg like it was an invading army. I didn't interrupt until she came to a temporary halt before taking on the tomatoes on the plate's far side.

'You look hungry,' I remarked.

'I only got here yesterday evening. By the time I'd found a bit of level grass and got my tent up it was practically dark. I'd planned to walk back up to Constantine for food but I couldn't find my torch. So I snuggled down with my chocolate, an apple and my Kindle. Then I fell asleep.'

'You must have been really tired,' I said. 'If you need to eat out again I can recommend this place. The chef here is something else.'

Sam wrinkled her nose. 'I might afford a meal at the end, but I can't afford it very often. The sponsors for my research are pretty tight-fisted. The breakfast is good value, though.'

'I'll get us both another coffee.' She was a pretty girl, tall, with almond blond hair. I returned a few minutes later.

'So what are you doing at this Settlement?'

'I'm an archaeologist, Harry. My PhD is about how Bronze Age folk lived in this part of Cornwall. I've got permission from a local landowner – after a huge struggle – to do some digging. See what clues they've left us, down below the mounds. How about you?'

For a second I struggled: which aspects of my research were draped in confidentiality and which could be shared? Telling this girl something was surely safe enough. She'd mentioned a PhD, must be a potential academic. She wasn't a journalist, anyway.

'I've been asked to look for documents from a shipwreck on

the Lizard.' The yarn sounded threadbare. I really should have pinned it down better. Was there any way to get hold of Stewart again?

Sam, though, was used to unpromising starting points. 'All I've got is a circle of raised grass in the corner of a sloping field. It's down to me to work out the most promising place to dig – where they kept animals, where the kitchen might have been and so on.'

'And this is . . .?'

'Three thousand years ago, give or take.' Sam shrugged her shoulders; she was working to a longer time frame. 'There are no written records from those days, of course. That's what makes it so tantalising.'

'Mm. You're here all on your own?'

'This is Cornwall, Harry. It's a bit remote but it's not Syria. My supervisor said he'd look in next week. If I'm lucky, that is. He's a busy man.'

I decided I wasn't in that much of a hurry. I wanted to get back to Poldhu Cove but I didn't need to be there at first light. Female company was always welcome. 'Would you like to show me?'

It didn't take us long to reach the Settlement. We walked a quarter of a mile along the road, then a similar distance on a footpath over the fields.

The signs which we passed showed the path led to Scott's Quay. I decided I'd go for a look after I'd seen what I could of the Settlement.

We had to diverge from the path to reach the ancient circle

itself, it was on the far side of the field. Sam's hiking tent looked lonely. There were no other buildings nearby.

Now we were here Sam seemed slightly embarrassed at how little there really was to see.

I did my best; the Lizard stretched out beyond. 'The geography won't have changed that much over the centuries, Sam. Whoever lived here had a good view of the Helford River. Did they have canoes three thousand years ago? Is that how the occupants of the Settlement got here?'

Sam took up the thought. 'We don't know when they first had boats. Like I said, there are no written records. But it would be one reason for building here. You'd see your enemies coming anyway. And if there was a battle you'd be starting from the higher ground.'

After we'd tramped the site for twenty minutes Sam was happy to accompany me to Scott's Quay. It was only another half mile. 'I might as well start to know something about the surrounding features.'

All we could see was a small jetty standing in a long stretch of mud with water beyond. I consulted my map. 'That's a limb of the Helford River. It's tidal, of course. Right now it must be low tide.'

Out in the middle of the water a small sailing boat was moored. Then Sam spotted a rowing boat tucked in beside the jetty. The owner must have come ashore for some reason.

'Maybe it's a fisherman with his catch,' I suggested. 'The quay is a convenient drop-point.' I glanced over my map. 'I can't see many other quays on the Helford anyway.'

Sam looked animated. 'Hey, perhaps this was the Settlement's source of food? I need to see if I can dig up some hooks there, once I've located the kitchen. Then maybe see if I can classify them, deduce what fish they were eating.'

I didn't want to dampen her enthusiasm but it sounded horribly tedious. It had been good to meet Sam, and I hoped to see her again.

But her remarks sent me back to my document search with renewed enthusiasm.

Church Cove and beyond Jangye Ryn, known as "Dollar Cove"

CHAPTER 14

The cycle ride to Poldhu Cove was easier today. I surely wasn't any fitter? Then I remembered that this time I hadn't come via Helston. No wonder it was easier, it wasn't nearly as far.

What I had to do was to follow in the steps of Sir Arthur Conan Doyle. "The Adventure of the Devil's Foot" had been intriguing enough to make me want to track it further.

The notion of finding a Lizard vicar with a good grasp of local history, especially struggles with shipwrecks, was worth pursuing anyway. Even if the idea hadn't come from Conan Doyle.

Trouble was, the more I thought about it, the more daunting the whole task seemed. I was after a very small needle in a very large haystack.

I puffed up the track to the former Poldhu Hotel, dumped my bike and sat down for lunch on the grass beyond.

For a moment I thought of asking the Hotel if they knew which room Sir Arthur had slept in. Assuming they did, dare I ask for access for a few minutes, to study the view from his window?

After a second I decided this was way over the top. Explaining my aim to the latest guest would be a challenge, even if they didn't have dementia. Right now I had the same view as the crime-writer, every time he'd come out of the Hotel. What might have grabbed his attention?

Once I'd eaten my sandwiches, I retrieved my binoculars and studied the view in more detail. Yes, there was no doubt. There was a small, stone building with a separate tower, built into the cliffs of the cove next door. My map told me this was Church Cove. The cove itself was sandy – indeed there were a few winter tourists trying desperately to enjoy it in the wind – but I could just see the cove beyond; and that looked decidedly rocky.

What was that called? My map said "Jangye-ryn". I wondered where I might find someone able to tell me what that meant in English.

If there was a church and it hadn't been abandoned it must have a vicar – even if he had half a dozen other churches as well. The simplest way to find where that man lived would be to examine the church itself.

Lunch over, I cycled back down the track into Poldhu Cove and then up the other side. There was just one cottage by the roadside at the top: was that where Holmes and Watson had started their fictional adventure? It fitted with what Conan Doyle had written; and made me even more interested in the vicar of Church Cove.

I spotted a path which led down to the cove. At the bottom I was on the beach, with a church on the far side. I took care to avoid sand in the chain as I headed towards it. A few minutes later I was at the church gate.

The notice board covered several recent events and one still to come. The place was certainly in use.

I pushed open the gate and strode through a densely-packed graveyard. The church door was closed. I gave it a shove: mercifully, it wasn't locked. Then I saw a sign asking visitors to close the door when they left, to avoid the place being swamped by wind-swept sand. There was a practical reason to keep it closed, they weren't being unfriendly.

I stepped inside. For a church in the middle of nowhere the building was a fair size. No seats, just wooden pews, but it could probably hold 100. Hard to imagine that many today – except, perhaps, for a major wedding?

Briefly I was reminded of my own celebration, many years ago. That was an equally attractive country church, though not as near to the sea. I shook my head in regret: that line wouldn't get me anywhere today.

Slowly, absorbing the detail, I walked around. The building had two side aisles. I paced steadily down the far one and past the pulpit at the front. It was raised up four or five wooden steps so the preacher could look down on the congregation, no doubt to put them in their place. Then I walked past the altar table and back up the other side.

The place was several hundred years old, but still felt welcoming. Some well-used hymn books were piled near the doorway. At the back I saw colouring books for children. That was a good sign, if the congregation had to allow for youngsters. Finally I saw it: a welcoming book for visitors.

I opened it to add my own name and saw that the book had been well used. Plenty more had been here before me.

Who was the earliest? I turned to the front, saw it had been signed by a vicar in 2002. So the book didn't go back very far. Not as far as one of my shipwrecks, anyway.

Would that be the current vicar? I recalled they'd given a location. I turned to it again and noted an address in Gunwalloe. That was the next village along, no more than a mile away.

I had no appointment but it was worth a try. I came out of the church, closed the door behind me (to keep out the sand) and set off up the road.

I tried to structure a line of enquiry as I cycled along. Even with rehearsal it wasn't very coherent. I could only hope for a sympathetic hearing.

Gunwalloe turned out to be a linear village of stone buildings beyond the next headland. The vicarage looked Victorian and was set back from the road. I parked my bike inside the gate and strode up to the front door. I was slightly disconcerted to see a surf board propped beside it.

I heaved on the heavy-weight doorbell. After a few seconds I heard someone inside shout 'Just a minute.' A minute later the door opened to reveal a slender, chestnut-haired woman of around forty, wearing a bright pink wetsuit.

'Good afternoon,' I began. 'I'm after the vicar for the church down in the cove.'

She gave a grin. 'That's me: Joy. I'm just back from my lunchtime swim. Would you like to come in?'

To be honest, I'd been expecting someone male and twice her age. I did my best to reconfigure my thoughts as I followed her down to the kitchen.

But I didn't need to talk yet. She indicated various utensils. 'Would you mind making us both a pot of tea while I go and get changed?'

It took her ten minutes to reappear. I guessed she'd had a quick shower as well as changing into jeans and a jazzy Christmas sweater. I could see this wasn't a vicar who cared much about the dignity of appearance.

'We might as well stay here,' she said. 'This is the warmest room in the house. I'll pour the tea and then you can tell me how I could help you.'

I settled in a chair close to the table. 'My name is Harry. I'm a historian at Exeter University. I've been asked by an acquaintance to look for an old document he has reason to believe came from a shipwreck round here.'

Joy looked at me with a twinkle in her eyes. 'And for some reason you reckon I might have got it hidden away in the attic?'

'Well, I've studied the list of wrecks on the Lizard. There are plenty near Porthleven. But my friend thinks that anything that came ashore there would have been seized by the authorities.'

'But my little church, next to the shore, might have been a sanctuary? A foreigner who was swept ashore might have crept inside for shelter? Well, it's an idea. The building's been there since the fourteenth century. It's the only one on the Lizard that's so close to the sea.'

'I had a look around earlier on, you see. The place wasn't locked.'

'It never is, Harry. Of course, we make sure there's nothing valuable left lying around. Don't want to add to temptation. We have a beautiful altar piece, for example, that's securely locked away.'

I paused to drink my tea and collect my thoughts.

'The idea might be crazy,' I said. 'But what occurred to me was that if someone was found in there, washed ashore, it might well be the vicar that would take charge of any documents they carried. And in that case there might be something which they'd put in the cellar, say, or the loft . . .?'

Joy didn't respond immediately. 'It's not that crazy. We have several gravestones of shipwreck victims washed ashore here, so that part of your theory is supported by evidence. This place has been the Gunwalloe vicarage, I believe, since the early nineteenth century. Is that old enough?'

'I'm afraid the document I'm after is probably older.'

Joy wasn't daunted. 'Obviously there must have been somewhere else where the local vicar lived before that, probably nearer to the Cove. But if there was anything valuable in the old loft, I'm sure they'd have moved it in here.'

Joy paused for further thought and then continued. 'D'you know, I've never had a proper look in the loft. I've only lived here for a couple of years, mind, but there's enough to do outside the vicarage without bothering with relics inside.'

She paused again. 'I'm afraid I'm rather busy this afternoon, Harry. I've got a sermon to write. But I'm free tomorrow. You've intrigued me. If you wanted me to help you search for it, I'd be happy to let you up there.'

CHAPTER 15

Wednesday morning was cold and windy. No incentive for a picnic lunch today, thought George, as she made her sandwiches. Cornwall in early January. What did she expect?

She was getting into the swing of the place now, she mused, as she navigated the Goonhilly Security Gates and headed for her office. There was a growing list of topics to look into. The Newquay Space Station, if it ever happened, would stretch everyone.

During one of her trips around the site, chasing yet another report, she spotted Anna filing. 'Too cold for a picnic today?'

'There's an off duty area in one of the rear huts,' her colleague replied. 'Have you found it yet? We could eat together there if you like – perhaps go for a stroll afterwards. If it's not raining, that is.'

It sounded good. Half an hour off site would clear her mind. The two women met for lunch at half past twelve.

As they ate Anna was full of apprehension about her forthcoming play.

'Tonight's the dress rehearsal,' she reported, 'we'll be in Trelowarren for hours.'

'Don't worry, I'm looking forward to it,' George reassured her. 'I've got my tickets. Two in fact, I'm coming with a friend. I'm told the tickets are selling well.'

'Well, it's our only planned venue. So far, at least. People who know us are aware of that and they don't want to miss it.'

Out of the blue George had an idea. 'I was once involved in a drama sketching the history of the Slate Quarry at Delabole. That was performed in January too: outdoors, under the cliffs, behind the car park at Trebarwith Strand...'

Anna knew the coast of North Cornwall, could guess where she was talking about. She wrinkled her face and shivered. 'Brr. Makes our play inside Trelowarren Manor seem like pandering to wimps.'

But George hadn't finished. 'The thing is, Anna, they got me to film the whole thing with my video-camera. Afterwards the Director took away all my material, hired an editor and turned it into a DVD.'

Anna considered for a moment. 'What a good idea. I guess that would cater for people who couldn't make the date.'

'Not only that. Your drama group will hopefully have a long-term future. A DVD could help publicise future productions. For example, your Director could send a copy to the Minack Theatre at Porthcurno. They'd be interested in a local drama group, surely? You know their theatre: it looks down on the sea. It'd be a fantastic place to perform.'

George realised that she was sounding far more proactive than she'd intended. What on earth was she doing?

'I'm sorry, Anna. It's only a thought. I'm not short of things to do on the Lizard. I'm not pushing to get involved, honestly.'

She noticed they'd both finished their lunch packs. 'Hey, it's still fine out there. What about that stroll you promised me?'

Once more they walked out of the gate and along to the Nature Reserve.

'There are paths round the back here,' said Anna. 'They go round outside the latest perimeter fence. Why don't we go and explore?'

It was like an industrial museum, thought George. There were plenty of footpaths through the heath land, besides the one next to the high-wire fence. In between the paths were bushes and trees. And other relics.

'Whatever's that?' asked George, pointing to a grass-covered mound about fifteen feet high.

Anna frowned, trying to recall the information board in the car park. 'I think it's an old service reservoir. Remember, this site was some sort of RAF depot during World War Two.'

Various brick huts were hidden between the bushes, some with even narrower paths going around them. George was intrigued. She led them round one or two, then they came to something more substantial: a hut with a rusty metal handrail around the top.

'I've no idea what this is,' said Anna.

The women forced their way round two sides. On the third, to their surprise, they found metal steps leading up to the roof.

'Can we try going up, Anna? I like mysteries.'

Carefully they climbed up and found themselves on a flat roof, thirty feet square. In one direction were miles of heath. In the other was a good view of Goonhilly Earth Station. George noticed illustrated boards attached to the railings on the other side.

She examined the boards carefully. 'Hey, look, Anna. This was where they developed a special form of radar during the war.'

Anna joined her. 'So this wasn't just a storage hut.'

George glanced downwards. 'Hey, d'you reckon any of the development work took place below us?'

'I doubt it. They'd need mains electricity to power their tools and measuring devices – and lighting. They couldn't just rely on candles. There won't be any link now.'

'Are you sure, Anna? They haven't bothered to get rid of these old huts. The power link might still be there as well.'

Anna shrugged. 'This hut must have an entrance somewhere.' She turned back to the steps and clambered down.

They had further battle with the bushes. After a while they found a passage leading to a doorway on the fourth side. But they were thwarted. It was firmly locked.

Anna tried giving it a good shove but it held firm. There was no way they were going to get inside.

'It's locked anyway. We'd better be getting back to the Station.' They turned and started to head back.

As they reached the Nature Reserve, a reflective George was looking puzzled. 'There's one thing that's odd about this.'

'What's that, George?'

'Everything else about that hut is, what, seventy years old. But that padlock was brand new. Whoever would do that? And why on earth would they bother?'

CHAPTER 16

In Helston Police Station Frances Cober was feeling frustrated. She'd spent Wednesday morning catching up on routine police work which had fallen behind, but her mind was on the mystery swimmers.

Any response to the media publicity about "Ms Loe", as she'd dubbed the dead girl from the Loe, would come to a call centre in Truro. There professional call-handlers would cross-examine callers and note details, pass them on to Helston if they seemed genuine. Nothing so far, but it was early days.

Constable Barwell had cycled the six mile path round Loe Pool that morning without noticing anything suspicious – no pile of women's clothing or abandoned bicycles, anyway.

He'd now contacted the owners of every car he'd found parked at night around the Pool. A few had been belligerent – one muttered something about a police state – but in every case he had talked, in the end, to a live human being. The constable was now working through all the owners of boats registered for use on the Pool.

Ms Loe's identity was proving really hard to find. Frances was ever more convinced that this wasn't simply a swim that had gone wrong.

By mid-afternoon she'd had enough of reading reports, needed to do something. She had contacted the supermarkets around Helston. There were several, but only Sainsbury's and Tesco had admitted to stocking swimwear.

This was one line of enquiry, Frances felt, that was probably best done by a woman. It might go nowhere but even that would be a form of progress. She seized the evidence bag containing Ms Loe's swimsuit and headed for the door.

There was no longer any need to hide the origin of the swimsuit. The death of Ms Loe had made it to local radio that morning and had caused quite a stir.

The manager of Sainsbury's knew of the case anyway.

'I can't personally identify every item we sell,' he admitted, 'but I know who's in charge of our women's clothing. Let me call her.'

A few minutes later they were joined by Yvette. Frances produced the plastic bag containing the swimsuit and explained to her and her manager the situation in which it had appeared.

Yvette took the bag and examined it carefully through the plastic. 'I'm sorry,' she said, 'we do sell swimsuits like these in early summer but we haven't sold any for months.'

The manager added that the store did use closed-circuit television to cover transactions at the tills. 'But we only hold onto data for a week. There's no way we could show you images of purchasers that far back.'

Half an hour later Frances was going through the same steps at Tesco. Much the same conversation ensued.

This time, though, there was more hope. The Tesco manager had summoned his female clothing manager, Polly. She had been more positive about the swimsuit Frances had brought in.

'I reckon this is one of ours. It's our basic range, no frills. If you wait a minute I'll fetch a matching item from our rack downstairs and we can compare.'

Polly reappeared five minutes later with three black swimsuits over her arm.

'This is all we've got left, ma'm. Two large and one small. The medium ones are the most popular, you see, they always run out first. Right, let's see if these are the same.'

Some space was cleared. Then she laid the costumes on the manager's desk, with Ms Loe's swimsuit in the middle. They all studied them carefully.

'They're the same make, I reckon,' said Frances.

'The one you've brought in is another in the small size,' observed Polly. The manager hastened to agree, although Frances feared he was simply trying to be helpful. Polly, though, sounded confident.

A pause as Frances, hiding her excitement, mused on the next question. She turned to the manager.

'Is it possible for your financial guys to track when the last of these – just the small size, obviously – was sold?'

He frowned. 'Should be. If it happened in the last week or two, anyway.'

'How quickly could it be done?'

'Right way, I should think.' He stepped over to his phone and made another call. A few minutes later a man in his early thirties appeared. 'I'm Hamil,' he said; he looked mustard keen.

Frances took the lead. 'Hamil, I'm trying to identify a swimmer found dead recently in the Loe Pool. It's possible the girl's swimming costume was bought in this store. Your staff have found this, it's a matching item. I'd like to know, please, when the last ones were sold.'

Hamil saw the problem immediately. 'We keep a copy of the last two weeks' data here in the store, ma'm, to settle arguments about what was paid, etc. I can look there right away. To go any further back we'd need to contact Regional headquarters. I'm afraid that'd take a lot longer.'

'The last fortnight would be a start, anyway. Right away, you said?'

A dead body of unknown identity was a serious problem; the manager could understand Frances' urgency. He turned to the financial guru. 'This is top priority, Hamil. If we can help the police, that's really positive. How long might you need?'

'I'll come with you if you like,' said Frances. She'd try anything that would maintain the pressure.

Hamil seemed happy enough to be accompanied, it was an unexpected chance to shine. He took a note of the black swimsuit stock number from Polly. Then he and Frances set off to the finance office, located behind the main store.

Frances was always glad to see more of life behind the scenes in Helston. What did financial controllers really do? She took a chair and sat back to watch him at work.

'This computer,' Hamil explained, 'takes data directly from

our tills. Then puts everything into a database we can use for our analysis.'

He leaned forward and started hammering the keys.

Ten minutes later he sat back with a smile. 'We've made a couple of sales, anyway. Just over a week ago: both at the same time, in fact. Is that what you expected?'

CHAPTER 17

Sadly there was no Sam to enliven my breakfast on Wednesday morning. Clearly a regular meal at Trengilly Wartha was beyond her means. Mind, I didn't feel too sorry for her. By now she would have plenty of supplies from Constantine.

But as I supped my second coffee there was a phone call from Sally, the Departmental Secretary in Exeter. She was obviously already at work.

'Morning, Harry. Hope I'm not disrupting your research?'

'That's alright, Sally, I've not started yet. What's the problem?'

'Well, I've just had an unusual phone call. I wanted to check it.'

I was puzzled. 'Go on.'

'Do you happen to know a woman by the name of Joy Tregorran? She claims to be a vicar down on the Lizard, some place called Gunwalloe. She wanted to know if we had any Harrys based in the Department. You're the only one I could think of.'

Now it clicked. The vicar I'd met yesterday was checking me out before letting me loose in her attic. What a sensible woman.

'Yes, that's alright, Sally. Joy and I met yesterday. I'm due to see her again this afternoon. She said she'd help me with some enquiries. If you could ring her back and reassure her I'm genuine, that'd be really helpful. It is research I'm doing, honestly.'

101

Sally sounded slightly unconvinced as she rang off. Of course, she knew more about my personal background than anyone else in the Department. No doubt she'd make me explain more when I got back.

I had spent the previous evening working through various lists of shipwrecks around Church Cove that I'd found on the internet. I needed to be as informed as possible when I saw Joy.

I'd also found more details on Jangye-ryn, the rocky cove around the headland from the sandy bay where I'd found Joy's church.

The place was also known as "Dollar Cove". That was because a Spanish treasure ship had been wrecked here "in the seventeenth century". Reading on, I learned that "silver coins had occasionally been found nearby".

This might be of interest to Stewart. The timing was right, anyway. Though if he wanted someone to help him find more coins, I reckoned he'd need to hire a metal detector, not a historian.

Thinking of Stewart reminded me I was working to a tight deadline. I had less than a fortnight to make any headway. I decided that I might as well do a really good job on researching Dollar Cove, now it had come to my attention.

One clue that Joy had mentioned yesterday that I'd not previously thought of was the graves around the church. I recalled there were plenty of those. It might take all morning to sift through them. On the other hand I was familiar with old English lettering, so I was sure I'd do a better job on this than Stewart – if he'd tried at all.

Once more I cycled up over central Lizard and down to Church Cove. The intermittent gusts made it hard work. This time I went via Gunwalloe, though there was no sign of Joy as I went past the vicarage.

I paused to look over Dollar Cove. There was a strong wind today and the sea was really rough. There were plenty of jagged rocks sticking up out in the bay, with wave after wave crashing against them. It was only too easy to imagine a sailing boat coming to grief here.

When I got to the church I saw even more graves than I'd remembered. I'd hoped there might be some logic to the layout, say with the older ones lying nearest to the church, but inevitably that hadn't happened. There was no pattern at all.

I could see no alternative but to conduct a complete trawl. I drew myself a plan of the churchyard, dividing it into sections using the various paths. After that I started examining the tombstones in each part, one by one.

The most melancholy ones were linked to recent deaths. Especially a few laid over youngsters who, the dates on the stone implied, had died in their teens or early twenties. I could only guess these had been local accidents linked to swimming. Fresh evidence that the sea round here could be ferocious.

I assumed – hoped – that Joy wouldn't be going for her swim today. Even with the limited protection of her wetsuit.

Plenty more stones belonged to couples with a desire to be buried side by side. Sometimes these family groups covered several generations. There might not be so many around now but there'd been plenty in the past. One or two family resting places stretched back over decades.

Then I found something that might be more relevant. A simple stone, hard to read and not very large. There was no name at all; maybe it was unknown at the time of burial? After a second I realised that was actually promising: it might mean it was a body that had been washed ashore.

The burial date itself was just about legible: April 20th, 1684. Maybe, later, I could pin this down to a particular wreck?

I continued my search for another hour but didn't find anything else that old. By now it was late morning and I was hungry. I decided I'd retreat into the church for my picnic lunch. Unorthodox, but it was too windy to sit outside.

There was no-one else in there. I took a pew near the back and made sure I didn't leave too many crumbs. As I munched I pondered. This place must have looked more or less the same for centuries. Was there really nowhere here that something like a document could be hidden?

After my lunch I had another wander round the church. As I passed the pulpit it occurred to me, how long had this been here? It was really old, might even be the original. In particular, I wondered, how accessible was the space beneath?

The pulpit was solidly built with seasoned oak. I couldn't see how a weakened wreck survivor, with a valuable document to hide but no tools, could possibly break it open.

I was still on my own. Some instinct told me this might be important. In desperation, seeking inspiration, I mounted the pulpit steps. This was the view that Joy would have of her congregation and they of her. She was a very attractive woman and crisply spoken. I couldn't imagine she'd have any difficulty in holding their attention.

It was as I came down the steps that I noticed a subtle difference in sound on the lowest step. I turned back for a closer look. Then I saw why: unlike all the steps above, this one wasn't properly screwed in, it was slightly loose. I gave it a heave and to my surprise it slid out. Behind was an inky black hollow.

I gave a whoop of joy. I had my torch with me – after all, I was going to explore a loft later. I pulled it out and shone a beam into the gloom.

In fine detail I examined every single corner beneath that pulpit but without success. There was nothing in there at all.

I sat back to reflect. This wasn't a failure, I told myself. I now had a mechanism by which a document could have been brought ashore and hidden – perhaps for centuries – in this remote church. Maybe I'd find more at the vicarage after all?

Joy wasn't in her wet suit this time when she came to the vicarage door. She wasn't wearing her best Christmas jumper either. But she did look like she was dressed for an expedition into a dirty loft.

She must have noticed me inspecting her and glanced down with a smile.

'My oldest respectable jeans, Harry. The oldest with no holes in the backside, anyway. Would you like some tea before we start?'

That was fine by me. I was in no hurry and enjoying Joy's

company. Plus I wanted to tell her about my finds in Church Cove.

We sat down once more in the slightly warm kitchen and Joy made us a pot of tea.

'I hope you won't mind,' she said, as she started to pour. 'I always urge my congregation to take care when dealing with strangers, so I rang up Exeter University to check you were who you'd said.'

'Very sensible,' I replied, 'Sally told me you'd rung.'

I took a sip of my tea. 'I might have made some progress on my search,' I reported. 'I've been hunting round your churchyard this morning. I found one gravestone dated 1684. No name on it, so that might have been an unknown sailor who was washed ashore. I'll do more work when I get back to my Inn, see if I can find a wreck that matches.'

I went on to tell her about the cavity I'd found beneath the pulpit.

'That pulpit's been there for a long time,' she commented. 'It could easily be three hundred years old or more. It creaks when I stride about. I sometimes wonder when I stand there how long it will last.'

'D'you preach there every week?'

'I have a couple more churches to look after but they have their main services in the evening. So I am at Church Cove most Sunday mornings. You'd be welcome to join us.'

I wasn't opposed to church but I didn't go very often. Her warm smile was very inviting. 'Maybe I could try this Sunday,' I mumbled. 'I'm only down here for a couple of weeks.'

The moment passed. Was it a move in our relationship? I had no idea. We finished our tea and Joy suggested we should head for the attic.

As we walked upstairs I saw what she meant about the kitchen being the warmest room in the house. There wasn't much competition; the rest of the place was absolutely freezing. I was glad I was wearing two sweaters under my fleece. Joy didn't look as warmly covered but I presumed she had acclimatised to the cold.

'To be honest, I've never been up there,' she said. 'I didn't fancy going up on my own.'

'I'll go first if you like,' I replied. I used my torch to spot the hatch on the landing ceiling. 'Right. Have you a chair I can stand on?'

Joy disappeared and came back a moment later with a solid looking chair. I placed it under the hatch, climbed onto it and gave a heave.

The hatch was stubborn but I'm fairly strong. It lifted slightly. A moment later I managed to slide it sideways and was able to peer into the loft beyond. But I could see nothing: it was pitch dark.

'I don't suppose there's a light up there?'

'There's a switch over here that I never use.' Joy reached round me and flicked it. Suddenly there was a feeble light in the attic. Someone had been there before, I could see an aluminium loft ladder straight ahead.

'Right. Stand clear, Joy.' I seized the end of the ladder and gave a pull. I thought it might have been seized up by years of neglect but it was still working. Slowly, inch by inch, I eased it through the hatch. Finally I released a catch to let down the lower rungs and the ladder stood on the landing carpet. I gave a tiny sigh of satisfaction.

'Look, Joy, I'm more warmly dressed than you. It's going to be really cold up there. Why don't I go up on my own? You can hold the ladder and act as my safe-guarder.'

'I go swimming in the sea nearly every day, Harry. Even in the depths of winter. I'm used to the cold. You go first and I'll follow.'

The woman certainly had guts. In any case it was too cold to argue. The sooner we got up there the sooner we'd be back to the warmth of the kitchen. I seized my torch and started slowly up the ladder.

Church and pulpit at Church Cove

CHAPTER 18

An hour later, Joy and I were back in the vicarage kitchen. No doubt the temperature was actually much the same as it had been before, but after the bitter cold in the loft it felt pleasantly welcoming.

A modern-day loft would have large sheets of chipboard laid across the beams to make it safe to walk across. There was nothing like that up there, and nothing to hang on to either. We both had to be extremely careful not to put a foot between the beams.

'It's only plasterboard below,' I warned. 'It wouldn't take our weight. And if you fell right through there's no guarantee where you'd land. It might be a nice soft bed – or it might be the hard edge of a chair.'

I wasn't sure if this advice was needed – was this something they covered on a course for vicars? – but I didn't want her to get hurt. Joy was a robust woman, used to living on her own, but she wouldn't thank me if she ended up with a broken leg.

Shining my torch, I saw a layer of insulating fibreglass between the beams, a valiant but doomed attempt by someone in the past to retain a fraction of the heat from the vicarage below.

'I don't want to be critical, Joy, but this lot needs replacing,' I commented. 'You need to get your churchwardens onto this. These days there are grants for this sort of thing. Fibreglass should be six inches deep, not six centimetres. There's no need to do it all yourself, there are contractors to help you. No wonder the rooms are so cold.'

We weren't moving around quickly so I was feeling colder than ever. I didn't say any more though I felt sorry for Joy. But she was a determined woman who wasn't going to give up easily.

It was a big loft but we searched every corner. Halfway round we came across a few cardboard cartons that raised our hopes but they were mostly empty. One contained a collection of hymn books. On close inspection, though, it turned out they had been published in 1870.

'We certainly don't need these,' said Joy decisively. I was glad to see she was a modern woman, not in thrall to the past.

It was in the far corner that we found a few wooden planks, lain across the beams. As far as I could tell, these had been left behind after some long-ago repair to the roof above. They weren't recent, anyway.

Then, behind the planks, Joy spotted a small casket, about the size of one of those boxes you'd use to hold half a dozen bottles of wine. Whatever was inside was not heavy but when I shuffled it I could hear a rattling. There was something.

It was our last hope. I shone my torch round the loft one more time but could see nothing else that could possibly help us.

'Let's take this back down to the warmth and see what we've got,' I urged.

Between us, moving one at a time and balancing the casket on one beam after another, we bumped our find over towards the hatch.

'Right, Joy,' I said. 'This is the awkward part. I'll go first. Could you pass it to me once I get halfway down the ladder?'

It was harder to reach the ladder from here than it had been to climb up it, but eventually I swivelled myself to stand on it.

I climbed down steadily until my head was level with the hatch, and then asked Joy for the casket. Slowly, carefully, she handed it over.

This was the hardest part. Cradling the casket with one hand and the top rung with the other, I stepped down, one foot at a time. I'd positioned the ladder more steeply than its designer had ever intended but it was too late to do anything about that now.

Step by step I descended. Finally I reached the landing floor. I turned away and rested the casket on the carpet, then called up to my companion.

'It's OK, Joy. I'm down now. Can you follow?'

I stood beneath the hatch to hold the ladder firm. Joy's trainers emerged first and then her lower body. Those jeans had certainly seen better days. She was on the ladder now, it should have been fine. Well, I'm sure it would have been if her hands weren't frozen after that hour in the loft.

With the result that, as she got the rest of her body onto the ladder, she lost her grip and came hurtling down towards me.

It was a mercy that I was positioned where I was. I clutched her as she came towards me and we both fell over, Joy on top and me underneath. I was glad of the natural padding of her bosom.

There was a moment of silence. I could tell she wasn't injured when she started to giggle. That made me laugh too, it was going to be alright.

A moment later we were both shedding tears of relief as we unwound ourselves from one another. We laughed and laughed.

Then I seized the casket which had caused us so much trouble and we headed downstairs towards the kitchen.

The first step was to fill the kettle to make us more tea. We were in urgent need of warmth: Joy looked absolutely frozen.

'Could I give you a hug?' I asked. 'Just to get you warm, I mean.'

She looked at me, smiled and nodded. The hug seemed to last some time. I don't have that much experience of vicars but she was the cuddliest one I'd ever held. Some warmth transferred, anyway. After a moment Joy asked me to let go so she could make the tea.

'Right,' I said, a few minutes later. We'd each had a mug of tea and were starting to feel warmer. 'Shall we see what we've found?'

Eying it more carefully, the casket was covered in what looked like tar.

'Maybe that was intended to keep it waterproof?' I mused. Supporting evidence, perhaps, that it had once been on board a ship. But it was waterproof no more. The top had already been opened.

Joy reached into a cupboard and found me a chisel in her toolbox. It was a fierce-looking tool for a woman of the cloth. Then, with Joy holding the casket bottom, I inserted the chisel into the groove near the top and gave a strenuous heave. Nothing happened, but with two more shoves the lid was prised wide open.

'This is more your treasure than mine,' I said. 'Would you like to look inside?'

Joy was as keen as I was to know the contents. Quickly she seized some old newspaper from beside the Agar and spread it across the table. Then she emptied the casket out onto it.

The result was, to say the least, disappointing. A huge number of desiccated, dark lumps, each a few centimetres across, fell out. Joy gave the box a thump and a vigorous shake but nothing else came.

I couldn't believe it. I grabbed the casket from Joy and peered inside. Was there anything stuck to the bottom? I even used my torch for a detailed search but I could see there was nothing at all.

All that encouragement, all that effort, and we had almost nothing to show for it. It was enough to make a man weep.

Half an hour later I was seated in a corner of the Halzaphron Inn, half a mile further down Gunwalloe. Like I said, it was a linear village.

There had been just one bounty from my afternoon's efforts. For as I'd left the vicarage I'd made Joy an offer: in response to all her help, could I at least take her for a meal one day? It would be a modest token of thanks.

She was a busy woman and I'd expected a polite refusal but instead she had directed me towards the Inn. 'I've various other things I have to do this afternoon, Harry, starting with a hot shower and a complete change of clothes. But if you really insist I'd love to join you for an early supper – say half past six?'

It turned out the Inn was a long-standing hostelry, open for drinks all day and offering its customers free access to the internet. The table I'd secured was close to a cosy log fire and for the first time that afternoon I was warm. I'd ordered a cafetière of filter coffee and used the intervening time for research on Lizard wrecks around 1684.

I'd expected to be drawn back to the Spanish vessel I'd read about earlier, with its cargo of silver coins. Instead the date forced me to consider the Schiedam, a Dutch trading vessel hired by the British Navy to make a journey from Tangiers.

It too had come to grief in Jangye Ryn ("Dollar Cove"), next door to Church Cove, in April 1684. There was no trace of the boat to be seen today and it was said there had been no survivors.

Once you have a theme to focus your research, the internet is a great resource. I was helped too that 1684 fell within the period covered by my PhD, so I knew much of the background.

I was quickly reminded that King Charles the Second had acquired this corner of Morocco as a dowry when he had married Princess Catherine of Braganza from Portugal in the 1650s. But it was a fragile inheritance and it was clear the Moors didn't much like it. The King had decided to abandon it completely in 1684. The Schiedam was the first of several vessels that had been chartered to bring the valuables of the Royal Court back to Britain.

I was still deep in the detail when Joy arrived. She'd certainly done me proud. It was the first time I'd seen her not in either wetsuit or jeans. Once she'd slipped off her cagoule and fleece I saw a long purple skirt and a sparkling cream sweater. She had no obvious makeup but she was wearing a discreet gold necklace. In short she looked gorgeous.

In contrast I was still in the same clothes I'd chosen that morning to explore her loft. I glanced down at my walking sweater and cords and felt bad. 'I'm sorry, Joy, I can look smarter, but I didn't bring any of it with me.'

She gave a disarming smile. 'Harry, it's you I've come to be with and your fresh view of the world. I'm not that bothered about what you're wearing. Right, what would you like to drink?'

That was how the evening started and it went like a dream. I hadn't enjoyed a meal so much for ages. I didn't say anything about my latest findings and we gave no thought to the loft. By silent agreement all that was ignored for the time being. Instead we each shared something of ourselves.

Joy, I learned, had once been a full-time science teacher at Penzance Comprehensive. She'd felt a call to full-time ministry when she was about thirty and retrained at Exeter. Gunwalloe and the surrounding two churches was the first parish where she was the vicar. Among her passions was a desire to help people link their personal faith to the scientific world beyond.

I inferred from various asides that she was single. 'Though that's not a vocation, Harry, it's just I've never met anyone that I really clicked with.' Her parents were still thriving; she saw them regularly on her days off. She had two brothers, both of whom worked on their parents' farm. She also had several young nephews and nieces.

'That's why your church is so child-friendly,' I remarked. I told her about the children's books I'd seen at the back of the church in the Cove. She seemed encouraged, pleased that I'd noticed.

In turn I sketched out my career, in and out of academia. 'So what were you doing when you weren't in University?' she asked. I recalled that this was the issue Stewart had tried to probe without success. With Joy, though, I felt no need to hold back. I told her about my life in the UK and my time in North Africa. Of course I didn't go into too much detail.

Two hours went by in a flash. All of a sudden we'd finished our coffees and our meal was over. As I went to the bar to ask for the bill it hit me: unless I could think of something there was no good reason why I should ever see Joy again.

That was when I saw a bundle of notices lying on the counter. They announced a forthcoming play, put on by an amateur drama group from Constantine. It was based on some book or other by Agatha Christie and was scheduled for later this week – tomorrow evening, in fact. The performance would be not that far away. It was in the middle of the Lizard at the historic mansion of Trelowarren.

After I'd paid I took a copy of the notice to show Joy.

'What's all this?' She read it slowly and her face lit up.

'Hey, Harry. I have Thursday as my day off. That means I'll be free tomorrow evening. Should we go?'

CHAPTER 19

George hadn't been able to see Dr Jim Harvey on Wednesday to ask him about the new lock on the radar-development hut. But she'd booked a short meeting with him for Thursday morning.

'Anna and I went for a quick stroll after lunch,' she explained. Then she told him about their accidental find at the radar hut. 'It might be perfectly innocent but I wanted to make sure you'd been informed.'

George stopped talking. What would he say? How concerned was the man about security at Goonhilly?

There was a pause as Dr Harvey pondered.

'Thank you very much for telling me, Mrs Gilbert. I must say I'm rather surprised. I've given no instructions to anyone in my security team that would cause a new lock to be fitted. So what might it mean?'

He stopped. Was he expecting her to provide the answer? George assumed not, she simply had to wait for him to continue.

'Goonhilly no longer has any say over these huts. They're beyond our security fence. So I suppose it's just about possible that a local – say, someone from that Nature Reserve – has seen the chance to claim cheap shelter for their equipment. The new lock might be completely harmless.'

George was about to respond when he continued.

'More worrying, though, it might have been claimed by someone who wishes Goonhilly harm.'

George furrowed her brow. 'Harm? In what way?'

'There are three types of harm that concern me. First of all, someone might decide to sabotage our signalling equipment, or threaten to do so. That's never happened but it would be easy enough to do.'

George suddenly remembered. Just before Christmas there had been massive disruption to passengers from a drone seen – or at least reported – over Gatwick airport. 'You're not thinking of drones?'

Harvey sighed. 'I wasn't till three weeks ago but it seems that would be one way. There's supposed to be gear in all commercial drones to stop them flying near sites like Gatwick – or Goonhilly. But it's obvious now that the kit can be removed.'

'Are there other means of signal sabotage?'

'Well, before Gatwick, if I wanted to cause trouble, I'd have used a model aircraft to drop strips of foil over our satellite dishes. The dishes are sensitive, you see, signals would be easy to disrupt. By the way, that's a lot easier to do near to the site than by interference further away.'

There was silence. 'You said you had three types of concern,' prompted George. 'So what are the others?'

'Ah yes. The second is someone breaking into our work here. A lot of stuff is confidential, of course. Guaranteed secrecy is vital to our brand. If one of our projects was ever broken into, that could be very damaging to the morale of all the rest.'

George was sceptical. 'But you've a high security fence with cameras on the top?'

'No, no. That part's been taken care of. I was thinking of electronic interception.'

George mused for a moment. 'But internet cables can be intercepted anywhere?'

'That's true. Eavesdropping from a listening gadget would be less lethal. On the other hand the risk would be easy to exaggerate.'

George considered. 'You mean reputational damage is also a problem?'

'Certainly. But there's also a third risk. We're a remote site, miles from anywhere. If someone really wanted to damage us and had the resources to hand, I'm sure they could wipe us out. There was a massive fire on the heath near here in 1976. A repeat of that could be far worse than just reputational damage.'

'Wow.' George started to see what made Dr Harvey so gloomy. He had plenty to worry about. 'Handling security is a really big job.'

'Being remote cuts both ways, of course, Mrs Gilbert. It gives us a lower profile, makes us a less tempting target.'

Harvey gave a sigh then continued. 'To be honest, that's one thing that worries me about Newquay Space Station. Bracketing it with Goonhilly is high publicity. Our Chief Executive is dead keen, of course, but I'm not sure if we can handle it.'

Dr Harvey was talking very frankly. It occurred to George that he might not have many colleagues here that he could talk with so easily.

Whatever was used would need to be brought down here. She made a mental note to ask Frances about local smuggling opportunities and their impact on the police. She'd be seeing her when they met for supper that evening, before the play in Trelowarren.

CHAPTER 20

On Thursday morning I woke and headed down for my luxury Tregilly Wartha full English breakfast with a rare feeling of excitement.

It wasn't as though my search was over and I'd found the missing document. If I'd ever been on the right track, it had gone forever. What was different was that oddly, out of the blue, I seemed to have found a friend. That was a delight; serendipity in motion.

I thought back. After our meal I had walked Joy back to the vicarage, pushing my bike beside me.

We had stopped to say goodnight outside the gate. 'Thank you very much,' she said. 'I'll be OK from here. I look forward to seeing you at Trelowarren, tomorrow evening.'

It was a long way back to my out-of-the-way Inn in the dark but for some reason it involved little effort. Or maybe my mind was elsewhere.

I reviewed my options as I munched my toast. Through the window I could see the weather was windy but fine. I had the day ahead of me.

One possibility was to cycle down to visit other coastal vicars across the Lizard. Maybe something similar had happened in their church as had happened in Church Cove? Certainly any one of them, near to Mullion or Lizard Point, could have seen a shipwreck. It was plausible that a vicar had asserted his authority, hiding away a washed-ashore document. After all, there was no police force to look after missing property in historic times. Not, at least, till the nineteenth century.

But I was more drawn to delving deeper into the history of the Schiedam. I was pretty certain that someone had been washed ashore in Dollar Cove, clasping a watertight casket that held something of value. I was a historian: surely I was as well-equipped as anyone to work out what that might have been?

Also the further question: why ever was it so important to Stewart?

After breakfast I retreated to my room and grabbed my tablet. Then I set myself to unravel the context in which the Schiedam had sailed. Was there anything in that which could add value to a document which one of its passengers might have carried?

I started delving into the history of the British Colony in Tangiers. It had only lasted for thirty years so didn't make the usual English history. Hardly anyone had ever heard of it. Even a professional historian like myself had forgotten it took place. So was there anything strategic that had happened in that short period of time that might still be relevant today?

For a while I browsed from one account to another. Then I came across a name I knew well. Dr Samuel Pepys, the hero of my own PhD, had spent several months in Tangiers during the 1680s. I was surprised: surely he would be too old? I found his life in Wikipedia and checked: no, he was born in 1633, he'd only be fifty. I kicked myself, I was writing him off too early. He wouldn't die for another twenty years.

I read that Pepys had been sent there as Secretary of the Navy, in charge of dismantling the Tangiers English settlement.

My phone rang. I scowled: who was this? The University knew I was away from Exeter doing funded research. It wouldn't be them. And I had no close family likely to bother me.

I decided to ignore it. A moment later it rang again. Whoever was trying was very persistent. Reluctantly, eyes still on the screen, I picked it up.

'Dr Harry Jennings here. Can I help you?'

My heart jumped as a silvery female laugh came down the airwaves. 'Harry. It's Joy, Joy Tregorran. Have you got a moment?'

I was tempted to say she could have as much of me as she wanted for as long as she liked, but I managed to resist. I had to stay calm.

'Joy. How nice to hear from you. I'm sitting at my desk doing some background research on the stuff we found yesterday. But I can easily stop for a few moments. So what gives?'

'Well, as you know, today is my day off so I can do what I like with a clear conscience. Nothing much happens in the depths of winter, anyway. I decided that I too would do some research on the casket.'

'Two heads are better than one, Joy. Does this phone call mean you've found something?'

'I might have. I've got some ideas, anyway. First of all I rang my old school in Penzance and talked to the Head of Chemistry.

He's still there and remembers me. He's agreed that if I can get the contents of the casket over to him, he'll turn it into a project for his sixth formers. See if they can analyse those black lumps, identify what they are. He sounded rather intrigued.'

'That'd be great. Is there any chance you can take it today?'

'I'm off there as soon as I've finished this phone call.'

'Wonderful.'

'The other thing, Harry, is that I've talked to the Bishop.'

'Sounds ominous,' I muttered.

'I decided he was the best person to ask: what happens to the contents of a vicarage when the place is closed or moved elsewhere? It turns out that it's quite an important question for the Church of England.'

'Ah. Is there some legal obligation to hang on to the contents?'

'It's something like that. I didn't understand all the details. Anyway, I told him a little about the search in my loft – I didn't mention your name, by the way. I said I'd found a casket but it had already been opened.'

'It's good you didn't mention my name, Joy. Well done. Did the Bishop offer any reaction to the fact that the casket had been opened?'

Joy paused. 'Well, it was slightly odd. I told him about the tar round the casket, you see. He suggested that might be some sort of waterproofing. Then he wondered if that meant it might have contained some missing document or other.'

It sounded like the Bishop's mind was running on much the same line as ours. 'Yes?'

'He told me that there's an old chapel on the Lizard where any such documents found here are stored. It's possible, he said, that was why the casket lid had been opened and the items had been taken.'

I mused. 'Right. They might not be lost after all. So the crucial thing is, did he tell you where you might find this chapel?'

'He did. And guess what, Harry, it's the chapel that adjoins Trelowarren Manor. So I gave them a ring. The place is not usually open to visitors but as a local vicar they'd be happy to let me in. With a colleague, of course. So would you like us to go there this afternoon?'

CHAPTER 21

It was the evening of "Then There Were None" at Trelowarren.

George was looking forward to talking to Frances about smuggling beforehand, as her friend came for supper ahead of the play. But when she arrived, Frances, too, had news to impart.

'You were right about supermarkets, George,' she began. 'Tesco's does stock basic swimwear, even in winter. They sold their last black swimsuit – one matching the one worn by the Loe girl – just last week.'

George had just taken the beef bourguignon out of the oven. 'We've only got an hour, Frances. We'd better eat as we talk. Right, tell me more.'

Frances outlined her search. 'So not just one but two swimsuits were bought, at the same time, late on Tuesday evening.'

'So you've got the name of the purchaser? Or a CCTV picture?'

Frances grimaced. 'That's the disappointing bit. The finance department found the transaction record all right. But the customer had paid in cash, so they've no idea who it was.'

'But Tesco's would have an image?'

'Oh yes. They overwrite their records every two weeks but they still had the data from last week. There was no trouble about giving me a copy. I've been running it at the Station.'

'And?'

'I'm convinced it's a man. You'd hope he would have a limp or something, but of course he doesn't – not even spectacles. As far as I can judge he's white, medium build and medium height, and wearing a bobble hat and thick scarf. Not that surprising, I suppose, in the depth of winter. Trouble is, it means you can hardly see his face at all.'

George tucked into the casserole as she pondered.

'It's evidence, surely, that the two cases are connected? A man buying one woman's swimsuit late at night would be slightly odd. Buying two at the same time is downright peculiar. Have you told your boss?'

'He's elusive, George. There's going to be a massive demonstration, either for or against Brexit, or maybe both, this Saturday in Truro. They are expecting thousands to march all round the town and end up in the Market Square. Television cameras will be there. I'm one of many officers drafted in from West Cornwall. My boss doesn't want it all to go wrong.'

George had tried to keep away from the Brexit debate but it was getting harder to ignore.

'Poor chap, he's got my sympathy. But can't you make a few more discreet enquiries while his attention is elsewhere? Give our girl from Coverack more attention, for example.'

Frances pulled a face. 'That would be nice. We've no trace on her at all. What have I missed?'

'Last Saturday we had no strong reason to worry about her. Now there's a possible link to a murder enquiry. Isn't there anything?'

For a few moments there was a baffled silence.

By now the women had finished their main course. 'Let's round off with lemon cheesecake,' suggested George. She got it from the fridge.

'Putting it all together, Frances, it seems to me that this set of crimes is anchored on the Lizard. Ms Coverack could come from Helston, might even have a flat there. That's one way she could melt away once she'd slipped out of the hospital.' George shrugged. 'She might still be in hiding.'

Frances nodded. 'You might be right. But how does that help?'

'I'm not sure. How about interviewing anyone who had contact with her last Saturday?'

Frances considered. 'Like the ambulance crew?'

'Well, they had half an hour with her on the way to hospital. Did the woman say anything? Even random mumblings might tell you something.'

'I suppose so. At the very least, we'd have a description. Someone must have seen her in a better light than we did.'

'Actually, there was something I wanted to talk about with you,' said George, as they sipped coffee a few minutes later.

'Go on.' Frances hoped she wouldn't be too demanding.

George outlined her find of a new padlock on the old hut and her subsequent conversation with the Head of Security.

'So potentially, you see, security is a big problem,' she concluded. 'Or it could be if the site had serious rivals. Not to destroy it, probably, but to make its businesses feel vulnerable to attack, so tempted to go elsewhere.'

'Alright, there's a problem. How's it affect me?'

'I wanted to ask about smuggling in these parts.'

Frances was a little surprised. George hastened to explain.

'It seemed to me, Frances, that several of the manager's worries could only be enacted by someone with specialised equipment. Drones, for example, or listening devices. Advanced kit, not the sort of thing you could just order over the internet. Or would want to risk carrying through customs.'

'Hm. Sounds like the stuff you'd find in a dark corner of Eastern Europe.'

'Exactly. So what I was wondering, Frances, was how easy it would be to smuggle stuff like that across the Channel and into the Lizard?'

Frances considered the alternatives.

'You have to remember, George, smuggling was a major industry in Cornwall for centuries. That goes with our distance from the rest of the country and the ruggedness of our coastline. We've hundreds of navigable coves; not easy to keep track of.'

'I guess that's true of the Lizard?'

'I'd say especially the Lizard.'

'So if an item was ordered for anyone round here you'd bring it ashore as close as possible. Not further up the coast?'

'That's right. You're not talking hundreds of items. It's specialist stuff, on a small scale?'

'I hope so. Alright, you've convinced me to take delivery on the Lizard. Which parts of the coastline should I use?'

Frances considered.

'You know, I wouldn't use the coastline at all. If it was coming on a small launch, I'd bring it in via the Helford River. That's sheltered from storms.'

'Dead of night?'

'Oh certainly. But not around full moon.' Frances pondered. What else would she advise?

'In the summer you must avoid tourists. They're hopelessly unpredictable, might decide to go for a midnight swim or fishing at night.'

'Right. So it would best be done in the winter?'

'Well, there are no tourists at the moment. But you'd still have to take note of the tide. I mean, at low tide you'd be wading through mud.'

George glanced at her watch. 'That's plenty to go on anyway. Thank you. The play begins in quarter of an hour. I've got tickets but I think we'd best get over there.'

Trelowarren Manor and its old chapel

CHAPTER 22

I had a light lunch at Tregilly Wartha before setting out. I felt a tremor of excitement, I was going to meet Joy again, even earlier than I'd expected.

I was getting used to the pull up past Gweek to central Lizard now. The Trelowarren Estate was a huge area, just off the main road from Helston to St Keverne. Even in the depths of winter the place looked dramatic as I turned off and cycled towards the Manor down the estate road.

I'd tidied myself up as best I could. After all, Joy and I would be here again this evening for the Agatha Christie drama. But being on a bike did rather limit the options.

I got to the Manor, padlocked my bike and headed for the main doorway. Inside was a massive hall with rows of chairs at one end and a stage at the other. Presumably this was the venue for the drama. Beyond was a reception desk. I headed over and dinged the bell.

A fierce-looking woman appeared, wearing a plaid skirt and gilet.

'Yes?'

'A colleague and I made a booking to see some of the chapel records this afternoon,' I began. 'I'm a bit early; I don't think she's here yet.'

The receptionist looked irritated. 'What was the name?'

'My colleague is the Revd Joy Tregorran. She's the vicar in Gunwalloe.'

The receptionist made a show of peering in the booking book as if it was written in Sanskrit. 'Ah yes. You must be Dr Harry Jennings? Perhaps you could wait until you're both here, then I'll take you round.' She indicated a seat nearby.

I like to think of myself as a friendly sort of guy. I relish the challenge of relating to people like that receptionist, anyway. I pointed back to the rows of chairs behind us.

'I presume these are for tonight's performance?'

Grudgingly she responded. 'That's right. The Constantine Players. They're very good. They come here every year.'

'Are you expecting a full house?'

'Most of the seats are booked. They normally are. It's only a two-night performance, you see. Of course, we have guests staying in cottages on the Estate. It's hard to tell how many of them will come.'

It had never occurred to me that the place might be full. 'Could I buy a couple of tickets for Joy and me, please?'

Attila the Hun was starting to thaw now I was spending money. 'Certainly.'

She peered at another sheet. 'There are a couple here near to the side. They're fifteen pound each.'

'That's fine.' I took out my wallet and paid in cash. I didn't want to risk more advanced technology.

I had just put the tickets in my wallet when Joy appeared.

132

Once again she was smart and feminine, a fashionable dress plus a stylish lemon fleece, no sign of a clerical collar. She smiled at the receptionist, who seemed to recognise her.

'Ah, Reverend Tregorran. Your friend has just bought tickets for this evening's performance. But I understand your first aim today is to visit the old chapel?' More animated now, she came out from behind the desk and led us through the Manor.

The way Joy had described it I had expected there'd be a small team in charge of records in the old chapel but it wasn't that complicated. Attila was our only guide. Mustn't think of her as that, I told myself. I wondered if Joy knew her real name.

The chapel itself was a medium-sized stone construct with stained glass windows. It was serene and very beautiful.

'It's sixteenth century, I believe,' said Joy. I could see she was in her element. I was happy for her to take the lead.

'I talked to the Bishop this morning,' she explained to Attila. 'He said that this building housed some of the older documents from various vicarages on the Lizard. I wondered if you had anything from the previous vicarage in Church Cove?'

'Let's see,' the receptionist replied. She seized a large, leather-bound volume from a side table. 'We keep a record of all the material stored. The documents themselves are locked in filing cabinets, out in the vestry.'

'I'm afraid I don't know when the transfer might have happened.'

'Vicars rarely do. Trouble is, it's never the current one that did the transfer. Tell you what, why don't I leave this volume with you. You can search for anything of interest. When you know what you're after, come back to the reception desk.'

After saying which she wandered off, leaving the pair of us to face a mammoth search.

This was Joy's bailiwick but I was an experienced historian. It would take both our skills to move this forward.

'Let's make sure we both know exactly what we're looking for,' I urged. 'Can you tell me, please, the name and address of the old Church Cove vicarage?'

'Mm. It goes like this.' Joy printed a name on a piece of white card from a table by the chapel doorway. She flicked through the data record. There were dozens of tightly written pages. 'This is all in date order, Harry. It's a real pity we've no idea when the transfer happened.'

Joy knew more about the documentary process but as a historian I knew plenty about records. The Church of England was a relatively tidy organisation. It wouldn't deliberately make things harder than necessary.

'Can I have a look, please?'

I took the leather tome from Joy and started reading from the back. I was right. I gave a grunt of satisfaction. For I'd found an index of all the vicarages mentioned in the front pages. And with each vicarage there came the page number (or numbers) where it was mentioned.

The vicarages weren't in any special order, of course. Each one only needed to appear the first time any document for it had to be listed. Some wouldn't be there at all: not every church had replaced its vicarage. In some cases the same place had served the church for centuries.

But the index made for a much faster search than we would have achieved, if we'd had to wade line by line through the whole volume.

I explained my discovery and handed the volume back. Joy could do this faster than me. It took only ten minutes before her face lit up. 'Got it!'

She dictated the page number, I wrote it down and we turned to the front. And there it was.

July 1879. Transfer from Church Cove to new vicarage in Gunwalloe.

Set of 3 documents, found in a tar-sealed casket in old vicarage loft.

Brought to Gunwalloe Church by a Moroccan seaman, 1684.

There followed a comprehensive file reference.

It was everything we had hoped for. Solid evidence of what we'd suspected. I pulled out my phone and took a photo. Then we headed back to reception to find Attila.

A few moments later we were back again to the chapel. The receptionist brought her vestry and cabinet keys with her. Joy showed her the entry in the record book, she selected the cabinet and then applied the keys. This was going to be it.

Only it wasn't. The filing system was sound. Second drawer down in Cabinet C. We found the folder mentioned in the record and looked inside. But it was empty.

I could see Attila wasn't happy. She went back to the leather-bound volume and double checked. This was certainly where it was supposed to be. In fact there was an empty folder hanging in the cabinet, just where we'd hoped to find our documents. But not the documents themselves. They had completely vanished.

CHAPTER 23

Joy and I sat in the snug at Trengilly Wartha having afternoon tea.

It wasn't the nearest tea shop to Trelowarren but it was one place that I knew would be open. In the second week of January that was by no means a given. Certainly there was nowhere to eat at Trelowarren.

For once it hadn't involved me in a cycle ride. Joy had a Volkswagon Polo of indeterminate age that she referred to as her "chariot of fire". Judging by the speed it chugged us along I think the name was ironic.

'This is a cosy little Inn,' Joy remarked, glancing around. 'You've done well to find this, Harry.'

I decided I wouldn't go into the details of Stewart's subsidy which I earned by coming here. I poured us both a cup of tea. No mugs here, of course: we had fine bone China cups and saucers, elegantly decorated.

'So what do we think?' I asked. 'How on earth did those documents go missing? Is this really the end of the road?'

'Mrs Chiswick seemed pretty stunned,' Joy replied. 'They must have gone before her time. In the last century, anyway – if not earlier.'

'She said the chapel was always kept locked,' I mused, 'I can believe that. You wouldn't want a place like that to be disturbed. So the thief would have to get inside there as well as into the correct filing cabinet. And to know what they were looking for.'

A pause as we both pondered.

'Let's think this through carefully, Harry. For a start, that leather reference volume which told us where to look had been there for decades. So if you came with an idea of what you were looking for, that would help you find it. And those filing cabinets might not always have been locked. They might not have bothered with that in gentler times.'

'That means, Joy, the hardest part would be getting inside that chapel. But if someone had broken in there would be signs of forced entry. Staff at the Manor would know that, even if it happened long before their time.'

'If it had happened then today, surely, Mrs Chiswick would have told us.'

We both drank some of our tea. I mused on other options. 'Do you reckon the place could have been opened up for some special event?'

Joy put her hand over her mouth. I sensed I'd sparked an idea.

'Harry, I've just remembered. I came here once, a long time ago. Twenty five years back, when I was still a teenager. It was a Saturday in August. My parents brought me and my brothers over for the day.'

I had no idea where this was going but I wasn't going to stop her.

There was a pause as she collected her thoughts. 'There was a mock battle, you see. Based on the one that took place at Trelowarren during the Civil War. It was staged in the Estate meadows and valley, just beyond the Manor.'

'A re-enactment, you mean?'

'That's right, Harry. It was a Sealed Knot event: Cavaliers and Roundheads, wearing redcoats or whatever, all armed with muskets or swords. And plenty of cannons firing – well, making a bang, anyway.'

I started to catch her excitement. 'Keep going,' I urged.

'I remember, Harry, it lasted all day. It was a big event: there were thousands here to watch. Well, all those pretend soldiers would have to get changed somewhere, out of sight of the crowds.'

'Joy, that's right. They could hardly travel here by train, dressed up as seventeenth century soldiers. Or take suitcases onto the battlefield.'

'They'd need a place to store their present-day clothes while the battle was raging.'

I saw where she was heading. 'So you're asking, might the chapel have been used as a cast room?'

There was a pause as Joy considered. 'The Estate would need every space they could find. One lot or other would have claimed the chapel.'

'Probably the Cavaliers – they were Royalists,' I suggested. 'In Cornwall they'd be the ones the Trelowarren Lord of the Manor would back.'

Joy looked at me quizzically. 'You mean, it would be natural to let them use the chapel as their base?'

'Well, that's probably what happened when the real battle

happened in 1648.' I gave a hollow laugh. 'There's probably a PhD on the subject.'

There was a pause as I refilled our tea cups. More thought was clearly required.

Just at that moment Joy's phone trilled.

She pulled the device out of her handbag and squinted at the dial. 'It's my old school,' she exclaimed, 'I'd better answer this.'

'I'll leave you to it,' I said. 'I need some fresh air.' A poor excuse but I didn't want to eavesdrop. I came back into the snug ten minutes later, to find Joy looking very pleased with herself.

'I hadn't expected that,' she remarked. 'They've managed to do it far faster than I'd dared hope.'

'Do what?'

'That was the Head of Chemistry at Penzance. D'you remember, I took him all those black lumps from the casket this morning. Well, it was the first week of term so he made the lump analysis the goal of the students' first practical.'

'Forensics on the cheap,' I commented. 'How did they do?'

Joy glanced down at the notes from her call. 'Well, one finding was that each of the lumps contained plenty of sugar – around 80% by weight. And the sugar was a mixture of glucose and fructose.'

'Yes?'

'Their second finding was that the main contents, leaving aside the sugar, were calcium, potassium and phosphorous.'

'Right. Did that lead to any firm conclusion?' I was no scientist, I wanted a practical answer.

'Oh yes. While the lads were weighing and measuring, the girls were chasing up ideas of what it might all mean via Google. I'd told them all that you and I'd been able to discover, you see. Then at the end of the lesson they put their combined results together.'

I was starting to feel impatient. 'Come on Joy, you're teasing me. What was their conclusion?'

My friend grinned. 'Harry, they reckoned the lumps were almost certainly a medium-sized collection of dates.'

I sat back and pondered. Yes, that would all make sense. Dates were plentiful in Morocco. It was plausible someone should bring a box to Britain, even three hundred years ago.

'I can believe that,' I responded. 'What's odd is to bring them all that way on a hazardous voyage – and then to hang onto them when the boat sank. You'd think they were gold sovereigns.'

Joy mused for a moment. 'You'd only behave like that if you thought they'd be even more valuable to you later . . . or to someone else.'

'Ah. You mean, if they were intended as a present? I guess they'd be rare in those days. You could hardly pop down for a box from Sainsbury's.'

There was a pause. It was a conundrum.

Joy was the first to speak. 'What the leather bound record told us was that "the casket was bought ashore by a Moroccan sea-man". But of course they couldn't be sure of that. They could tell he was North African, probably, from the colour of his skin and his hair; but the seaman bit was just a guess. But what if he was more than that?'

I could see where she was going and took the thought on. 'Was

141

he some sort of servant, perhaps? I could just about imagine a servant wanting to bring a present of dates to someone in England. But to hang onto them like that it must have been intended for someone really important.'

There was silence. It was an interesting idea, but had we taken this as far as was possible?

'Just one more thought,' I said. 'We've been treating the documents as the key content of this casket. But they might not be that at all. Dates are rather sticky things and they didn't have plastic in those days. So . . . '

'The documents might have been old sheets of paper or parchment that the servant used to pack the dates – to keep each layer apart.'

'No, Joy, that can't be right. Remember, someone bothered to steal the sheets from the chapel. They couldn't have been blank.'

'But Harry, doesn't that strengthen the idea that this was a high-up servant? They weren't just blank sheets. Was that because they were early drafts of some sort, ones that he lifted from an official rubbish bin?'

We went round and round for some time. In the end I tried to summarise where we'd got to.

'So the sheets probably didn't matter to him. He only cared about the dates. But for some reason which for the time being we can't even guess, they were and are very valuable to someone now living on the Lizard.'

142

CHAPTER 24

George had not set foot in Trelowarren Manor since she'd collected her cottage keys from reception the previous weekend. Then the place had seemed dull, even boring. This time she was pleasantly surprised to find it had been transformed by the Constantine Players to make it ready for their two nights of drama.

The main hall, with its rows of seats in front of a curtained stage, was already fairly full. Not many, though, had felt warm enough to remove their winter coats. For these Lizard locals, whatever the weather, this was a treat not to be missed. George hoped their anticipation was justified.

She bought a programme from a warmly-dressed usher and took a seat on one side of the auditorium with Frances beside her.

The cast included the original names of all those that George could vaguely remember from the BBC Christmas Week broadcast, three years ago. The list included Anna; she was playing a servant called Ethel, working at the mansion on Soldier Island.

She pointed out the name. 'I know her. She works at Goonhilly on security. She was with me when we found the new padlock. It was her enthusiasm that made me want to come.'

Now they were here, George had misgivings about what the police officer would make of it. She didn't recall the police com-

143

ing well out of the story. It was, after all, based on an Agatha Christie crime novel from the 1930s. By then Christie was notorious for unexpected endings, some more plausible than others. Not many, though, were due to police brilliance.

A few minutes later the performance began.

George recalled that the television version had started with the ten guests being transported on a small launch across a placid sea to a mansion on Soldier Island.

The stage version started just after that. The guests included a doctor, a retired policeman, a lawyer and a former soldier. It seemed that none had met before and soon became clear that each was hiding something from their past.

Their first meal together was disturbed by a voice from the study next door. 'You are all guilty of murder.' But there was no-one in there. Not the most welcoming of greetings.

The story had been published in 1939 and would give its readers little comfort. There was no Hercule Poirot tucked away on Soldier Island to solve the mystery and provide reassurance.

George was dragged back to the present by a death on the stage. It looked like a poisoning. Shameful events from the guest's past, maybe inviting such a punishment, started to emerge.

In normal circumstances, even in 1939, a suspicious death would lead to a call to the police. George started to appreciate the cunning of the author in making it clear that this could not happen.

The play was set on a remote island with no ferries and, of course, no mobile phones. No easy access to forensics to make sense of the death. And an impending storm meant the guests would all be trapped there for days.

George could sense tension mounting around her as the story continued. Soon there came a second suspicious death, this one servant Ethel, from a massive overdose of sleeping pills. George was sad that her colleague's part in the play was so truncated.

Once again facts about the victim came into focus. The theme of unconventional justice started to emerge. And the earlier role of one guest, a former high court judge, came into the conversations.

Another guest was a retired soldier. Before long he had been distracted, hit from behind and killed. Subsequent dialogue revealed that this man had once sent his wife's secret lover to his death on the battlefield.

Guest after guest came to an untimely end. One death was even relayed as having taken place on a beach.

It was a bleak play, George thought. She would be glad of a break. It had run for nearly two hours. She glanced at her programme for interval details but none were specified.

Tension in the audience continued to rise.

By now the guests on the island were desperate. How could the killings be stopped? The island was searched, the guests went out in groups of three – no-one wanted to risk being one of a pair – but no-one else was found. It had to be one of them.

The killings seemed unstoppable. The fatal methods were never the same. One guest was stung; another was shot. In the end only one person was left. Was this the killer?

No. The last guest was a former games mistress. It was alleged she had lost one of her pupils, when they'd been allowed to swim out too far and had drowned. The woman went out to the hall, put a noose around her neck and committed suicide.

In the stunned silence that followed the stage curtain closed.

The lights came on and a middle-aged man appeared. 'There will now be a ten minute intermission. Don't worry, ladies and gentlemen. The second half will be extremely short.'

'I guess we've got a few minutes to work out who the killer is and how it was all done,' murmured Frances. 'What d'you think?'

'This makes Midsomer Murders look benign,' replied George. 'People say that's murder-ridden but it never has more than two or three deaths per episode. Christie is positively gung ho.'

The analyst considered her friend's question. 'Presumably one of the deaths must have been fake. Which one, d'you reckon?'

Frances wasn't sure. 'The doctor certified them all as dead, didn't he? Maybe the killer had to be him?' She frowned. 'But why on earth would he do so?'

George mused for a moment. 'It might not be the doctor. Maybe it was two of the guests, operating in tandem?'

'The trouble is, George, we were told at the start that the guests didn't know each other beforehand. Once you're forced to consider that things you've been told aren't true, it's hard to make any progress at all.'

The ten minutes passed quickly and Act Two began. In the end a plausible solution emerged.

'So it was the judge,' concluded George, as they slipped on

their coats. 'With a motive to resolve various miscarriages of justice that he'd come across in his career.'

'He knew he was about to die anyway,' added Frances. 'It's not impossible. As fiction goes it's moderately convincing.'

'It was well acted anyway.'

They had just reached the doorway when Anna joined them.

'George, have you ten minutes to come and talk to the Director?'

George frowned. 'If that's what he wants. I'm not far from home, anyway.'

Frances knew any talk might last for some time and decided to slip away. 'Thanks very much George. It's been a fun evening. I'll ring you tomorrow. Maybe we can go for another walk on Sunday?'

Battling against the audience as they streamed out, Anna led George to a room at the back of the stage. George saw she was to meet the character who had announced the interval, a cheerful-looking man in his late fifties. He smiled a welcome as Anna made introductions.

'My name is Charles. Thanks for coming, George. I have a question. It's a shot in the dark but if you don't ask then you'll never know.'

Whatever did he want? George suddenly recalled her aside to Anna about filming dramas to make them accessible to a wider audience. She smiled at him politely.

'During a break in dress rehearsal,' he began, 'Anna was telling me about your comments on the benefits of filming dramas. She said you'd done it yourself at least once. She completely convinced me. I can't think why I'd not thought of it before.'

'It was only an aside over lunch, Charles. I enjoy filming but it's only a hobby.'

'The thing is, George, we're got our second performance tomorrow evening. Is there any chance that you could film us in action?'

George pondered. It was her first week on the Lizard. Her work hadn't yet spilt over to the evenings. It would be good to have something else to get her teeth in to.

'I'd love to,' she replied. 'I'll be back from work by five thirty. I'll come straight over. Start to work out the best angles and so on. Thank you very much indeed.'

CHAPTER 25

At half past nine on Friday morning the taxi came to Trengilly Wartha to take me to Truro railway station. Thus I started the long journey that would take me to Cambridge. I'll tell you how that happened as I go.

By the time Joy and I had stopped our analysis on Thursday afternoon it was after five. But I had a cunning plan. 'Joy, the play doesn't start till half past seven. They serve evening meals here at six. Please would you join me for an early supper?'

The question was slightly rhetorical. I'd already booked a table for the pair of us when I went for my stroll in mid-afternoon.

Of course Joy said yes. I don't think she'd thought about where she would eat at all. Probably she was used to doing without, or lasting till she had a toasted sandwich when she got back to her chilly vicarage. I thought she deserved better.

By unspoken agreement we left discussion of missing documents for the time being. I won't dwell on the food, which was out of this world. Maybe being on cloud nine makes a good meal taste even better?

It was as we started on desserts that Joy made her left-field connection. She'd been asking me about my PhD thesis. It was part of a wider discussion about the arts and the sciences and how far they overlapped. Was the great divide into the two cultures unique to Britain?

This was a topic that she'd thought about. After all she'd been a science teacher who'd evolved into a vicar: she had experience of both sides. I'd been explaining how I had become interested as a student in Samuel Pepys, the famous diarist of the Great Fire of London.

'He covered the chasm. I mean, he had comments on the causes of the fire and also on the social consequences.'

I went on to comment on how this event – though hugely dramatic at the time – was a mere sideshow for a man who was to spend so long on the edge of seventeenth century politics.

It wasn't her field but Joy had a wide knowledge of life, was interested in people and had an instinct for remote connections.

'So your prolific Mr Pepys was also a friend of the King Charles of his day?'

'He was. Of course the aristocracy didn't spread so far in those days. Everyone of note would know each other. And both these men had catholic tendencies, you might say.'

Joy persisted. 'So he would know about this tug of war over the territory in North Africa and whether it was worth Britain holding on to?'

'Certainly. I was looking it up only this morning. Actually, I read, Samuel Pepys was sent to Tangiers in 1683 to help prepare for the repatriation.'

Joy ate silently for a moment. I thought she was catching up with the Eton Mess. Mine was finished and I'd found it delicious. But no, her thoughts went wider.

'So is it possible, Harry, that Mr Pepys met this servant – our survivor on the Schiedam – while he was out there?'

I hadn't previously made a direct connection and considered for a moment. 'I suppose so. I mean, Pepys was the sort of man who would talk to anyone, high or low. He'd even make an entry on the meeting in his diary, provided they were interesting enough.'

'He's the most famous diarist ever, isn't he?'

That was what my PhD had alleged, anyway. 'For his time, I guess. He was a very clever man.'

Joy paused then gave a sigh. 'Harry, how else might we know what those documents were about? Except if someone who knows his way round the writings of this famous diarist, a man who was present in the place at the time, goes to see what they recorded.'

Joy stopped for a moment and then continued. 'It would be the final version, of course, of what was first drafted in our documents. But might it not still give us a clue?'

At that moment the waitress had arrived. There hadn't been time to take it further, not if we wanted to see the Agatha Christie drama from the start. And if there's one thing to be said about a whodunit, it's that you have to see it from the start. That's where all the best clues are hidden.

It was an entertaining performance. But that has been written about elsewhere. My mind was largely on my own mystery, not a whodunit so much as a what-was-really-said?

Was it really worth a trek all the way to Cambridge, just for another trawl through Samuel Pepys' diary? Logically it was ridiculous, the most remote of long shots.

On the other hand, I had a remit which I'd followed this far. What else was there left to try?

I mentally replayed this conversation as the train trundled through Cornwall and then South Devon. It started speeding up once it reached Exeter. By early afternoon I'd travelled by Underground across London and was heading for Cambridge.

Pepys was a graduate of Magdalene College, one of their most prestigious alumni. There was even a library there in his name. I'd spent much time in the place when working on my PhD. That was a long time ago and no doubt all the staff would have changed.

On the other hand, they had a copy of my thesis – it wasn't a best seller, it was one of only four copies in existence – resting on their shelves. Or, to be precise, in one of their back rooms: accessed on request. The work had earned me free access to that library for the rest of my life.

I had enjoyed my toils at the time (how could anyone not enjoy time spent in Cambridge?) but I had never before thought it would do me the slightest good.

It was as I'd got onto the train at Kings Cross that I first got a slight sense of being followed. It was strange.

You are probably thinking I've gone crackers. Loopy. You might even be right. The thing is, I'd had some experience of trailing others, and of being followed, during my time away from academia. I'd even been trained by professionals to watch for telltale signs. I'd absorbed an instinct about when it might be happening, an instinct I hadn't felt for years but which was now raising its ugly head again.

Various lessons flooded back. The first thing was, don't give away any sign that you recognised there might be someone on your trail. For example, don't start looking around like a demented chicken, head twitching from side to side. For the time being I should be content to be followed. It wasn't as though I was going anywhere sinister.

But I could give whoever was after me something to think about. I'd planned to take a taxi from Cambridge station into the town. After all, I would be presenting all my expenses to Stewart. He didn't know it yet but he would be funding the entire trip to Cambridge.

It would be much more entertaining, though, to get on a bus. There was a regular service heading for the town centre. One was just about to leave.

I leapt on as it started, the door slamming behind me. The driver was slightly annoyed. I paid my fare and made sure I was the correct side to look out of the window and observe various fellow passengers. Most were wandering about on the forecourt. None gave any sign of frustration at my departure. I hadn't disrupted anyone's plans. Maybe the whole thing was fantasy, the result of an overdeveloped imagination?

By now it was almost four o'clock. I got out in the Market Square and headed down past Sidney Sussex towards Magdalene. I'd rung on the way to check the place was open – 'We don't just open in the undergraduate term, sir,' I was told – but I wanted to appear there in person and find out about weekend openings in early January.

I had my Exeter University credentials ready to prove who I was. There was only one person in attendance, a serious-looking woman with heavy glasses, her hair in a bob, of around my own age. I wondered, for a second, if I had once known her as a student.

She didn't admit to recognising me, anyway. There was no small talk here. I explained I wanted to pursue some of the later writings of Samuel Pepys and I was directed to shelves over in the far corner.

I learned that the library would be open next day – Saturday – from nine thirty to three. Not that long but I was content. It was surely enough time to tell if Joy's bright idea had any merit.

CHAPTER 26

George was rather pleased she'd got a non-work project to keep her busy on Friday evening. When working away from home it was very easy for consultancy work to expand to fill all waking hours.

She had had lunch once again with Anna. This time they hadn't got further than the foyer at the back of Goonhilly, but they'd used the time to plan out filming details. George had been pleased to discover that Anna was also keen on photography – perhaps that was why she'd passed the idea on? But it also suggested other options.

'Anna, you're only needed for the first part of the drama. I mean, you're almost the first one killed. Would you be able to help me with the filming once you're dead – if you see what I mean?'

Anna had grinned. 'Don't see why not. I'd better check with Charles but it should be OK.'

'The thing is, we want as many angles covered as possible, even if, in the end, they're not all used.' Between them they'd planned it all out.

'I'm going to suggest that Charles sets up his own camera at the back of the hall to take a standard view of the whole play. And some microphones near the front. That'll give us a basic version

155

of the whole thing. That can be interleaved afterwards with whatever pictures we take as well.'

Anna had brought a copy of the script with her. It was dog-eared and coffee stained. 'From when I was learning my lines,' she admitted.

They'd gone through the play scene by scene, working out the best angles to film from. Some scenes would need to be covered from both sides.

'Have you ever done this sort of thing before, Anna?'

'Not really. Mostly I've just been shooting my nephews and nieces.'

'Right. The thing is, don't jerk the camera. Only go for close-up shots on longer speeches. Otherwise keep wide-angle so we've got the whole scene from one angle. I'll do the same. Charles can hire an editor afterwards to pull it all together.'

As they chatted George recalled the television version. 'It's a pity we can't take some opening shots of the cast in a launch, going over to an island. That'd make for a dramatic beginning.'

Anna started. 'That's possible, you know, George. We had to watch the BBC version at first rehearsal. Turns out that was filmed on the Lizard, going across to Mullion Island. But you'd need permission from the National Trust. No-one lives on the island, it's a bird sanctuary.'

'D'you know anyone in the Trust?'

'I don't – not been round here for long enough. Charles will. He's lived in Constantine forever. I could ring him if you liked?'

George left work promptly at five – that seemed to be what

everyone did on Fridays. She got back to her cottage, changed into trainers, dark jeans and a black sweater and had a snack. Then she headed over to Trelowarren Manor with her video camera.

It was only ten to six but most of the cast were there already. There was a hum of anticipation. The Thursday night performance had gone well and it was hoped Friday's would be even better. The fact that it was going to be filmed added to the buzz.

George had hoped that being directly involved would give her a chance to make new friends. For some reason that wasn't how it worked. Probably it was too late for someone new to fit in. No-one knew who she was or much cared. Her dark, unobtrusive clothing didn't help.

George identified places from where she could stand and film, on one side or another. She also sought ways to go behind the backcloth invisibly, passing from one side to the other.

As she passed to and fro George caught fragments of conversation from various dressing rooms. She took little notice, had no idea who was talking to whom.

'Thank you for getting back to me . . . so you're happy for us to come tomorrow . . . about half past ten . . . what's that, there's a lad that can take us to a sandy beach? Wow, that's great . . .'

'The last night at last, eh . . . Yes, I was doubtful too, but I'm glad I've been in it . . .Predictable? I wouldn't say that . . .Well, I'm sorry it's all over. Wonder what we'll do next? Will we all still be here? . . .'

'I've got all I need now . . . I'll see you tomorrow evening . . .'

'Our last night, Nat. Thank goodness . . . Well, I couldn't take much more. Not with all the other things we've got on at the moment... Right, best of luck with that, then.'

'Can you believe it, Sandra, it's practically over. Is there any way we could twist the ending? ...Make it a shock to everyone .. . Hey, suppose we swapped lines so you were the murderer? ... How much d'you bet? ... Go on, then, what'd we have to do?'

George spotted Anna coming out of the furthest dressing room, dressed as the mansion servant. She hastened to catch her, pass on her ideas and the filming positions she'd identified.

The atmosphere was taut: nerves backstage were tightening. George could hear a few people talking in front of the curtain. It was only twenty minutes till the play would begin.

The analyst had planned it as best she could. From now on it was out of her hands.

Two hours later the whole cast were receiving rapturous applause. The drama had gone even better than the night before. George felt proud to have been there, even if she'd made only the smallest contribution.

The actors who had mused on revising the final scene had thought better of the idea – or had got cold feet. For better or worse, warts and all, Agatha Christie's solution reigned unchallenged.

As the audience streamed away, a party was laid out on the stage. Modest celebrations were certainly in order. George was happy to be included.

As the cast and crew seized glasses of champagne or apple juice, Director Charles climbed onto a chair.

He raised a glass. 'Well done, everyone. Better than I'd dared to hope. Brilliant! Constantine Players' best production so far.'

George could see that Charles was a perfectionist. Even at this late stage he made one or two comments on points for the future. Then he reached his final announcement.

'As you know, friends, this performance has been filmed.' He turned towards George. 'Thank you, George, for coordinating that. I have a media friend in Truro who will pull the various strands together. I am sure that it will come out really well.

'There is, though, just one more finesse that could move the film from good to excellent.' He beamed round the stage.

'As we all remember, the television version of this drama started with guests travelling across to Mullion Island. Would it not be really good if our modest film could do the same?'

George noted a mixture of excitement and apprehension on actors' faces. But Charles was a leader and they would follow.

'I have a good friend in the National Trust. She has given special permission for us to visit the Island tomorrow morning; even arranged for launches to take us all out from Mullion Cove. So what I would like, my friends, is for all of us to be down at the Cove tomorrow morning, in our costumes, dressed as guests as they sail for Soldier Island. And George, I hope you'll be there to film us.

'This is the last lap for this year, ladies and gentlemen. But it will, I hope, lay a marketing base that will underpin all our future productions.'

CHAPTER 27

I'd arranged to stay that night with Simon, a fellow history don that I'd known for over twenty years, but not seen face to face for a decade.

He'd certainly pulled out all the stops, even lent me a suit and arranged for us to eat at High Table. There was an academically respectable bunch there tonight, including a former Cabinet Minister.

It was the weekend before that Brexit vote – the one that was promised as the "final vote on the deal". I wasn't fully convinced it would happen. We'd had one "final vote" already, only the month before.

Of course, Cambridge as a whole was strongly opposed to Brexit and many at that table would love to see the policy discarded. But others were mindful of the risks to democracy if a popular vote was ignored simply because it was inconvenient or expensive. As one of the fellows remarked, this was the first time Britain had registered a referendum vote that was unexpected. Would it actually be followed?

Someone else muttered that only a Prime Minister from Oxford could have contrived a popular vote that was so unpopular. 'If he'd given the matter ten minutes thought, he'd have seen that any change to an existing policy should require a solid majority before it was enacted.'

I'd had an early start and a busy day, was happy enough to sit and listen. It was encouraging to hear a profound difference of views being expressed in a collegiate manner. The habit of listening to one another hadn't died out altogether. I recalled that Cornwall had voted for Brexit, although the County received strong funding from the European Union. That didn't make much sense. But much else didn't make sense either.

Simon's flat was out on the Chesterton Road, not far from the town centre. It was good to have a breath of fresh air as we walked back.

Once in the flat, Simon opened a bottle of Baileys that he'd been given for Christmas and gave us both a glassful, larger than I'd expected. Then he started the gentle interrogation: what on earth I was doing in Exeter, when I'd had such a glittering career ahead of me in Cambridge?

All very enjoyable, and I'd like to think I gave him some solid answers. But it meant I didn't get to bed till well after midnight and didn't wake up till nine on Saturday morning. Simon was still asleep as I gathered my belongings and slipped out the door. I'd thank him later for his hospitality.

There were not many in the Pepys Library when I got there shortly before ten. There was an old buffer at one of the tables with a notebook, and a couple of women, half his age, at the far end of the room. They were conversing quietly. I couldn't possibly complain it was too loud.

The details of my PhD started to come back. It had practically all been based on published material. As Joy had surmised two days ago, Samuel Pepys was highly prolific. Most of what he'd intended for publication, which covered all manner of topics, was still in print. And if it was, there would certainly be a copy on the shelves here.

My thesis had been concerned with Mr Pepys' early life. How had he made his way into the establishment? What tricks had he pulled? Which well-known figures had he befriended? What had been the result?

Now though I was interested in his later years. In particular 1683, which was his only known visit to Tangiers.

First I tried the main shelves: had his diary persisted that late? It seemed nothing had been published. Pepys' diary fame, which was well-deserved, arose from the 1660s, helped by the Plague and the Great Fire of London. It was probably his genius at covering these events which eased him into the Establishment.

So what might the man have written in Tangiers? I was in a hurry, had no time to spend on an exhaustive search, so I put the question to the serious-looking librarian. She seemed to blossom as her expertise was mined.

Half an hour later I'd been handed a box of manuscripts written by Samuel Pepys, dating from 1683. 'I'm afraid they're not well catalogued,' she admitted. 'But everything we have for that year is in there.'

I had four hours before the place shut for the weekend. This was going to be a race against the clock.

I claimed a table of my own and laid everything out. Wisdom was now needed to find the best prospects. I was still after a needle in the haystack but the haystack had got much smaller.

On one pile I laid manuscripts that listed quantities. Most were assessments of the costs and benefits of holding the North African territory. Interesting for a PhD student, but I couldn't see it being of value to Stewart.

A second pile – almost as huge – was made up of receipts. The man had bought plenty of wine and run up huge hospitality bills during his few months there. Probably, though, these had been on some sort of tab. Pepys was a generous man, no doubt used to easing his way with donations of one sort or another.

The third pile consisted of published papers, augmented with caustic comments. Might these be something of longer term interest? I resolved to come back to them if I had time.

The final pile held everything else. I seized it with enthusiasm. Especially when I saw that Pepys hadn't totally given up writing his diary, even though it was no longer polished for publication. If there was anything, that was where it was most likely to be.

I put the diary items in date order and started to wade through them. Each day covered the events of that day, great and small. I could only skim through and see if anything rang bells.

Pepys' lettering was hard for a modern reader to interpret. I battled on for nearly an hour but I could see I wouldn't get through it all in time.

Then it occurred to me, was there a photocopying service? It turned out there was. No machine for customers but they did have a staff facility. Quickly I went back to my table and scooped up the diary fragments. Then back to the counter.

The librarian counted the pages – there were twenty five – then glanced at the clock. 'Hm. I'll start straight away. If you're lucky I might get it all done before we close.'

I gave her my best smile. Then I wandered back to my table. How to make use of the intervening hour? I decided to have a look at Pepys' caustic comments.

I'd got halfway through the pile when I came across something of interest. For Pepys had managed to acquire a secret document relating to Gibraltar. And it had clearly interested him, he had plenty to say.

I did my best to absorb his commentary but it was hard work. I daren't ask the librarian to do any more. They had strict rules at the counter about not using a camera – they feared the cumulative effect of bright flashlight on old volumes. Very sensible. But surely photographing a couple of pages wouldn't make much difference?

I glanced around. One or two of the morning's researchers had gone home but the cast was mostly the same. The old buffer was still at the far end, as were the toilets.

Quickly I grabbed my jacket and slipped the required pages inside. Then I headed for the toilet. There was no trouble and I was back at my table, feeling only a little guilty, a minute later. I retrieved the pages, put them back on the pile and had another attempt to read Pepys' comments.

I was still at it when the librarian announced they would be shutting in ten minutes. I seized the box and started stacking the various piles back inside, then took it to the counter.

'Have you managed to do my photocopying?'

'Just finished, Dr Jennings.' She handed a bundle of sheets over and I stashed them in my rucksack. 'That'll be twelve pound fifty.'

I handed the money over and she gave me a receipt. I headed on my way.

I'd checked the train times. All being well I'd be back in Cornwall late this evening. And at Joy's church tomorrow morning. For a few seconds I was totally distracted.

Would I later regret that lapse of concentration?

CHAPTER 28

George awoke excited but slightly apprehensive about the prospect of filming the cast of "None" on their voyage over to Mullion Island.

The previous evening's work, filming a well-rehearsed play, was something she had done before. Really, not much could go wrong. On the other hand, filming a voyage in a small boat across a mile of open sea was a challenge. Why on earth had she pushed for it?

It was a pity Frances wouldn't be with her. She was busy today, helping to police a Brexit march in Truro. George had no idea if the police officer was good with a video camera, but she would be safe hands in an emergency. She shook her head angrily. Where had this defeatist thought come from?

There had been no time to plan anything after the final performance party. So George had arranged to meet Anna early at Mullion Cove. They could at least have a conversation about options and issues.

It wasn't possible, George found, to park at the Cove itself. The nearest car park was quarter of a mile up the road and charged for the privilege, even in the depths of winter. Everyone would need to park there. That would add a delay: they'd do well to start the voyage on time.

The Cove had a small harbour, mooring half a dozen boats. There was a café but it wasn't open yet. George perched on a stone wall while she waited for her colleague and tried to make a plan. There would be no chance of repeating anything that went wrong. The analyst had to predict the best filming locations before she'd even set foot on the island.

She considered the sequence to be filmed: the guests' first arrival on the island. Then she realised: Anna was not in the party to be taken over. The logic of the play meant she began on the island, ready to welcome the guests. It was an important role to fulfil, set the scene for the whole story.

George hadn't paid much attention when Charles had talked logistics. She had no idea how many boats he planned to hire.

She glanced across. The boats in the harbour were small, they'd need at least three to hold all ten guests, maybe four. There weren't just the guests, there was also Charles and her. So how many boat owners were around? She saw one, bailing out over-night rain, and wandered over for a chat.

'Morning,' she began. 'My name is George. I'm one of the party hoping to go across to Mullion Island this morning.'

'Argh. We wuz told to expect a crowd. Fred, Joe and Ben are going to help as well. Does 'ee want to go straight away?'

As he spoke she saw Anna walking down the road. If the man took them now they'd at least be in the right location. 'That'd be great,' she responded.

Five minutes later they had launched on the journey to the island. There was some swell but the sea was reasonably calm.

'There'll be wind later,' the boatman told them. 'Best not to be there too long, I reckon. Two hours at most.'

As they voyaged George did her best to film the approach to the island and the view across to the coast. She couldn't tell which would work best but it was good to have alternatives.

Even though the wind was light it was very cold. George was wearing a cagoule over a thick sweater. She suddenly realised Anna was wearing just her servant uniform. 'Aren't you freezing, Anna?'

'I didn't want to be carrying extras. I forgot about wind chill. Is there much shelter on the island?'

The boatman could see the problem. 'Not much. Our landing cove is out the wind, mind. Will you have to go anywhere higher?'

'I hope not.' Anna did her best to snuggle down inside the boat. George hoped for her sake that the rest of the cast wouldn't be too long.

Half an hour later there was a burst of activity in the harbour. Three boats were setting out, each holding three or four passengers, dressed in pre-war clothing. One or two looked apprehensive: probably not just an enacted façade.

Slowly the boats headed towards them. George had a small tripod, she filmed their whole journey, some in close-up and the rest panoramic. She felt sure it would make a good opening scene.

As they arrived Anna (playing servant Ethel) came down to greet them. George had retreated to the side and captured every moment. She even managed to comply with Charles' insistence that he stayed off camera.

That's the lot, thought George.

But Charles had other ideas. 'There's one scene that takes place on the seashore,' he reminded them. 'It involves soldier Lombard being forced out to sea. You've already got the dialogue. I'd like us to try it, please, here in the cove. Humour me, folks, just the once.'

George sensed the actors were being pushed to the limit. She was warmly clad but the cast were dressed for their parts. They had no extra layers. Thick waterproof cagoules did not exist in pre-war years.

The actor playing Lombard, Nathan, was particularly un-happy. The scene would involve him paddling about in the icy cold water, being gradually driven out from land by one of the other guests.

Clever camerawork was needed so the second actor was not identified, shown only in profile. But George could see what was needed, was confident it could be done. There would certainly be no chance of a repeat here. Nathan had winced as he dipped his toes into the freezing water; there was no chance of him stepping out much further or making the scene longer than it need be.

The rest of the cast sheltered from the wind at the back of the cove. Anna tried to be useful, climbed up at the rear and filmed the whole scene at a distance. It was all over in ten icy minutes.

'Right folks, that's it. Let's get back to the warmth.' Charles had some empathy, didn't want to invite open rebellion. Gradually the actors started to head back towards the boats.

One or two realised that Nathan needed help. They stayed to dry his feet, helped him put on socks and boots and dragged him to his feet.

George could see opportunities slipping away.

'Anna, I'm on that first boat. I'll get useful pictures of the others and scenes at the far jetty. We haven't got any of those yet.'

'What should I do?'

'Would you mind waiting till last? Maybe hold back, take one or two shots of everyone leaving?'

The event was over now. George pushed onto the first boat ('camera girl's privilege'). She got good shots of the boats trailing behind her and later of them milling about near the jetty.

Once in the harbour the analyst noticed the café was open. A moment later she was inside, ordering a hot chocolate. Various actors followed her example while others headed straight for their cars. As a final gathering it was rather untidy.

George had hoped to swap notes with Anna before they left but she must have missed her. No doubt she would see her on Monday. She didn't know the make or colour of Anna's car.

If she had, she'd have noticed that this car was still parked in Mullion Cove as the analyst headed home.

CHAPTER 29

The various train times were tight but collectively manageable if there were no major holdups. I'd ordered a taxi to the station and was there in fifteen minutes. Just in time to buy a late-lunch tuna baguette and a large mug of Costa coffee before the train drew in.

It was the fast Saturday afternoon train to Kings Cross, fairly crowded, but I managed to find a seat. Travelling alone has some benefits. After finishing my lunch I opened my rucksack and started to peruse the photocopied diary I had recently collected. The librarian had very kindly put all twenty five pages into an official cardboard folder. I smiled wryly; there were some benefits to having a PhD after all.

Trouble was, Pepys' writing hadn't got any more legible during the process.

By now I was feeling tired. It had been a late night with too much to drink, first at the High Table and later in Simon's flat. Maybe I was out of condition for the Cambridge lecturer lifestyle? More to the point, perhaps, I was finding it too hard to concentrate in the crowded train.

I put the papers down and allowed my mind to roam. What would Joy be doing now?

I guessed she was probably putting the finishing touches to her

171

sermon – or sermons. We hadn't discussed her ministry at all. I didn't know if she would repeat the same material in the evening or had to prepare two different talks for different congregations on each Sunday. Anyone could do that from time to time, but it was hard work if it happened every Sunday. Especially if she had little support or encouragement from her colleagues. Mind, I didn't know for certain if that was the case.

You might well be wondering why I didn't just give her a ring. The simple answer is that we had agreed not to phone one another while we were apart. Each of us would be busy with our separate activities and a call might be too much of a distraction. With a bit of luck we wouldn't be apart for long.

I was hoping to be in Church Cove next morning to hear her sermon. Was it going to be funny? Or thoughtful and serious? I reminded myself that those ideas weren't necessarily in conflict. Jesus had managed to do both, often at the same time. Would the talk be relevant to the needs of her congregation – or even to me? I was thinking nonsense, of course. But I was looking forward to being with her again.

The thought came, unbidden. It was a long time since my wife and I had got divorced. She hadn't been able to cope with all the times I was away with my fieldwork. Or at least, hadn't been able to cope without finding another man to distract her.

Angry, shying away from the emotional rollercoaster, I forced my mind to move onto something else.

I had travelled the width of the country to collect and make sense of some very old handwritten documents. True, that should earn my department in Exeter a few thousand pounds and raise my accreditation slightly, but what else would it achieve? The question was still at the back of my mind: what on earth was Stewart after?

By now the train had reached the outskirts of London. I realised that I couldn't answer that question without at least looking at one element of what I'd found in Cambridge. I decided that would be my goal on the longer leg of the journey, after I'd got to Paddington.

I had hoped that the Great Western express out of Paddington might be less crowded but of course it wasn't. It was still Saturday afternoon.

In fact my new fellow-passengers took up just as many seats but were more rowdy. I gathered from the various posters they carried that they had been on a march down to Parliament Square and College Green, relating to Brexit. They were after a "People's Vote". Was their implication that last time, in 2016, it hadn't been "people" voting at all?

There was another group who had something to do with Brexit and had come up from Cornwall to say so. Their posters were confused and I couldn't even work out which side they were on. Get your ideas straight, guys, I thought to myself.

As before, I'd managed to get a seat, this time with a table to work at. I told myself it wasn't my business to judge my fellow-citizens. At least the marchers were doing something. They wanted to make a difference.

It was all far too complicated. I sighed and pulled out my sheets of Pepys' critique that related to Gibraltar. At least most of this was printed. Only Pepys' part had been handwritten; and by the look of it, this had been done at speed. He was obviously a man whose brain worked faster than his hand could record.

I peered at his thoughts, took out my pen and wrote a more readable version alongside. Then sat back to consider the great man's arguments.

I struggled to remember the status of Gibraltar at the time. When had it become British? I knew it was somewhere around then. I connected to the Great Western Wifi and consulted Wikipedia. It turned out that, in 1683/4, Gibraltar wasn't even British; it was land that belonged to Spain.

So what was the gist of Pepys' comments? I reminded myself that this had been written while he was staying in Tangiers, tasked with planning the next move for the Royal Navy. As it happened I'd been to Morocco myself. On a clear day you'd be able to see Gibraltar across the twenty miles of straits which marked the western end of the Mediterranean.

I read Pepys' comments again. They made a bit more sense now. He was comparing Tangiers with Gibraltar from the point of view of the British Navy. Assessing which of these two Mediterranean ports would be of more strategic value. And he came to the uncomfortable conclusion, for someone writing in 1683, that Britain would do far better to own the port that was positioned on the European side of the water.

Pepys concluded that the country needed to find a way to legally annexe Gibraltar, even as we prepared to depart from Tangiers.

There were wars going on across Europe. The Dutch, the Spanish, the French, the English, and several other countries as well, were all at loggerheads, slowly building Empires around the rest of the world. Pepys' notes suggested various ways that this conflict could be exploited so our strategic goal was achieved.

I returned to my tablet and scoured my internet sources once more. Gibraltar had been acquired by Britain, I read, in 1714. It was the result of an International Peace Conference. And we had held it ever since, despite regular complaints from Spain. Even when both countries were members of the European Union.

Gibraltar had performed a vital military role for Britain in World War Two. In more recent time there'd even been a couple of referendums, each asking which European country the population wanted to be attached to. Both had been easily won by the British. They were more English than, well, the English.

With this background I thought once more about Stewart and my own project. Could this possibly be what he was after? Had the Moroccan castaway brought to Cornwall, by pure chance involving dates and shipwreck, a first version of Samuel Pepys' explosive comments?

Reading it afresh, it seemed to me that Pepys' comments made our links to Gibraltar less innocent than I had always presumed. He had his ups and downs but he was a leading politician of his time. It hadn't just happened – it wasn't an accident of history – that the Rock was linked to Britain rather than to its immediate neighbour, Spain.

One further thought came to me. Pepys' comments were handwritten. They had never been published. One result of that was there was no easy way that they could make their way onto the internet. If I hadn't managed to dig them out they could have been hidden away forever. Might that make them explosive if they came to light at the right time?

Thinking of a possible reason for Stewart's commission brought me back to my own vulnerabilities.

I was on my own. I'd had no further sense today of being followed. Maybe that had just come out of unspoken anxiety about a "last throw of the dice" trip to Cambridge? Even so I needed to be wary of losing the items I'd gained from the Pepys Library.

It was too late for more analysis. The train was starting to empty now, just two more hours to Truro. Maybe a short nap would be sensible?

I packed my valuables into my rucksack and nestled it down on my lap. Then I stuck an arm through the straps. I wouldn't lose it on a busy train. The main risk was falling asleep until I'd gone way past Truro.

But even if I did, it wouldn't be the end of the world to land up in Penzance, even if it was the end of the line. A taxi to Trengilly Wartha from there was affordable. Tired but content I let my eyes close.

I was awakened by the noise of the train screeching and squeaking to a halt. I looked out of the window and saw that I'd reached Truro. By now the carriage was fairly empty. I had a final slurp of my coffee then grabbed my rucksack and leapt from my seat. I'd just managed to get out of the carriage as the platform guard signalled for the train to restart.

Maybe it was a recurrence of the panic from yesterday. But for some reason I sensed that, once again, I was being watched.

There was nothing I could do. I grabbed my phone and looked up the number of the taxi service that had brought me here from the Inn yesterday morning. 'We'll be with you shortly, sir.'

Sure enough, a taxi came along within a minute. Half asleep, I opened the rear door and climbed in. I was slightly surprised to see that there was someone inside already.

'Trengilly Wartha?' the driver asked.

'That's right,' I confirmed. 'It's just outside Constantine, that's a village on this side of Helston.'

I sat back. I was safe now, could go back to sleep for half an hour. As I laid my head back on the headrest I was aware that my fellow passenger was leaning towards me. They had some sort of cloth in their hand. Then they thrust it over my mouth. I was caught completely by surprise. I must have blacked out.

I can tell you nothing more about what happened after that for many hours. For a while others would have to tell the tale.

CHAPTER 30

It was Saturday evening. George and Frances had agreed, the day before, to meet for a meal out. 'It's not fair for me to keep relying on you, George. This time it's my treat.'

Frances had suggested they meet at the Ship Inn, a gastro-pub in Mawgan. 'That's midway between Gweek and Trelowarren. It won't be overcrowded in January. I'll book it for, say, seven thirty? Whatever the marchers get up to I'll be back from watching them by then.'

As the afternoon went by, George found she was increasingly worried about Anna. Had she been left behind on Mullion Island? She recalled that the girl was dressed merely as a servant. She wasn't wearing thick layers of waterproof, capable of withstanding biting winds; and George had heard that the forecast tonight was for freezing fog.

In late afternoon, as darkness approached, George had driven back to Mullion Cove to check the car park again. It was almost empty, just one car, a purple Kia. George was almost certain that had been there when she'd gone home from the Cove for lunch.

She made a note of the Kia's registration: maybe Frances would be able to work out the owner? It would be reassuring if it didn't belong to Anna.

When she reached the Ship Inn, George was pleased to see that the place was pleasantly full. Frances had already claimed a table in an alcove close to the log fire. She looked weary, she'd obviously had a long day. But she cheered up when she saw George.

'Hi, George. They've a low alcohol cider that I'd recommend.'

George forced her way to the bar and returned a few minutes later. She smiled, it would be good to talk to someone on a similar wavelength.

Frances pushed a menu in front of her. But before ordering anything George had something urgent she needed doing.

'Is there any chance, Frances, that you could do me a favour?' Her friend nodded.

George explained how she had ended up filming on Mullion Island and feared that her associate might have been left behind. 'I've got the number of the only car in Mullion Cove car park. Is there any chance one of your colleagues could check it out, find out who it belongs to? It'd be a huge relief to know it's not Anna's.'

Frances could appreciate the need for urgency and was soon on the phone to Helston.

'Give us a ring back, Dennis, when you've got something,' she concluded. 'Thanks very much indeed.'

'He'll ring me straight back. The DVLA are quite efficient. Right, George, I'm hungry. What do you fancy?'

Twenty minutes later the pair were tucking into helpings of sea bass with a range of vegetables. 'This is really good, Frances,' George observed.

'Fish meals are excellent around here. It's part of the Lizard culture.'

A pause and then George asked, 'So how was your day in Truro?'

'It was busy, George, very busy.'

Frances reflected for a moment. 'This Brexit thing is really hotting up. It's like . . . well, it's almost a new spectator sport. I doubt anyone really understands the issues, but they've taken sides anyway.'

'You mean, it's "I'm backing my team, win or lose"?'

'More or less. With a similar disregard for the rules and the ref. Actually it's even worse, it's almost tribal. Somehow or other there are huge loyalties on both sides which have little to do with traditional politics. Established politicians simply aren't cutting through. That makes everything a lot less stable. My boss is really concerned.'

A pause as both women ate more of their fish. 'So what were the marches today about?'

'One of 'em was the usual Brexit crowd. You'd think from the way they talk that the European Union is evil personified, the cause of everything that's ever gone wrong in this country. And also that the day after Brexit is completed, all will be sweetness and light.'

'Right. But they didn't have things all their own way?'

'Oh no. There was a separate march, starting on the other side of Truro. It was smaller but rather more civilised: that was the Remainers, also known as the People's Vote. They didn't shout as loudly but I think they were no less sincere.'

'Except that this lot didn't believe the result of the Referendum; wanted to wish it away.'

'Or else keep running it until it came out differently. Quite.'

'So that was it: Leave versus Remain?'

'Not quite. There was also a third march, with a message between the two.'

'What on earth did they want?'

'I didn't fully understand, George. It was some peculiar mixture, with a third ingredient thrown in as well.'

George mused as she finished her fish and set down her cutlery. What else might grab people in this end of Cornwall?

'Hey, was it the restoration of the Cornish language?'

To her surprise, Frances nodded. 'Well almost. What they were after seemed to be full Cornish independence.'

George gaped at her in amazement. 'What – '

But their conversation was interrupted by a beep on Frances' mobile. She glanced at it. 'Got to take this, George. It's Dennis from the Station.'

Frances turned away and held the phone close to her ear. She frowned, wrote something on a scrap of paper. A few seconds later the call was over.

She turned back towards George. 'I'm afraid that's not the news you were hoping for.'

'Go on.'

'Dennis says that the Kia is owned by someone called Anna Campbell. He's got us her address. It's down near St Keverne.'

'We need a dessert to help us think this through,' said Frances.

The waitress came and two brown sugar meringues were

ordered. The women held back from further debate until these had arrived.

'OK George, what might have happened to Anna?'

George began with her big fear. 'That somehow or other she got missed off the last boat back from Mullion Island.'

'But is that likely? I mean, she was part of the cast. They all knew her. The only way it could happen was if she'd fallen a long way back. But even then one of the cast would miss her, wouldn't they?'

Frances was reassuring; George was no longer certain.

'Alright, what else might have happened?'

George mused. 'Maybe Anna got back to Mullion Cove with everyone else, decided to go for a walk. Say she had walking gear already in the car. Then something happened on the walk, perhaps she slipped. Hey, she might still be out on the Coast Path.'

'OK. I can see that's possible. Though the path is very popular, even in winter. She would probably have been found by another walker. And we've no idea which way she would be heading. Even if we contacted the coastguards, they wouldn't start any search before it got light. So are there any other possibilities?'

George forced herself to consider the question calmly. 'I suppose that by far the simplest is that one of the cast invited her back for lunch. Maybe they went to the cinema? A bit like the way you left your car in Coverack.'

There was silence as both women tackled their meringues. George could see she might have been worrying unnecessarily. There was nothing she could do at this time of night, in any case.

'What are your plans for tomorrow?' asked Frances as their

meal drew to a close.

'Not got any at the moment.'

'Well, I'm off duty. Are you interested in another cliff walk?'

'As long as the weather is fine. Have you anywhere in mind?'

'I was just thinking we could park near to Kynance Cove and then walk up to Mullion Cove.'

George frowned. 'What makes you suggest that?'

'For one thing, it's a fabulous cliff walk. Kynance Cove is the finest view in Cornwall. It's probably the walk Anna would have done from Mullion Cove, going the other way. So when we got to Mullion, we could talk to the boatmen, see if any of them remembered bringing Anna back from the island.'

'You mean, Frances, it's another walk in search of clues on a missing female.' She smiled, 'Our usual Sunday exercise, in fact.'

The Lizard's fabulous Kynance Cove

CHAPTER 31

George Gilbert awoke on Sunday morning to discover that the view from her cottage window could be summed up in one word: fog. It made for a dismal setting. The context – her worries based on Anna's abandoned car – didn't help.

She had no idea how long the fog would last or how far it stretched. But it was hardly an excuse to spend the morning in bed. She forced herself to get up, cook some porridge and then prepare a couple of tuna sandwiches for lunch. How early dare she phone Frances to plead for a change of plan?

Her anxieties were cut short by the arrival of the police officer. Despite the gloomy weather she looked cheerful.

'Hi, George. Still happy to explore?'

'I'm OK if you are. But will we see much? Will we see anything?'

'This sort of overnight fog doesn't usually last too long. By the time we get to Kynance it might be starting to lift.'

George admired Frances' determination. Once she had a plan she wouldn't easily set it aside. But she presumed the police officer had plenty of experience of the Lizard in fog, knew what she was doing.

They decided to go in George's Mini Cooper as she had better fog lights. It was barely half past eight when they set out, not many other cars on the road. George drove watchfully: this was not the time for idle chatter.

They headed towards Helston and then turned left down the main road across the Lizard, heading towards Lizard Point. George wondered if the fog was getting worse. At the very least it was patchy. Occasionally it might be starting to lift and then it got thicker.

They had nearly reached the entrance to the side track that led to Kynance Cove when they were almost driven off the road by a large car, holding grimly to the centre of the highway. Probably its driver had assumed there'd be no-one else about. Frances, ever diligent, tried to take down its number but was thwarted by the dense fog.

Then they were onto the track to Kynance. 'We won't meet anyone travelling from the Cove this early,' said Frances. 'There's a National Trust car park at the far end,' she added. 'There won't be anyone there yet, we'll just drive in. I belong to the Trust anyway. I'll leave my membership card in the windscreen.'

George hadn't been to this part of Cornwall for years. She had a vague memory of a fine view down to the Cove in summertime. Just as well, since there wasn't any view this morning. She parked the car and slowly, fingers struggling in the cold, they put on their walking boots and zipped up their cagoules.

'Hey, I think it's starting to lift,' observed Frances.

George thought this was a triumph of hope over reality. Then she realised it was true: she could see a little further than when they'd arrived.

'We'll start over there,' said the police officer, pointing towards the cliff edge. 'That's the classic view.'

She led the way and George dutifully followed. She had to admit Frances was right: there was no doubt the fog was clearing. It was more of a mist now. Probably the wind was helping blow it away. They tramped through barren heather and finally reached the cliff edge.

'The finest view in Cornwall,' claimed Frances.

George stood beside her and peered down.

Kynance Cove was in its early morning tranquillity. No doubt it would have looked more spectacular in bright sunshine, but the remaining wisps of mist added to the air of mystery.

There was a bar of beach far below them, leading to a rocky promontory beyond. The cliffs where the women were standing dipped and then continued on towards Mullion. A white building nestled in the enclosed valley below.

'In summer time that's a popular café,' said Frances. 'But it's closed for the winter, I expect.'

George continued to examine the scene. It was well worth studying. She could see several small caves that could be reached from the beach.

'So what does all this look like at high tide, Frances?'

'Oh, you wouldn't see any beach at all. That far rock would be totally inaccessible, it's called Asparagus Island. Those caves down there would all be submerged. But there are steps. Would you like to go down?'

A fine footpath wound its way, twisting and turning, down through the cliffs, alongside the summer café and onto the beach. The National Trust at its best, thought George.

'You know, it's well after low tide. The water is starting to come back in,' said Frances.

'I wouldn't mind exploring the beach, even if only for a few minutes,' replied her friend.

'Make sure we don't get cut off then.'

George headed to the furthest end of the beach. From here there were cliff views on both sides, north up towards Mullion and south down towards Lizard Point. She was close to several caves.

Suddenly her eye was caught by something just inside the furthest opening. A large rounded rock, was it, or something more significant?

'Frances, look.'

Her friend followed her arm, could see where she was pointing. 'Hey, what's that?'

Quickly they headed towards it. It was a body. For the moment it was safe on the dry sand inside the cave, but George could see it wouldn't stay dry for long.

She gulped; was this going to be her last sighting of Anna?

Running, they reached the cave in seconds. The waves were lapping close to the entrance now, they didn't have long. Frances knelt down, put her hand inside the body's scarf and felt the neck for any sign of a pulse. 'He's still alive. Can we drag him up the beach between us?'

George felt a sense of relief that it wasn't Anna after all, it was a man. But whoever it was still needed to be rescued.

There was no time for finesse, they didn't have a stretcher. Each of them seized an arm. Then they hauled the man out of the cave entrance and steadily up the slope, towards the highest point on the beach.

'We can't stop here, George. See that seaweed. The tide will come right up to these rocks.'

'We've got a few minutes though. Hadn't we better check if he's got any broken bones?'

George turned and studied the man properly for the first time. She gave a gasp. 'Frances, I know who this is. I haven't seen him for a while but we were friends at College. This is Harry Jennings, he's a history lecturer.'

'Thank goodness for that. At last – a victim that we can name.'

Frances gave the man a rapid assessment. 'I've no idea what's going on inside him but I can't feel any broken bones.' She turned back to George.

'We've not got many options. All we can do is to choose the least worst. If we can manage to pull him up to the bottom of those steps we came down then we're probably clear of the tide. Once he's safe, one of us can stay to watch him while the other climbs back to the car. With a bit of luck the higher ground will give access to a mobile phone link. '

George agreed. They knuckled down and heaved Harry by his arms once more. Twenty minutes later they had reached the bottom of the steps.

George retrieved car keys from her cagoule pocket. 'You'd best phone the ambulance, Frances. You can tell 'em exactly where to come. Then stay warm in my car till they get here.'

Frances set off up the steps and George turned to Harry, still slumped unconscious on the lowest step. She peeled off her hat, scarf and gloves. 'Oh, Harry, what scrapes you get yourself into. Now then, dear friend, is there any way that I can make you more comfortable?'

CHAPTER 32

It took half an hour for the ambulance to reach Kynance Cove from Helston through the mist. It wasn't yet ten o'clock; George's car was still the only one in the car park. The ambulance drew up alongside.

As the driver jumped out, Frances realised that she knew him. It was the same crew as had attended their victim at Coverack, the week before.

'Well, well. We meet again!'

'Hi. It's Sergeant Cober, isn't it? Is this your weekend hobby?'

'Only in January. Are you the only guys ever on call?'

'The best ones, anyway. Right, where's our patient?'

Frances pointed down into the Cove. 'We had to move him to keep him out the water, got him as far as the bottom of the steps. It's a haul back up, I'm afraid.'

'Don't worry. There's a track round the back they use to take supplies to the café. We can drive down most of the way. D'you want to hop in?'

Five minutes later, George was surprised to see the ambulance looming out of the mist. The crew jumped out, recovered a stretcher and strode towards her. Frances followed more slowly.

'We got to him just before the sea did,' explained George. 'He was in a cave. He's breathing but not conscious. Not too cold and

190

we think no broken bones. He'd not been lying there for long.'

The ambulance driver knelt down beside him. 'Well done for finding him, ladies. We'll take him to Truro Hospital. They'll work out what's wrong.'

The ambulance crew settled the stretcher and gently transferred Harry onto it. Then they laid a thermal blanket over him, tucked it in and carried him carefully back to the ambulance.

'You know, I'm not so bothered about that walk now,' said Frances. 'I've lost one victim in a local hospital before I had chance to talk to them. I don't want to lose another.'

'Harry is an old friend, Frances. He's a responsible guy, won't run. But I'd like to be there when he wakes up. We'd better hurry back up those steps.'

Ten minutes later George and Frances were struggling to keep up with the ambulance and its precious cargo as the crew drove him carefully up the Lizard to Helston and then on towards Truro Hospital. The patchy mist made blue hazard lights irrelevant.

George wanted to stay close to her old friend. Frances had no direct link. Her motivation was a desire to get to the bottom of what looked like a serious crime. Her interest was heightened by the similarities between this find and the women they'd found a week ago.

'It was a close call, you know, Frances. I was watching. That cave was under water before the ambulance got here. If you and I had come half an hour later he'd have been dead, probably swept out to sea.' It was only with a struggle that she held back her tears.

'No point in calling up Scene of Crime then,' observed Frances. 'There must be some connection with the swimmers from last week – goodness knows what. This is worse than Agatha Christie.'

The name reminded George that they had set out today to find Anna. But for the time being Harry was her priority. He was tangible. She would just have to hope the woman turned up next day at Goonhilly.

'What's in your parcel?' she asked. Frances had appeared from the ambulance carrying a plastic bag. The police officer smiled.

'It's the first break we've had, George. You saw it was the same ambulance crew?'

'Yes?'

'Well, you know how the NHS is strapped for cash. It turns out this crew hang on to old thermal blankets in one of their lockers – in case they run short. They let me have the one they used last week on Ms Coverack. So I might be able to get her DNA after all.'

'Great. Let's hope her DNA is also somewhere on your database.'

The mist was clearing now and the ambulance ahead could go faster. George didn't want to lose him so didn't speak for some time, focussed on keeping up. But she could still ponder. And think outside the box.

Suddenly she had an idea. 'Frances, d'you think it's time for the police to start playing the criminals at their own game?'

Frances turned, gave her friend a careful glance. No, she wasn't joking.

'What were you thinking of?'

'Well, let's assume Harry wasn't trying to commit suicide. In that case, someone left him in that cave to drown.'

'I'd say that's almost certain. So?'

'What if you waited for twenty four hours and then called another press conference? Take a photo of Harry while he's still unconscious. In fact, given what happened to Miss Coverack, I took a few while I was waiting. One of them would do.'

'Go on.'

'Tell the media that another person's been found drowned on the Lizard. Show them Harry's photo. You could work out the most likely place for him to end up – maybe a short way up the coast? Make up some story about how he was found. And then appeal for suggestions on identity.'

Frances considered for a moment and then shook her head doubtfully. 'I don't understand, George. I'm not used to telling the press lies. What good would that do?'

George was still thinking the idea through. 'Well, for one thing, it might help us find out where he's been staying. I mean we don't know how long it'll be before he's conscious. It could be days. Don't you need to search his accommodation as soon as possible?'

'Come on, George, I wouldn't need to say he was dead for that. I could say he was still unconscious.'

George hadn't finished. 'The second reason for the trick is that it would stop you having to keep guard on him in Truro. Isn't that what you'll have to do otherwise, if you think he's a murder victim? Whereas if whoever left him in the Cove thinks

193

they've finished him off, they won't feel any need to try again.'

There was silence. Frances didn't want to go down the road of deceiving the press. A deliberate con was a slippery slope. But George was right: the logical alternative had to be keeping guard on Harry. She could do that by herself today but would need Inspector Marsh's approval and more resources if the vigil went on much longer.

'We can't do anything today, George: the local press don't work on Sundays. In any case, if our story is that he's been washed out to sea and then washed up again somewhere else, we'd need to allow time for that to happen.'

Frances paused and then continued. 'We'll leave it till tomorrow. If Harry is fully conscious then we can discuss it with him. I mean, the poor bloke might not want to be declared dead. We don't know what he's doing down here, he might prefer just to slip away.'

The police officer concluded, 'In any case I wouldn't want to do it without discussing it first with my boss.'

George sighed. Her main priority had been to keep her friend safe. Maybe Frances was being wise. It was hard to be completely dispassionate when you were a little emotionally involved.

CHAPTER 33

'Make sure, George, that we don't give reception Harry's real name. There's no point in making it too easy for whoever wants to kill him.'

The ambulance had reached Truro just after eleven and the patient had high priority. George and Frances had trailed after Harry into Accident and Emergency, their roles ill-defined.

Frances was aware that she didn't have the same power over hospital staff in Truro as she had in Helston. She would just need to be patient. The two were discussing their tactics while Harry was given preliminary triage. Eventually he was put on a trolley and taken off into the depths of the hospital.

'So who is this and what happened to him?' The reception nurse was looking at them sceptically.

George responded. 'You've been looking at Harry . . . Harry York. I'm George Gilbert, an old friend of his. Frances Cober here is a Helston police officer. We found Harry two hours ago, lying unconscious on a Lizard beach.'

'Hm.' The nurse mused, then decided to take them seriously. 'Our staff suspect he's been drugged. We'll need to do blood and urine tests, see if we can work out what substance was used, before we can decide on the best treatment. These days our labs are open seven days a week, so that shouldn't take too long.

195

D'you want to wait?'

'Yes, please.'

'Right. We're sending him to Penryn Ward. It's a backup ward for the A&E Department, on the top floor.'

The signs were less confusing than those in Helston, they found the ward without difficulty. At least Truro on Sunday was quieter than Helston on Saturday evening. Harry was lying at the far end of the ward, curtains closed around the bed.

The ward nurse explained, 'We're taking samples right away. Harry is still not conscious. You can sit over here if you like, till he wakes up. But you might have a long wait.'

George and Frances took their seats. Fortunately there was no-one else in the side room and they could talk freely, although they made sure they kept their voices down.

'Let's assume that someone drugged him, one way or another,' said Frances. 'Then left him to drown at Kynance. That's attempted murder. You know him. Where d'you reckon we should start looking?'

The question reminded George of something. 'Ah. While I was waiting for the ambulance I checked Harry's pockets.'

'Oh, well done. What did you find?'

'There was no phone that I could find. And no wallet, either.'

'That makes sense, George. His assailant would take them both. Either would have told the police exactly who he was, once his body was washed up. As we both know, not knowing an identity really slows down an inquiry.'

George nodded. 'That's what I thought. I did, though, find something in his top jacket pocket that the searcher probably missed. It's this.'

George reached deep into her cagoule inside pocket and brought out a train ticket. She flipped it over and read out the details.

'It's a return ticket, Frances, from Truro to Cambridge. That's a long journey. It's recent: out on Friday and back on Saturday - yesterday. It looks like something happened to him after he got back to Truro.'

Frances mused for a moment then opened her smart phone. 'OK. I've got the current rail timetable here. Let's see what train he might have been on – he wouldn't have had much choice.'

She pressed various keys and examined the result. 'Right. The latest he could have left Cambridge to get back last night would have been about four o'clock. That would get him to Truro just after eleven pm.'

'Do they have CCTV cameras outside the station here?'

'They certainly do, George. As long as they're still working.'

Frances frowned, checked a list and then dialled a number. 'Cornwall Police here,' she began. 'Can I talk to the security officer please?'

There was a short delay before someone answered. Frances identified herself and explained briefly the nature of her call. 'D'you have a camera at the front of the station?'

The answer was yes. Frances continued, 'I'm investigating a man who came off the eleven pm train from London last night, probably drugged. He's unconscious so I haven't been able to narrow down the exact time he was drugged yet. But I want to move on this as quickly as possible. Could I come over and check your recording? . . . Right away if possible . . . Thank you very much. I'll be there in about fifteen minutes.'

Frances turned to her friend. 'Is that OK, George? I'll leave you on guard while I go and check the CCTV. Could you email me your best picture of Harry, please?'

Frances had been in such a hurry to catch her security contact at the railway station that she hadn't left George precise instructions. What on earth did "on guard" really mean?

George sent on the photo of Harry and then pondered. There would be no harm in making sure the ward nurse was alerted too.

Fortunately there was a lull right now in ward activity. George wandered up to the desk and caught the nurse's attention. Her name tag said she was Megan.

'Any lab results through yet, Megan?'

'Not yet, I'm afraid. The first results shouldn't be long now. Your friend looks peaceful enough at the moment. Don't worry too much.'

'Can I tell you my real concern?'

The nurse looked at George carefully. Some instinct told her this was a sensible woman, she must take her worries seriously.

'Go on.'

'We were setting off on a walk when we spotted Harry in a cave in Kynance Cove, completely on his own. With the tide coming in. My friend's a police officer, she believes someone was trying to kill him. The thing is, if they find out they've failed, they might want to try again.'

The nurse looked shocked: this was well beyond her comfort

zone.

'So what can I do?'

'Well. Could you make sure no-one except known medical staff goes anywhere near him?'

The nurse considered. 'This is an emergency ward, we don't get many visitors. I suppose I could invent some medical reason or other to tell visitors to keep away: risk of cross-infection or something.'

'That'd be really good,' said George. 'Once Harry's conscious, the risk will go down. It's today that worries me most.'

George felt slightly relieved as she wandered back to her side room. And especially glad she'd given a false name for Harry at reception. But she hoped that Frances would not be too long. She was finding guard duty extremely stressful.

CHAPTER 34

While on her travels around Truro Frances had managed to call Constable Tim Barwell. He'd been doing some bike maintenance at home; last week's trip around the Loe Pool had taken a heavy toll.

'I'm not too busy this afternoon, boss,' he said. 'I can live without my bike if I have to. Where would you like me to come?'

Frances had explained the problem at some length.

'I'd be glad to take my turn on guard duty for Harry,' he responded. 'I can stay at the hospital overnight if you want.'

He came into the ward half an hour after Frances had returned from the train station. That was convenient: at least there was no problem with George having to try, cautiously, to make sense of who he was. She was pleased to meet this embodiment of youthful virtue. His eyes shone with the mere prospect of action.

But in other respects progress was slow. She and Frances each checked from time to time but there was no sign of natural recovery. Harry was still unconscious and the lab report on the drugs in his body was "still awaited". Treatment could not yet begin and the staff refused to speculate on how long that might take.

By late afternoon, frustrated, the women had returned to George's cottage at Trelowarren. Neither was keen to leave Harry but they had to prepare for busy weeks ahead.

'Would you like to share another convenience meal, Frances? I've got some chicken supreme. It's not much fun eating on my own.'

'If you really insist, George. I've nothing at home anyway. I'd been banking on us eating out. Thank you very much.'

Twenty minutes later, both more relaxed, they were tucking into chicken and rice and enjoying small glasses of cider.

'I don't want to pry into police details, Frances, but did you get anything useful from the station CCTV cameras?'

'I did get something. But it's not much use until Harry can add some comments of his own. Here, I'll show you.'

Frances walked out to the hall, fetched an envelope from her inside cagoule pocket and handed it over.

George saw half a dozen pictures of the station forecourt, the time stamp in the corner showing they'd been taken every twenty seconds. She recognised Harry easily. He was as distinctive as ever, looking cold in his sports jacket, just as they'd found him earlier today.

On the first two pictures he was busy on his phone. On the last one he was staring at a dark-coloured car as it came towards him.

'That was the last one I could find with him on it. I guess he got into the car. It's probably a late-night taxi.'

'Can you read the number?'

Frances shook her head. 'It's too fuzzy. But I'm getting the electronic version sent over. We've some enrichment kit at the Station that might tell us something. In due time that could be a big step forward.'

They continued eating, reflecting on the day's events.

'I'm afraid we didn't get any further on our search for Anna,' observed Frances a while later, thinking back to the day's original goal.

'No. I'm hoping she'll be back in the office tomorrow,' replied George.

'And if she isn't?'

'Her boss is Head of Security at Goonhilly. I'll start off with him. He should have her contact details and probably a decent photograph. Don't worry, Frances, I won't hesitate to raise the alarm if necessary. If it's clear that she's disappeared then you'll be one of the first to know.'

George made sure she was at Goonhilly early on Monday morning. Apart from her concerns over Anna, and also her worries for Harry (there'd been no call from the hospital, he was presumably still unconscious), she had plenty of work connected with the Newquay Space Station to get her teeth into.

Goonhilly was a research establishment; it didn't run on precise working hours. The analyst didn't want to raise any concerns for Anna until it was well past the time when she was normally in.

She gave her till half past nine and then wandered down to the open plan area, where she knew the girl was based.

Anna's desk was empty.

'Isn't Anna here yet?' asked George.

'She's not often the first in,' one of her colleagues remarked.

He didn't seem remotely concerned.

'But she's not phoned in sick or anything?'

He glanced around with a questioning frown. But no-one had taken any call from her this morning.

'Could you ask her, please, to call me once she gets here,' asked George.

'Sure,' said the colleague. He scribbled a note and put it on her desk.

George crept back to her office and knuckled down to her various project tasks. But she found it hard to give them her undivided attention.

An hour later George decided that she'd given Anna long enough. She rang Dr Jim Harvey and found he could give her a few minutes straight away.

'I fear something's happened to Anna,' she began, once she'd taken a seat in front of the security man's outsized desk.

George recalled her deep conversation with him on Friday. Mercifully, it seemed, that had encouraged him to take her more seriously.

'Tell me what's happened,' he responded.

Quickly George outlined the filming trip to Mullion Island on Saturday and the uncertainty over which boat Anna might have come back on.

'But the thing that really worries me, Dr Harvey, is that her car – it's a Kia – was still in the car park at Mullion Cove on Saturday evening.'

'Hm.' Dr Harvey gave the matter some thought. 'And she's

not here this morning?'

'She's not at her desk, anyway. As far as I can tell, no-one's heard from her.'

'Right. The first thing we need is a thorough search of the Goonhilly site. It'd be very embarrassing if someone had sent her off filing in a remote hut. I'll get Admin onto that straight away. Then I'll get her file and ring up every contact we've got listed.'

'Is there anything I can do?'

Harvey considered. 'Could you go to Mullion Cove and talk to the boat men? At least you'll know who they were. Can any of them remember bringing her back? If none of 'em are sure then I guess we're into a search of Mullion Island. Let's hope it doesn't come to that.'

George drove away from the site a few minutes later. She was gratified that Dr Harvey had taken her seriously, but apprehensive for what that meant for Anna.

Half an hour later the analyst was parking once more in the Mullion Cove car park. The purple Kia was still in the same position. George walked down to the Cove, wondering if any of the boatmen would be around on a weekday or if they'd all be off fishing.

Ben was there anyway, tinkering with his boat.

'Hi,' she greeted him. 'I'm George. I've links with the Constantine Players. You gave us all transport over to Mullion Island on Saturday morning. Would you be able to help me?'

'I'll do what I can, miss. What's the problem?'

Mullion Cove and Mullion Island

George reached into her cagoule and produced a photocopy of the photo of Anna which she had been given by Dr Harvey.

'This is an office photo of Anna, she's one of the people that went over there on Saturday. She's disappeared. Her car is still in the car-park up the road but she hasn't turned up for work. I'm sure of that much, anyway; she and I both work at Goonhilly.'

Ben looked puzzled at this potpourri of data. 'So how can I help?'

'What we don't know is if she came back, or if somehow or other got left behind on the Island. It will affect where we start the search, you see.'

'Ah.' Ben took the photograph and examined it carefully.

'As I recall, it wuz windy on Saturday. None of the girls looked anything like as smart as this. Course, they wuz all in their drama rigouts.'

He pondered for a moment. 'Hey, wuz she . . . wuz she one of the ones doing some filming?'

George felt a glimmer of hope. This was progress. 'That's right. I was the main camera woman and Anna was my assistant. I came back on the first boat so I could film the rest of 'em at sea. Anna was going to come back on the last one. She was doing the final piece of filming on the Island.'

'In that case, I might be able to help you, George. It wuz me piloting the last boat back, see. I recall someone a bit like this Anna, I think, she wuz in our boat. She had ginger hair. She wuz almost left behind, mind, but she made a big fuss and they all insisted I waited for her. My eyes wuz mainly on the weather, see. It's only a small boat, I didn't want to get caught in the next storm. So I'm sure she's not on the Island. Well, almost sure, anyway.'

'Ben, that's a huge relief. Thank you very much indeed.'

The Mullion Cove café wasn't open this morning so she couldn't even buy Ben a coffee to say thank you. But as George walked steadily back up to her car, two further thoughts came to her.

Firstly, the copied photograph she had shown Ben was only black and white. It gave no clue on hair colour. Anna didn't have ginger hair, it was auburn. But one of the other girls did. Ben was probably thinking of her. His testimony was driven by an unconscious desire to please. It was inconclusive, to say the least.

But never mind Ben, she was an idiot. There was one data source that had been in her own control all along that she hadn't thought to look at. One that ought to be conclusive, one way or the other.

She would just have to make a short detour on her way back to Goonhilly.

CHAPTER 35

Monday morning had been almost as hectic for Frances. She got to Helston Police Station early, checked her latest emails and then called Tim Barwell in Truro General. No, there wasn't any change to Harry, he reported. At least the nurse hadn't said he was any worse. They were still waiting on the lab results before they could start treatment.

'I'll send Dennis over straight away to replace you,' she said. 'Take the rest of the day off, Tim, and get some sleep. If Harry doesn't wake up today I might need you back there again this evening.'

Then she hastened to bring the newly-arrived Dennis up to speed before sending him off to Truro.

After that she despatched the thermal blanket that she had retrieved from the ambulance – the one they'd used a week before on Ms Coverack – over to Forensics. She added a note, pleading for urgent DNA analysis. She had no idea how this data might fit in to anything else that was going on, but there could be a link of some sort.

Finally, she tried to phone Inspector Marsh. She couldn't get through, but his secretary squeezed in an interview for her with him later that morning. A face-to-face briefing would be better anyway. Marsh might be sceptical about a girl found drowned in the Loe, but he would take the case of an almost-drowned Harry Jennings more seriously. Wouldn't he?

Frances had relaxed a little by now, was just working through some of the background tasks that had built up over the past few days, when there was another call. She picked up her desk phone somewhat reluctantly – the switchboard normally screened her from random calls. She was the last resort, not the first port of call. She put on her calmest voice.

'Hello. This is Helston Police Station. You're talking to Sergeant Frances Cober. How can I help you?'

A female voice came down the line. 'Hello, I want to report a missing person. Well, he might not be missing but . . .'

Whatever was coming next, she sensed some reassurance was needed. 'Let's go from the beginning, madam. What's your name, for a start?'

'I'm Joy, the Revd Joy Tregorran. I'm vicar at Church Cove. I'm ringing from the vicarage at Gunwalloe.'

Frances scribbled the name in her notebook. As far as she knew she'd never met the woman.

'And have you a name for the person that you think is missing?'

'It's Harry . . . Harry Jennings. He's a history lecturer at Exeter University. You see – '

Frances glanced at the clock on the station wall. Surprisingly it was only showing nine o'clock. Gunwalloe was the near end of the Lizard and this could be vital information. It might even explain what Harry was doing in this part of Cornwall. She computed: if she rushed, she could fit in a brief visit before heading to Truro.

'Joy, can I come and see you – straight away please? I'll be with you in about twenty minutes.'

She recalled what had nearly been done to Harry and a horrible thought occurred to her. 'In the meantime, please, could I request that you don't open your door to anyone? That's probably way over the top but I do have a reason. I'll explain once I get to you. Just hang on, Joy, I won't be long, I promise.'

The Monday morning rush hour was still active. It took Frances twenty five minutes to reach the vicarage in Gunwalloe. The officer had decided to drive over in her own car, there was no point in signalling police concern by having an official car parked on the road outside.

Once at the door Frances pulled on the heavy-duty doorbell, then stood two paces back with her warrant card open.

Twenty seconds went by and then twenty seconds more. Frances started to worry. Then the door opened a few inches, it was on a chain. A stressed-looking woman looked out, saw the warrant and gave a timid smile. Then she opened the door.

'Good morning, madam, I'm Sergeant Frances Cober.'

'I'm Joy Tregorran. Do come in. Would you like a coffee?'

A few minutes later the women were seated in the slightly warm kitchen, mugs of coffee in their hands.

'Right,' said Frances, 'let's start this conversation again. Tell me what you know about Harry and why you're so worried about him.'

'OK. I met Harry for the first time last Tuesday.'

So this wasn't a long-standing relationship. 'Where was that?'

'He was doing some project or other which led him to this vicarage. He thought there might be something hidden here. I was busy, but he came back on Wednesday afternoon and between us we searched the loft. Later we had a meal together in the local Inn. We found that we were enjoying one another's company. So much so that on Thursday we went to a play together. That was at Trelowarren Manor.'

'You mean the drama "Then There Were None"? Based on the book by Agatha Christie? What a coincidence, I was there too. It was good, wasn't it?'

Joy nodded. 'Trouble was, that was the last time I saw him.'

Frances nodded, though reflecting Thursday was now four days ago. If there was something the matter, why hadn't the woman reported it earlier?

'So what makes you think he's disappeared, Joy?'

'He had to go away for a couple of days: more enquiries relating to his project. But he promised me he'd be back in time for the Sunday morning service at Church Cove. He said he wanted to see a modern church in action. To be honest I think that, really, he wanted to hear me preach.'

'But he wasn't in the service?'

'No.' Joy paused, looking downcast.

'We'd agreed we wouldn't bother phoning each other, you see, while we were busy and a long way apart. I didn't want to interfere with his research.'

There was a pause, then Joy continued. 'I assumed that he must have lost interest in me, decided he didn't want to hear me preach after all. So at first I did nothing. Walked back home for a solitary lunch.'

'Till something else happened?' Frances could see that Joy needed encouragement.

'That's right. In the afternoon, I decided I'd ring Harry anyway. I mean, there was no point in me pining away if the man had completely lost interest. But I needed to know.'

Of course, Frances knew that Harry was not in any position to take her call by then anyway, but she wanted to learn all that she could from Joy.

'So what happened?'

'I got through to someone. Another man. But it certainly wasn't Harry. He sounded surprised that the phone had rung. I said I must have got the wrong number and dialled off.'

'So then you tried again?'

'Not straight away. I mean, if I was going to leave a message for Harry it had to be carefully worded. Then I rang the number.'

'What happened this time?'

'I just gave my name: Joy. I didn't give my surname or say I was a vicar. I didn't want to leave any clue on who I was. I said I wanted to leave a message for Harry. He already had my number. Please could he ring me at his convenience, I was in all afternoon. Then I rang off.' She gave a nervous laugh. 'After which I started to worry like mad.'

'So what made you call the police?'

'This morning I forced myself to stop feeling sorry for myself and to think clearly. I concluded that something unplanned must have happened to Harry. That's when I decided to call you.'

Joy stopped speaking and looked hard at Frances. 'If this was all new information I doubt it would warrant a personal visit. So, Sergeant, what can you tell me? And why ever do I need to lock my door?'

Frances needed a few minutes to work out what she could say. 'Before I begin,' she asked, 'is there any chance of us having a second mug of coffee?'

As Joy busied herself – this time it looked like she was going to provide biscuits as well – Frances mentally ran through the options.

First of all, she judged it impossible that Joy had anything to do with Harry's disappearance. If she had, to ring the police would have been the last thing she'd have done.

The choice was how much detail the officer could share. The trouble was, the less Joy was told the less she would be on her guard. She couldn't be expected to lock her doors without understanding why that was sensible – especially given her pastoral role.

Conversely, the more she knew, the more inclined she'd be to share with the police. Frances hadn't yet got any detail on Harry's project. Joy must know more than she'd said so far.

Frances concluded that full disclosure was the only viable option.

Joy brought two mugs to the table. 'Right, Sergeant. Here's coffee; help yourself to biscuits. Now then, what d'you know about Harry?'

'Everything I'm about to tell you, Joy, is in strict confidence.'

'Of course. I am used to keeping secrets, Sergeant.'

'Right.' Frances collected her thoughts and then launched in. 'I'm sorry to have to tell you, Joy, that Harry is currently lying unconscious in a bed in Truro Hospital.'

Frances realised as she spoke that this wasn't the kindest way of sharing such shocking news. She should have been more gentle.

But Joy's experience as vicar had given her resilience. She put her hands to her face and gave a gasp of alarm.

For a moment there was silence in the kitchen. Then the vicar looked up. 'What happened? Was Harry involved in an accident of some sort?'

'That's why I warned you to keep your doors locked, Joy. It seems likely that someone was trying to do him harm.' Frances went on to outline how Harry had been found by chance in a cave at Kynance Cove and had been pulled back from an incoming tide.

'That's why I wanted you to take care, Joy. Whoever did that to Harry probably thinks he's dead and washed out to sea. Until we catch them I fear they might want to do something similar to you.'

Joy continued to look shocked.

Frances glanced at her watch, saw it was already half past ten. She was due to see her boss in less than an hour. She'd better not be late.

'Is there any chance I could go and see him?' asked Joy.

'I have a twenty-four hour watch on Harry, Joy. And I have to get to Truro right away. I'm hoping he'll recover consciousness today. Once he's with us, I'm sure he'd love to see you.'

The police officer gave her a smile and then felt in her pocket. 'In the meantime, Joy, here's my card; and that's a direct line. Call me any time, day or night.'

Frances concluded, 'If you could organise yourself to stay inside the vicarage today, that would be very sensible. Ring me if anything happens here that seems at all suspicious. Stay calm.' She smiled, 'I'll be back this afternoon for a longer chat.'

CHAPTER 36

'I hope you haven't come to nag me about a fat swimmer in a sparse swimsuit,' began Inspector Kevin Marsh, as Frances Cober took the only spare seat in his modest office.

'Not today, sir. I've something more serious than that.'

'Go on then.'

As briefly as she could, Frances told her boss how she and a walking friend had stumbled on the body in a Kynance Cove cave, early on Sunday morning.

'By pure chance my friend recognised him. He was Harry Jennings, an old student friend of hers, now a University lecturer. He was breathing but not conscious. The tide was coming in. We had to pull him to higher ground between us, or he'd have drowned. Once we'd done that, we called an ambulance, got him to Truro General within the hour. They're still trying to work out what's wrong with him.'

'Hm. So what do our wonderful health experts suspect?'

'The most likely cause, they say, is that Harry has been drugged. They are still waiting on lab results based on blood and urine samples. But if that is the case then –'

'You might well have stumbled on the last phase of an attempted murder. Right, Sergeant. I see what you mean. This is serious.'

216

Marsh sat back and pondered for a moment. 'So what steps have you taken so far?'

'I made sure we didn't give the man's correct name to the hospital, sir. He's in there as "Harry York". I stayed with him all afternoon. I put one of my constables on guard overnight and there's another one there as we speak. The thing is, sir, if it is an attempted murder that failed, and that becomes widely known, whoever did it might want to try again.'

'Good, good. That sounds sensible, at least for a day or two.'

'I'm off to the hospital next, sir. I'm hoping they'll be in a position to start treating him soon. Once Harry is conscious he might be able to tell us a lot more about what happened. Also, maybe, to tell us what he was investigating that led to the attack in the first place.'

Marsh looked more alert than Frances had seen for years. Maybe for once he was going to say something useful?

'Have you any suggestions, sir?'

The Inspector was silent for a moment.

'The thing is, I don't much like coincidences, Sergeant. You say it was "pure chance" that your friend recognised this man. From a long time back. But don't you think that's amazing? The man is hidden away on a remote beach and your friend is there at the right moment to find him. Are you really sure about her? You haven't just been set up?'

Frances was shocked. This wasn't what she was expecting at all. Inside she was fuming – how dare her boss set up in judgement on her friends? –but she did her best to keep her voice neutral. 'I'm certain that she was as surprised as I was, sir.'

He frowned. 'Well, just keep the thought in mind, anyway. Don't involve her any more from now on unless you really have to. This is a police matter, remember. And she's not part of the force at all.'

There was silence as fresh thoughts were collected.

The Inspector continued, 'We can't do anything until the blood test results are in. We need confirmation that drugs were used; and we need to know which ones they were. Our only advantage right now is that Harry is still alive, not washed up on some far off beach. Trouble is, until he can talk about what happened, that doesn't do us much good.'

Frances recalled the idea which George had floated the day before. Best though not to say where it came from. 'Could we do a press conference, sir, claim that his body has been found dead, washed up further along the coast or something?'

For a second Marsh almost smiled. 'That's a cunning idea, Sergeant. Really smart. But I'm not sure precisely where it would get us. Harry might find he had to pretend to be dead for days, or even weeks. And if he wouldn't play ball on the idea then we'd be horribly embarrassed.'

He considered for a moment. 'There might be some other sort of trap we could set, though. What if we claimed the drugs had caused him to lose his memory?'

'It's not clear that they haven't, sir.'

Reluctantly, Marsh nodded. He thought his idea had sounded rather clever. 'That's true. OK, let's keep that between us as a last resort – a trick to use if all else fails. In any case, I'm behind you on this one, Sergeant. We'll keep it from the media for as long as we can. Let me know what happens and tell me if you need more resources.'

The last word reminded him of his wider problems and he sighed. 'Mind, we're horribly stretched at the moment. I'm fearful that all these political marches that our fellow officers had to supervise on Saturday will start mingling and fighting before too long. If we're not careful we could end up with a local civil war.'

He concluded, 'It's the Westminster "meaningful vote" to-morrow, I think. The latest one, anyway. They say it's the Prime Minister's last stand. Let's hope that our wonderful MPs can find some way to get their collective acts together.'

When Frances got to the emergency ward at Truro General she sensed a ripple of excitement among the staff, though in the far-end bed Harry looked as inert as ever.

Constable Dennis Penhaligon saw her arrive, came out from the side room and brought her up to speed. 'They've just had the lab results back, boss.'

Frances was aware professional niceties had to be respected. She would need to wait till one of the staff nurses was in a position to share the news.

'Has anything else happened?' she asked him.

Dennis pulled a face, 'Quiet as a grave, boss.' Then realised this was perhaps not the best phrase for this context.

'Right, Dennis. Why don't you go and find yourself some lunch, I'll wait here till you get back.'

Dennis wandered off in search of signs for the hospital canteen and Frances eyed the staff; which one of them could she push to tell her what they had now found?

Ten minutes later her patience was rewarded. The staff nurse they had dealt with yesterday, Megan, came to sit beside her in the side room.

'We've just had the lab results for Harry,' she said. 'They say he's been given a severe dose of Gamma-Hydroxy Butyrate. You probably know that as GHB.'

Frances frowned. 'I've come across it. Isn't it what's used on date rape?'

'That's right, though that's not what happened here. GHB depresses the central nervous system. There's no odour. It's more or less undetectable when mixed with a drink – an ideal way to spike someone's drink and make them vulnerable. And it's not that hard to get hold of. If you wanted you could certainly find it in Truro.'

'So he wasn't injected?'

'Not as far as we can tell. We can find no needle marks on Harry's body, anyway.'

'What's its effect?'

'A mild dose of GHB will make you feel euphoric. The trouble is, a bigger dose will cause dizziness or blurred vision, even loss of consciousness. In extreme cases, with a large dose, it can be fatal. We think that's behind what happened here.'

'Right. No reason, then, to think it was an accidental overdose?'

'I don't think so, Sergeant. And it's not something you'd take to commit suicide. It's not sufficiently predictable, there are easier ways to do that. No, I think you can safely assume that, somehow or other, Harry has been assaulted.'

Frances mused. 'So . . . moving forward?'

'Now we know what he's had, there are treatments, though they may take a while. We don't know exactly when he was given the drug or how big a dose he had. The Consultant says it's important we don't over-treat it and make everything worse.'

Frances frowned. 'You mean, he might be unconscious for days and days?'

'One or two, anyway. But don't worry, we'll get him back in the end.'

Frances recalled her earlier discussion with Inspector Marsh. Would there be any side effects? 'Is there any risk of memory loss?' she asked.

'That's not usually a consequence of GHB. By tomorrow or Wednesday he'll probably be as right as rain.'

So all they had to do was to guard him for a couple more days. And in the meantime to start work on identifying his attacker.

Once she was back in Helston, Frances decided that it was time for a longer conversation with the Revd Joy Tregorran. She now had more news to share about Harry and many more questions that needed answers. This was the start of a major enquiry.

She gave the vicar a call but got only a voicemail. That was slightly odd. Frances left it for ten minutes and then rang again, with the same result.

Probably the woman had some commitment or other in Gunwalloe. She was, after all, a professional woman. Maybe she always turned off her phone during pastoral visits?

No need to get alarmed, the police officer told herself.

Frances hadn't been taking notes during her conversation with Joy. At first she hadn't realised there would be anything to record. Now, belatedly, she did her best to summarise what she'd been told.

Joy and Harry had been out for a meal at the local Inn; and to the play, "Then There Were None", at Trelowarren Manor.

Frances frowned. If anyone had been keeping track of Harry before they attacked him, Joy could have been seen with him in either location. She assumed they weren't brazenly fondling one another or anything. Even so, it might be easy to mistake the relationship. Moreover, Joy was the local vicar: she'd be well-known and easy to recognise.

Frances decided that she would not worry about the woman for the rest of the afternoon. On the other hand she would certainly call on her on her way home this evening.

CHAPTER 37

It was fortunate, thought George, that Trelowarren Estate was practically on the way from Mullion Cove to Goonhilly Earth Station. She could drop in to her cottage on the way back to the office.

What she was after was her video camera. In particular the film she had taken of the voyages back from Mullion Island. For that would give a more accurate record than she'd had from Ben: had Anna come back with the rest of the party, or was the poor woman still stuck on the island?

It wasn't possible to tell from the camera's viewfinder: that was too small. In its image every figure was only a tiny dot. But it didn't take long to connect the camera to the large-screen television that came with the cottage. That was better, it substantially enlarged the image.

By now it was almost lunch time. George made up a tuna sandwich to munch as she watched. She hadn't had time to edit the film over the last forty eight hours, so it wasn't the slickest footage she had ever viewed. But it was relatively sharp. No mist on the Saturday, anyway.

She ran the film on from the first boat trip across to Mullion Island. That showed the rocky foreshore. The beach where they

223

eventually landed was the only place where a landing seemed remotely possible.

The film ran on to show the other boats setting out from the Cove. Then the sequence which Charles had insisted on, in which poor Nathan had to stand in the freezing seawater as he was edged out into the deep.

Finally came the film of the return journey. Two of the other boats followed her own launch fairly quickly. She paused the film once or twice to check the occupants: no sign of Anna there.

That left the fourth boat. George saw she'd done her best to zoom in as it pulled away from the shore. It was slightly shaky. But there, sitting alongside the boatman, was the auburn-haired Anna, filming away on her own account. There was no problem: wherever the girl was now, she had not been left behind, drenched, cold and hungry on Mullion Island.

George made a pot of tea in celebration. It was just possible that Anna had rounded off her Saturday by going for a walk on the Coast Path and had a fall. But even in January the Path had regular walkers, especially at weekends. Someone, surely, would have seen or heard her.

The most likely explanation was that she had been invited back for lunch with another member of the cast. That worked as far as it went. But it still didn't explain everything: why hadn't she come back for her car and why wasn't she back in the office today?

George had only got involved in the play on the Friday, and then just to wield the camera. She hadn't spent time with the rest of the cast, had no social connection. Anna was the only actor she knew and the only one for whom she had a phone number. She puzzled for a moment: how could she reach one of the others?

Charles was in charge of the whole thing. He would have contact details for the rest. She resolved to try and find his address.

Google was consulted. What did it say about the Constantine Players? After a few minutes she found the website, which was rather anodyne. It linked the Players to Constantine Museum, with some opening times but not much else.

Then she recalled Anna saying that Trelowarren was their only venue for this play. So currently they had nothing else to advertise. No wonder it didn't say much.

George felt frustrated. She was about to close down her tablet and head back to the office when she had a thought. When was the Museum open? She found the website again. It claimed to be open for a couple of hours on Monday afternoons.

She might as well pay them a visit. A Museum would at least have someone in charge. With a bit of luck they'd be able to give her details on Charles – or some other member of the Players cast.

She'd lost her enthusiasm for work on Goonhilly Security in any case.

Constantine, when George reached it, was an efficient, pretty-looking village just beyond Gweek. It didn't sprawl far and had fields on all sides.

There was a ridiculously large church with a high tower in the centre, a few shops and then, further down, a burnished-stone building that she guessed had once been the Methodist Chapel.

The sign outside proclaimed "Constantine Museum and Arts Centre". George parked her car and wandered in.

A notice inside told her that she'd reached an exhibition, made up of work by local children over the years and entitled "Secrets of the Lizard". It was a mixture of drawings, paintings and diary entries. Most were handwritten, though one or two recent entries had been produced on a computer.

George stood at the entrance. For the moment she couldn't see anyone in charge.

If there was no-one to take the money, maybe the exhibition was free? George wandered up and down. It had been well-done, certainly. There were plenty of pictures of caves on remote beaches, one or two stone circles and a couple of fogous, which she gathered were small underground chambers. George had just come across a rather odd article entitled "Python's Pad" when someone else arrived, a middle-aged woman who looked like she was dressed for an arctic winter.

'Good afternoon,' George greeted her. 'Are you another visitor like me, keeping out of the cold, or are you in charge?'

The woman laughed. '"In charge" would be putting it too strongly. I come in to make sure nothing is trashed or stolen. Not that that's very likely. But it needs taking care of; it's taken us months to assemble.'

In truth George didn't have much interest in a children's exhibition but felt she had to ask a couple of questions before moving onto the Players.

'How far back do the entries go?'

'They're all post-war. Mostly 1960s or later. We've tried to focus on the more unusual places. Mercifully the Lizard doesn't change much over the years, so something that was seen fifty years ago is probably still in place today.'

George pointed to the stand she'd just reached. 'So what on earth is Python's Pad?'

'I have no idea. The designer behind the exhibition might know. He's never here on Mondays but he's usually around on Thursday afternoons.'

'Right. To be honest, what I really came for wasn't the exhibition itself, it's someone who might be able to tell me about the Constantine Players. I saw their play last week at Trelowarren Manor.'

'Oh yes, they've got some good actors – for a cast of local players, anyway. They put something on most years. They could do with a wider audience. It's a pity they're not better known.'

'D'you have any contact details? I had one or two questions, you see. I'm after a longer chat with Charles. He's the Director, I believe.'

The woman shrugged. 'I'm afraid I don't, I'm just a volunteer guide. But the Players have an office round the back. Maybe someone there will be able to help you.'

George found her way to the back office. It was musty and untidy, certainly wasn't intended to be seen by visitors. Today, though, there was no-one there at all.

If it was still relevant she would have to come back and talk to the curator later in the week.

George rang in to report to Dr Harvey of her limited progress on

Anna – it turned out that he'd not got anywhere on his phone calls either. Then, her energy sapped, she decided to spend the rest of the afternoon working in her cottage.

Later on she tried phoning Truro General for news on Harry. But evidently the police operation to protect him had been tightened up. Despite her best guiles, and even the claim that she was the one that had found him, she was unable to learn anything.

She resolved to ring Frances after work. She had no reason to think her friend would hold back, anyway.

CHAPTER 38

On Tuesday morning Frances decided that she would make sure the routine work was properly delegated within Helston Police Station; she was heading over to Truro later on. The longer she left it, the more chance there would be that Harry had recovered consciousness and was able to talk.

Dennis Penhaligon was once more despatched to swap with Tim Barwell, who had spent a second night keeping an eye on Harry.

She'd had a quick phone chat with Tim but he'd seen no signs of a major breakthrough. He confirmed, though, that the medical team were now active on the case. But he warned, 'Treating for drugs is not a precise science, boss. It's simply a matter of us being patient.'

The previous night Frances had visited Gunwalloe on her way home but there was no sign of Joy in her vicarage and the lights were all off.

Frances had peered through each ground floor window in turn. There was no sign of forced entry and nothing suspicious to be seen. For the time being the police officer had decided not to break in. She had no warrant to cover such a step; and no chance of obtaining one on what she knew so far.

229

At worst, something horrible might have happened. Frances thought of Harry and shuddered. Perhaps Joy too was now lying in a flooded cave.

But there was another possibility. Joy might have decided to take herself off for a short holiday for a few days and chosen to tell no-one where she had gone. After all, she might feel she had no more reason to trust police officers than anyone else.

Frances had gone home and agonised over what to do. At one point George had rung but she had been short with her, though she did tell her Harry was now being actively treated. Frances wasn't much bothered by her Inspector's worries. Even so, she hesitated to share her latest anxieties over Joy at this stage.

But even if the worst came to pass, she had not the faintest idea on where to start looking. Moreover, if something had happened to Joy, it had to be linked to Harry. Solving his case was the best way forward for Joy as well.

Whatever the case, public appeals for information on Joy would almost certainly be counterproductive. She had given her personal phone number to the vicar and reassured her she could ring day or night. But the inter-personal chemistry between them was weak. There was only one occasion when the two had met.

Sooner or later, she hoped, Joy would be in touch to explain where she had gone and when she would be back. She could only hope that this call would come sooner rather than later.

Midway through the morning, Frances received a call from Forensics. The specialist had managed to identify DNA on the thermal blanket they had been sent yesterday. So now they had the DNA record for "Ms Coverack".

The trouble was, it didn't match or link to the data for any known person on the Police National DNA database.

Frances pondered. She wished Tim Barwell was here to bounce ideas off, or that she could go and talk to George.

For a few seconds she considered another meeting with Kevin Marsh. But she recalled that he had been scathing about swimsuit victims and not much better on George. It would be best to stay on good terms by sticking to Harry. There was no point in rekindling his earlier ridicule.

The National DNA database contained data on all recent UK criminals. It also held the DNA for suspects on live investigations. So Ms Coverack was not known to the police, in the UK at any rate.

Suddenly Frances had an idea. She had already asked herself if there was a connection between the two swimsuit victims she had come across a week ago: Ms Loe and Ms Coverack. Would it not be sensible to check if there was any link between them on their DNA records?

Quickly she called back Forensics and explained her idea. It was not ridiculed, at any rate.

The Department confirmed that they had both sets of DNA records, although they had not so far been looked at together.

'We'll have a look,' said the local scientist. 'They're both here. It won't take us long.'

Twenty minutes Frances received the call. 'You're hunch is correct, Frances. Your swimsuit victims from the Loe and from Coverack are related. They've strong familial links. In fact they're not just distant cousins; they are sisters.'

'Great. Thank you very much indeed.'

For a moment Frances felt she had made a major break-through. Her suspicion that the girls had some personal connection or other was now proven. It didn't just rest on a coincidence of identical swimsuits, sold together at the local late-night Tesco.

Then the reality hit her.

What difference did this make? In truth they'd made little progress on Ms Loe, despite calls to all owners of cars parked around the Loe Pool and a media appeal. And no progress at all on Ms Coverack. They hadn't even managed to hang on to her for long enough that she could be interviewed.

The fact that the two girls were sisters might eventually account for their swimsuit-clad bodies both being found at much the same time. It might one day point to a common motive.

That was eventually. In the short term Frances was no further forward.

The problem continued to bother Frances as she carried on with routine tasks.

Then she recalled that today was Tuesday: it was a week since her only press conference on Ms Loe. Surely she could repeat that, but add the new information? It was an excuse for a fresh appeal, anyway. Maybe she could widen it to include a reference to her sister.

But could she be more subtle? Frances recalled that she had taken a few backup pictures of Ms Loe, when she and Tim had first been called out. Maybe one of these could be shown to the press this time – though perhaps fudging which woman was being shown? Someone might even recognise the swimsuit?

Frances could see that this press conference would be less straightforward than the one she'd called last week. But it was surely worth a try. She'd promised to keep the journalists in the loop, anyway. She gave a sigh, called the Public Relations officer and booked the event for later that afternoon.

By now it was late morning. Time for her daily trip to Truro. There must be something happening to Harry soon. Surely?

CHAPTER 39

Frances decided that she didn't need to brief Inspector Marsh again until she had something fresh to tell him. So she drove straight to the hospital and was soon in Penryn Ward. Dennis Penhaligon was waiting in the side room.

'Any news?' she asked.

'Well, you know that we put a gadget in the ward to track any incoming calls asking for Harry?'

Frances grinned. That had been Tim Barwell's suggestion. 'Hey, has it given us something?'

Dennis shrugged. 'It's inconclusive. There have been two calls to the ward asking for Harry in the past twenty four hours, both yesterday evening. And both from women. Trouble is, neither of 'em left a name.'

Frances pondered for a moment. 'One of 'em was probably my friend George. She was the person who first spotted Harry, she knows him from college and she's the only reason, actually, that we know who he is. She rang me last night but I was too busy to talk.'

'And the other?'

Frances mused. 'It might have been Joy Tregorran. She's the vicar in Gunwalloe that I talked to briefly yesterday morning. She's a more recent friend of Harry. It might imply that she's taken a break to keep out of the way but wanted to know how he was. It's a pity she didn't ring me directly. I'd like to talk to her again.'

'Or one call might be from the assailant or his girlfriend. Wanting to check if Harry is still alive, for a start; and to see if he's started to talk.'

Frances nodded. 'That's true. Pity the device isn't smarter, you know. There must be a way of capturing incoming numbers even if the caller had withheld their identity. If Harry doesn't wake up soon I'll get Tim to look for an upgrade.'

She turned towards the patient's bed. Harry was still lying peacefully but somehow – perhaps it was just wishful thinking? – there seemed to be more hint of life than there'd been yesterday.

She turned back to her colleague. 'Go and get some lunch, Dennis. I'll hold the fort till you get back. I'll see if I can winkle anything out of the nursing staff.'

Megan, the nurse that she and George had first encountered on Sunday, was on duty once again. Frances reckoned that she was the best chance for an unofficial briefing. The police officer waited until there was a period of calm in the ward and then grabbed the nurse's attention.

'How's it all going with Harry, Megan?'

'He's certainly improving. We're gradually stepping up the remedial dose and it's having some effect. He might come round any time.'

'No outside visitors?'

'No, thank goodness. We've made sure all the nurses are aware of the risk. And of course the police presence is an extra re-minder.'

'Once Harry is awake, how long will you need to keep him in?'

'Not long, I expect. If he woke up this afternoon, say, he could be out by this time tomorrow.' She laughed. 'Then he'd be your problem and not ours.'

On the whole that sounded reassuring. Frances went back to the side room but sat on the edge of her seat, where she could keep an eye on Harry.

A few minutes later there were a few more signs of life. Harry's body started to twitch and the bed clothes were moving a little.

And then, for a second, his eyelids fluttered.

Nurse Megan was equally alert for signs. She walked over and peered at the patient closely.

'Hello, Harry,' she murmured. 'Wake up dear, you're in hospital.'

It took a while before the ward staff were satisfied that Harry was fully conscious and that there were no hidden problems that they might have missed. But Frances was watching carefully from a distance and saw that his eyes remained open.

Eventually Nurse Megan came over to her.

'We think it'll be alright for you to have a few minutes with him. Not long, mind. He'll probably want to go back to sleep soon.'

'Thank you.'

Frances walked over and took the visitor's seat beside the bed. She gave the patient her biggest smile.

'Hello, Harry. My name is Frances. I'm a police officer.'

Harry looked slightly confused. He blinked a few times.

'I'm not sure how I got here.'

'What's the last thing you remember?'

He frowned. 'I was in a train. Coming back to Truro. It was late evening, I got out but there was no-one else around.' He paused.

'I came out of the station, you see, and then I called a taxi. On my phone. One came along very quickly so I got in. Then . . .'

He frowned again.

'Yes?'

'It was odd. There was someone else in the back seat. They reached out towards me. Then something happened and I must have blacked out.' He shook his head. 'I don't remember anything after that.'

He stopped and stared around him. 'What on earth am I doing here?'

Frances wasn't sure how much she should say at this point. In her peripheral vision she sensed a nurse moving towards them.

She had had her few minutes of face to face contact. There could be plenty more later. For the time being it would be best to stick to the hard facts.

'You're in hospital, Harry. In Truro. I'm afraid you've been drugged. But you're on the mend now. You're probably feeling very tired. Why don't I come back and talk to you again a bit later?'

237

CHAPTER 40

After her disjointed Monday, George Gilbert had made sure she would be in Goonhilly early on Tuesday morning.

The analyst was still worried about her friend Anna but for the time being that was not her direct responsibility. She had convinced herself that Anna hadn't been left behind on Mullion Island –that was the only place where, as chief film-maker, she might have had some personal culpability.

George had no idea where on earth the girl had got to, but there was no reason to connect her to any criminal activity on the Lizard. George had an important job to do at Goonhilly, for the moment Anna would have to be parked.

But she hadn't been in her office for long when there was a call from Dr Harvey. Could she come along to see him, please? She made her way to his office straight away.

'Thank you for coming, George. Also for all your endeavours yesterday in search of Anna.'

He saw she was standing a little uncertainly in the doorway. 'Please, George, do sit down. And from now on call me Jim. We'll leave Anna for now. There's something else that's come along that I need your help on. It affects security at Goonhilly, you see. You seem to be the only person around here that appreciates my underlying concerns.'

Intriguing. What was coming next?

Harvey continued. 'First of all, I've some news on the radar hut just outside the Station that you told me about last week. I told one of my operators about it. He got over there yesterday.'

'So what did he find?'

'He tells me that it was an immensely strong padlock, nothing like ones we use. Which means it was nothing to do with us. But he needed our strongest bolt-cutter to break it open – and it took him a long time.'

'And when he'd done that, what did he find inside?'

'That was the puzzle. The first thing was a live power link. Presumably that's connected somehow or other, via an underground cable, into Goonhilly.' He shrugged. 'But that might have been in place for half a century. We can live with that. The Station's electricity costs are massive anyway.'

'But what was it powering?'

'That's the really worrying question. It was a sophisticated battery charger, George. With every slot on the device full. It had a complete quota of fully recharged batteries.'

George was puzzled. 'Have you any idea what they're intended for?'

Harvey looked perturbed. 'Not sure. But remember our chat last week. We were talking of various ways the Station might be disrupted or eavesdropped. Listening could be done off the mains supply but one possibility that would need batteries is a large drone.'

George considered. 'But why would someone keep the batteries in the hut, but not the drone itself?'

'I can't be certain. Maybe someone plans to bring the drone along at the last minute, with another set of batteries. Then to attack the Station from the roof of the hut. The ones we found might just be intended for rapid replacement.'

There was a moment's silence. It sounded convoluted and rather sinister.

'So right now, Jim, you think it's possible that there's a large drone hidden somewhere on the Lizard, probably not far from Goonhilly. Which is intended to disrupt the satellite monitoring devices at the most embarrassing moment?'

George stopped. There was an obvious follow-up question: dare she ask it?

'Let's split the problem in two, Jim. Firstly, when is the next time that the Station is most vulnerable? How long have we got?'

Jim nodded gloomily. It was the question he had been asking himself, before he had decided to share with George.

'I would say it's the time when we have a senior visitor, a prospective client, that we are trying to impress. Especially if that means showing off our space monitoring capability and boasting about our security.'

'OK. And the next time that'll happen is . . .?'

'This coming Friday. There's a new Chief Executive Officer at Newquay, Kelly Symonds. She's coming over to meet our top management and to get her head round the Space Station concept.'

George recalled that she had been given the date before she started work at Goonhilly. She'd forgotten that Symonds was coming so soon. That was certainly a moment of potential risk.

'Right, Jim. So let's take that as our deadline. The other issue is, where should we be looking? How big are these drones? How easy are they to detect, in flight and in storage? And if you had one, where might you hide it?'

'Hey, slow down, George. To be honest, I don't know. Not the up-to-date answers, anyway. The trouble is, drone technology moves on so fast. The "facts" which I now recall are probably five years out of date.'

He paused and then concluded, 'Why don't we come back to this after lunch? You can carry on with your routine work. In the meantime I'll talk to some of my security friends elsewhere. Someone must have some up-to-date facts on the problem.'

George went back to her office but found it hard to settle. Of course, Jim Harvey might be mistaken. Or paranoid. But she recalled that no-one had taken much notice of the drone threat at all until Gatwick had been closed down for three days just before Christmas.

George assumed she'd be having lunch on her own. But as she headed for the communal hut at the rear – the nearest Goonhilly got to shared eating – she saw Anna was already sitting there, tucking into her yoghurt. Feeling quite aggrieved, George strode over and sat down beside her.

'Anna, where on earth have you been?'

Anna smiled. 'I had a day off yesterday. That is allowed, you know. Even in these stressful times.'

'But what about your car? The Kia you left in Mullion Cove. I saw it there and spent half of yesterday talking to a boatman. I feared we'd left you on the island.'

Anna put her hands to her mouth. 'Wow. George, I'm so sorry. My car has a dodgy battery. It wouldn't start after we'd finished filming. So I called the RAC, hid the key underneath and then cadged a lift over to Falmouth with one of the other Players.'

Her mouth opened wide. 'Oh, gosh. Have I caused a problem?'

George sighed. 'Just a few. The main thing, though, is that you're safe. No injuries or anything?'

Anna laughed. 'Apart from frostbite from the time in the wind on the island, you mean. No, I'm fine. We'd better get together and review our films. Could I come round to your cottage, perhaps, this evening?'

In the afternoon George went back to continue her security discussion with Jim Harvey. He was reassured to learn that Anna was now safe and back at work.

'I've made some headway on drones,' he told her. 'There are small ones, intended as toys for grown-ups, but they're all tiny – half a metre across, and weighing perhaps half a kilogramme. And they've a device built in to prevent them flying near to a sensitive site like Gatwick – or Goonhilly.'

'So they'd be easy enough to get hold of but probably not much use?'

'I think so. But there are also commercial ones, designed for heavy lifting; or for use by professional film makers or the Military. You could fit one inside the radar hut, but you'd need to take the arms off to get it in there. It would easily fit into a domestic garage.'

'What do these weigh?'

'Not too much. My friend reckoned it could be carried by one person, but you wouldn't want to haul it very far. It's a bit awkward with its long arms and rotors.'

George thought for a moment. 'Do these bigger one have any built-in detectors?'

'He wasn't sure. They'd usually build them with a transponder, a bit like the police use to track cars.'

George frowned. 'Would that work if the drone was switched off?'

'I'm not sure. It probably would if it was being charged. I've ordered a tracking device, it's due here tomorrow. So if you're up for it, I need someone to drive around the Lizard to see if it can detect anything.'

It sounded desperate but for the time being neither of them could think of anything better.

CHAPTER 41

Today, Wednesday, was the day her attempted-murder inquiry on Harry could begin, thought Frances. This time she didn't even go into Helston but headed directly out of Gweek towards Truro.

She had rung the hospital before setting off. Harry had slept well, reported the nurse, even declaring that he was 'ready for a proper interview'. She had also talked briefly to Tim Barwell. He was tired but game to stay on for the conversation. Having guarded Harry for three nights he had a stake in his long-term survival and was keen to be involved.

Half an hour later, clutching a large mug of Costa coffee, Frances had reached Penryn Ward. Her first shock, when she got there, was to see that Harry's bed was no longer occupied.

But it was alright. He was already dressed in the shirt and chinos that Tim had brought in for him and was seated in the side room, chatting to Tim. That was good. She'd been thinking it might be difficult to conduct a confidential interview in the open ward. Bedside curtains were hardly soundproof.

Frances also recalled Nurse Megan saying that Harry might be able to go home later today. Obviously that was the trajectory he was now on.

A few minutes later Harry had been settled into an easy chair in the far corner of the side room. Frances and Tim sat in two seats opposite. The police officer took out her notebook and the interview began.

'Right, Harry. I'm Police Sergeant Frances Cober and this is Constable Tim Barwell. We're both from Helston Police.'

'Pleased to meet you both. I'm Dr Harry Jennings, a senior history lecturer at Exeter University.' He paused. 'There seems to be a bit of confusion, though. The hospital has got my name down as Harry York.'

'Ah. We did that for your protection, Harry.' Frances saw that she needed to explain.

'You're in here because you've been drugged, Harry. That might have happened because someone wanted to kill you. I had to play safe. I didn't want to make it easy for anyone to try again.'

Harry struggled to make sense of it all. He looked shocked, then shaken and finally resolute. 'Oh, right. I suppose I should say thank you.'

There was a pause. Frances could see Harry pulling strands together. He was more alert today. Recent events were starting to make more sense.

'Yesterday, Harry, you told me that you got out of a train here at Truro late on Saturday night, phoned for a taxi, got in when it turned up. Then someone put something over your face and you blacked out.'

He nodded. 'That's right. After that the next thing I can remember is waking up in here. What day is it, by the way?'

'Today is Wednesday. It's about half past nine.'

'Wow.' He blinked. 'So I've been out of circulation for three days.'

There was a short pause. Frances selected her next question.

'Can you tell us anything about what happened during those days?'

Harry considered.

'Not much. I must have been semi-conscious at one point. It was dark. I couldn't see anything but I could hear two of 'em arguing. One said something like, 'We'd better finish him off.' Then I drifted back to sleep. Hey, how did I get here?'

Frances realised that she knew a lot more of the later story than Harry did. Briefly she told him how he'd been found at Kynance.

'So they left me on the beach to drown? Bastards.'

'That's why we've been so worried about you, Harry. Why Tim's been here on guard. And that's why we need you to remember all you can.'

There was silence for a moment. It didn't look like Harry was going to remember much more about his time in captivity.

'Let's take you back a little,' said Frances. 'What can you remember about the taxi at the station?'

Harry considered. 'I didn't give it much attention, I'm afraid. The driver drove up, leaned out of his cab and said "Trengilly Wartha". I said yes and jumped in.'

Frances, sensing something important, started to write down what he'd just said. Tim saw a chance to intervene.

'Can you remember the number you called, Harry?'

'It'll be on my phone.' He started to feel in his pockets, then realised his phone was no longer with him. 'Damn, it's not here. They've taken it.'

'I'm afraid that's one thing that you have lost, Harry,' said Tim. 'It's gone for good, I should think. We'll lend you a spare for a day or two.'

Harry looked bemused. He'd lost a vital part of his life.

Frances took over again. 'Let's go back to Truro station, Harry. The taxi driver already knew where you wanted to go?'

He nodded. 'Yes. But so what? That's what I'd told them when I called up the taxi in the first place.'

'Right. But tell me, how quickly did it come?'

'Oh, it was quick. I hardly had to wait at all.' Harry paused and reflected.

'In fact, you know, it was a damn sight too quick. They must have been waiting for me up the road, drove up as soon as they'd seen me come off my phone.'

'But the driver still knew where you wanted to go. He was the one that said Trengilly Wartha? It wasn't you?'

'That's right. I'm sure I didn't tell him.'

'OK, Harry. And exactly how many people knew you were staying at Trengilly Wartha?'

'Ah.' At last Harry saw what she was driving after. 'I see what you mean. Let me think.'

Half an hour later Nurse Megan interrupted them. 'The hospital snacks lady is here: would you all like tea or coffee?'

As they paused the interview for a few minutes, Frances glanced down at her notebook. She nodded to herself: the next stage of her inquiry was shaping up nicely.

Once they started again she read out the highlights.

'So, Harry, we've learned that you were staying in Trengilly Wartha because your client suggested the place and gave you a discount to stay there. You first arrived at the Inn a week last Sunday.'

'That's right.'

'No-one back in Exeter knows where you've been staying?'

'No.'

'It's possible you mentioned the name to C.T. Wicks, antiquarian bookseller of Helston, when you called on Monday.'

'Possibly. I gave him my phone number, anyway.'

'And the only person that you took there as a guest, you say – that was for an evening meal on Thursday – was Joy Tregorran. She's the vicar of Church Cove.'

Harry nodded again.

'And that's it. It's not very many, Harry. You sure there's no-one else?'

The interviewee scowled, concentrating. He'd been keeping his details as quiet as possible during his research, felt he'd been asked to do so.

Then he remembered Sam.

'Last Tuesday I met a PhD student who was studying a Settlement, called Sam – I don't know her surname. We had breakfast together at Trengilly Wartha. Afterwards I walked down to see her dig, then we walked on to Scott's Quay. I can't remember exactly, but I told her a little about what I was doing. Not much though. I really think that's the lot.'

Frances, though, was far from finished. Her next questions were about why.

'OK Harry. We'll check these people out. Now I want to get to motive. Can you think of any reason why anyone should want to finish you off? Any idea at all?'

Harry considered.

'As far as I know I've no long-term enemies. I've rubbed one or two colleagues up the wrong way over the years but not that much. I suppose the most likely thing is some aspect of my current project.'

'I understand this is confidential, Harry. But if you want us to find your would-be killer we need to know more. Who's the client, for a start?'

'Ah. He came to see me in Exeter. He called himself Stewart. The main thing I remember is that he had a magnificent beard.'

Frances had been writing as he spoke. 'And his address?'

'It was odd, now I think about it. He didn't say. He paid me an opening deposit in cash and said he would be in touch, once I'd started, to keep abreast of my progress. Trouble is, I haven't seen him since.'

'He sounds a bit suspicious, Harry. Would you recognise the man without his beard?'

'I very much doubt it. I only saw him the once, you see. The thing is, I had to say yes. I was desperate for some paid consultancy. My professor had insisted. The History Department is in a financial mess.'

'I see. So can you tell us, please, what this consultancy is about. The highlights, anyway.'

Harry was looking very uncomfortable. 'Stewart was keen that I kept it all secret. You do understand that?'

249

Frances nodded but her question remained.

'Stewart told me that he was after a document that was brought ashore in a shipwreck on the Lizard. It had some information relevant to him.'

'Hm. Is this why you'd been to Cambridge?'

Harry looked at her, amazed. 'How on earth d'you know that?'

Frances smiled. 'Elementary, my dear Watson. We found a return train ticket in your jacket pocket. Out last Friday and back on Saturday. I assume this had something to do with your project?'

Harry nodded glumly. He hadn't been nearly as secret as he had hoped.

'So who else knew about that?'

'No-one.'

'No-one,' repeated Frances. But he could hear the doubt in her voice.

'Well, no-one except Joy. It was her idea, you see. It came up during our meal at Trengilly Wartha on Thursday. So I got the first train to Cambridge from Truro on the Friday morning.'

This was the second time that Joy's name had come up this morning. Frances had no reason to suspect anything was wrong – not many vicars were aspiring murderers – but the question needed to be asked.

'How long have you known Joy, Harry?' she asked. 'And have you solid reasons for confidence in her?'

Later Frances was thankful that Tim Barwell had provided

physical support during the interview. Harry did not attack her but it felt like he was tempted to do so. Obviously her question on Joy had provoked him intensely.

It had never crossed the officer's mind that a relationship that had only run for a week (for half of which he'd been unconscious) could possibly be that serious.

It was clear, though, that Harry could not countenance the idea that Joy might have anything whatsoever to do with his downfall.

'Go and meet her,' he urged. 'She's an angel: strong, kind and caring. And wise. I would trust her with my life.'

Frances thought it unwise to admit that she'd already met Joy; or that Joy was another Lizard woman that for the time being had gone missing.

Eventually, with multiple reassurance from Frances and Tim, Harry calmed down. But he was starting to look tired.

'Seems to me, Harry,' Frances concluded, as the interview drew to a close, 'that the first person I really have to see is Stewart. Can you suggest how I could do so?'

'The only place where he'll know to find me,' replied Harry, 'is at the Trengilly Wartha.'

He gave his tartan shirt a look of disdain. He might be the same size as Tim Barwell but he had very different tastes. 'That's where the rest of my clothes are. I'd better go back and stay there.'

'Aren't you afraid they'll come for you again?' asked Tim.

'The thing is, Tim, before Saturday I had no reason at all to be suspicious. I was just doing a piece of academic research. Now I'm on my guard. I'll be alright.

'In any case, I've paid the Inn in advance for two weeks accommodation. Might as well get value for my money. Apart from anything else, the food there is out of this world.'

The upmarket country Inn of Trengilly Wartha

CHAPTER 42

Whatever his other foibles, Inspector Kevin Marsh was a man who kept to time.

Frances had made an appointment with him for late morning. She'd not expected to have to wait before reporting back on Harry, but when she got to the Station her boss was still out.

'He's not usually this busy,' she remarked to the Inspector's secretary.

'It's all these political shenanigans, Frances. As of today, Inspector Marsh has got direct orders from the Chief Constable.'

'That sounds exciting,' Frances responded. She was no political enthusiast, had managed to stay aloof from the Brexit debate. She'd not even followed yesterday's latest "meaningful vote" in Westminster, which had left the Prime Minister in disarray.

'Yes. Our Commander in Chief in Exeter wants every political leader, ranging from the one who's after a rapid Brexit to the one who's for a long delay, to be spoken to. Plus any in between.

'"March as often as you like," is his message. "Shout if you want to, wave your banners, grin at the cameras." But note that "violence will not be tolerated". And to go out of your way "not to shock or antagonise your opponents".'

To Frances that sounded a forlorn hope. Wasn't that what marchers hoped for? But their conversation was broken, anyway, by the flustered arrival of the Inspector. He didn't like being late either.

'So, Frances, where've we got to with the attempted murder?' began Marsh, once he'd sorted a few items with his secretary and then ushered the Sergeant into his lair.

Frances did her best to bring him up to speed. She'd now had two interviews with Harry, a brief one yesterday and a longer one this morning. What had happened to him after he'd reached Truro now seemed clear.

She went on to explain how, it seemed, his assailants had prior knowledge of where the lecturer was staying. The taxi driver knew where to take him. 'It's an old Inn just outside Constantine,' she said. 'It goes by the name of Trengilly Wartha.'

'Not many people had any reason to know that,' she added. 'We'll be talking to all the ones Harry can think of later today.'

The Inspector declared that he hadn't heard of the place. But it was quite a way from Truro.

'Trouble is,' she added, 'it's the only place Harry can go where his client will be able to find him. He told him to stay there, you see. Harry's lost his phone, of course. So he insists on going back there from hospital.'

Suddenly Marsh was alerted.

'But you can't let him do that, Frances,' he protested. 'I mean, you've convinced me that this was attempted murder. It didn't work last time, but won't that give his attackers every incentive to try again? This just makes that too easy – especially if he's been stupid enough to go back to the same place.'

Marsh stopped talking, trying to think through the alternatives. Frances did not try to argue. She had found from bitter experience that direct confrontation with her boss was seldom productive. Best to let him work it out for himself.

'But you say his client chose to put him in this Inn, eh? And in any case you want to speak to the client? So . . . you think he might have something to do with the attack?'

Frances shrugged. 'I need another interview with Harry, sir. To be honest, I'm not sure how well his research has been going. It's possible that he'd found out too much. Or else, maybe, he'd found out something but it wasn't what was expected – the client might want to suppress what he had found.'

Silence and then Frances continued. 'Maybe all he'd wanted to do was to seize Harry's phone to see how far he'd got? So he drugged him but something went wrong: he gave him an overdose. Then he thought Harry was dead, so he wanted to get rid of the evidence?'

That wasn't a bad idea, thought Frances. Perhaps, bizarrely, being with Inspector Marsh was giving her inspiration?

'So you think it'd be worth having a chat with him, anyway? You're probably right.' Marsh nodded, he liked to appear decisive.

'Well how about this, then, Frances? Why don't you allow Harry to go back to Trengilly Wartha, but send one of your staff, or maybe even go yourself, to act as guard? For the next couple of nights, anyway.'

Frances looked relieved. At least he hadn't kyboshed the whole scheme. 'Thank you, sir.'

Marsh could see his sergeant still had reservations. 'I'm happy for you to put all the costs on expenses, Frances. Meals as well. Goodness knows, we're clocking up the overtime with all these marches. A couple of nights spent on guard duty in a local Inn will be lost in the noise.'

Actions agreed, there was a satisfied pause.

Suddenly Marsh had a further thought. 'Hey, Frances, maybe I should go over there myself? I haven't guarded anyone for years. Harry might like to converse with an older man.'

Frances had to think quickly. 'That'd be really good, sir. But I've already interviewed Harry twice. We're starting to get to know one another. Wouldn't it be quicker for me to carry that process forward?'

Marsh nodded, a tad reluctantly. 'You're right of course. In any case I've got to spend all my time with all these bloody politicians. I've seen Mr Brexit and Miss Remain and their acolytes. But I've still got to find whoever is in charge of "Remain Detached in Cornwall". You wouldn't think it would be that hard, would you?'

Frances had a word with Inspector Marsh's secretary on her way out.

'I've got to go back to the hospital. I need to share a few things with the person we're looking after before they let him out. There'll need to be one or two changes. But could you do something for me?'

'Sure. What is it, Frances?'

'Well, the Inspector has sanctioned me to stay in an Inn near

256

Constantine for two or three nights, starting tonight. On expenses. It's a place called Trengilly Wartha. Could you look it up and book me in please? But don't mention the police, if you don't mind. It's a sort of undercover operation.' She grinned conspiratorially.

The secretary smiled back. Marsh was not known around the office as a generous man, either with his own money or with anyone else's: what was he playing at? Frances was half a generation younger. Should she book her a double room? Perhaps the political pressure was getting to her boss? Just do what you're told and be thankful, the secretary told herself. Frances was making headway on winning Marsh round, anyway.

At about the same time, George Gilbert had set out from Goonhilly with Jim Harvey's newly-arrived tracking device in her car. She had left straight after lunch and had undertaken to traverse as many roads as she could across the Lizard.

Her aim was to see if the device could sense any sort of drone, either within a house or inside its garage, as she passed by.

It wasn't what George had planned for her time in Goonhilly. On the other hand, if there was some sort of drone attack – especially this coming Friday, with the Newquay Airport CEO paying a visit – it would raise big questions on the Earth Station's reliability. She could hardly ask hard questions in her final report if she'd been in a position to protect the Station and failed to play her part when asked.

George had first headed towards St Keverne, passing a number of farmhouses and isolated cottages on the way. But these weren't that promising. If the drone was as awkward as Jim Harvey had suggested, it wouldn't be that easy to slip it in or out of a garage so close to a main road. Not while keeping its existence secret, at any rate.

When she got to St Keverne she trailed up and down the side roads systematically but without hearing any beep. It was possible that the drone she was seeking had no tracking device anyway. But her assumption today was that it was detectable, provided she was near enough.

The side roads were all quiet enough, not many cars. On the other hand there were a few random pedestrians. If you were fiddling with a drone in your garage, how could you anticipate a time when no-one would pass by?

George concluded that it was unlikely the drone was anywhere in St Keverne. That logic held in any other village too. Not one with footpaths, anyway.

So what did that leave?

There were caves scattered around the coast. But the drone needed to be accessible. You'd need to find a cave close to a track – like, for instance, the cave where she had found Harry Jennings, with the jeep track supplying the beach café close by.

But if you did that, how could you be sure the drone wouldn't be found by another coastal explorer?

George concluded that the drone's hiding place would have to be lockable and private, as well as away from any centre of population.

The only thing which she could think of was an isolated farmhouse. She got out her map. There were plenty of buildings like this, scattered over the Lizard. All isolated. It would take days and days to drive past them all.

George was just pondering what she should do – was it worth even trying? – when her phone rang. It was Frances.

'Hi, George. Am I interrupting key analysis?'

'Not at the moment, Frances. I'm driving rather aimlessly around the Lizard. I'm on a wild goose chase and I don't even know if there's a goose. A lost cause. So what can I do for you?'

'I wondered if you'd like to come for a meal out, George, either tonight or tomorrow?'

'I'd love to, tonight would be fine. My social life is fairly limited – to be honest, it's non-existent. But isn't that extravagant?'

'I'll explain when I see you. I'm paying anyway. You'll need to get to the Inn at Trengilly Wartha. It's on a road near Constantine.'

'That's alright. I know where Constantine is. I was there on Monday.'

'Great. Seven o'clock, say?'

'Thank you very much indeed, Frances. I look forward to seeing you later.'

CHAPTER 43

Frances had returned almost at once to Truro General, stopping only to buy a baguette on the way. There she found Harry reading a newspaper at the far end of the side room.

She'd told him the nub of her recent conversation with her boss but it hadn't gone down well. Harry was not over the moon at the thought of having a police guard at Trengilly Wartha, even if it was only for two or three days.

'Is whoever's coming there going to protect me or to spy on me?' he asked angrily.

Deep down, Frances suspected he was sensitive to his client's need for confidentiality. Harry probably feared that any publicity might lose him his consultancy fee.

'This project's already cost me plenty,' he went on.

Frances wasn't sure quite how to respond. He'd been paid to cycle round the Lizard and to stay at an upmarket Inn. Not a bad way to earn a living. And he'd found a new friend in Joy. That might be the biggest gain of all.

She hadn't dared admit to him, yet, that Joy was no longer to be found in the Gunwalloe vicarage.

'My boss says that the guarding officer can be me if you like,' she added.

'Hey, that's not so bad,' he conceded. 'How will that work?'

'For a start, I've asked my boss's secretary to book me in. But I've told her to say nothing about any connection with the police.'

'Hm. Sounds good to me.'

'So I'll go home now, Harry, dump my uniform and pack my suitcase, then drive over to the Inn as soon as I can. Once I'm there I'll have a scout round, skim the visitors list and make sure there's nothing blatantly wrong. I'll ring the Station in Helston to check if I have to.'

Harry nodded. She had a plan, anyway.

'After that I'll ring you here, Harry. You can come over by taxi.' Frances smiled. 'But please do make sure there's no-one else in the taxi before you get in.'

She paused, awaited his nod and then continued.

'I'll sit in the Inn foyer so I'll know when you're back there. Once you get to the Inn you can ignore me completely. But once you're settled in I will need to continue our interview – we can do it in your room if you like.'

'That'd be fine: it's number 17,' he told her. 'Upstairs in the main block. I'll look forward to seeing you.'

Frances' home in Gweek was only three miles from Trengilly Wartha. She was home half an hour later, changed and packed, then was back at the Inn within the hour. While she was at home she'd rung her colleagues in Helston to tell them she'd be out of the office for a couple of days. She didn't say exactly where. Of course, they'd be able to get hold of her on her mobile if they really needed to.

Trengilly Wartha was certainly off the beaten track. But the owners hadn't used that as an excuse for lower standards of appearance. The place had a charming air, it must have been an isolated cottage once, but it had been substantially enlarged.

There was plenty of space for parking. Frances grabbed a spot at the front. She noticed a racing bike – possibly Harry's – parked round the side. He wouldn't be using that for a few days. Frances booked in and was pleased to see that she'd been allocated room 15. Great, that was only two doors down the corridor from Harry.

The officer unpacked her suitcase and then phoned the hospital. The place was ready for Harry when he wanted to come.

Frances got out her notebook and seized an easy chair in the foyer. She was right out in the country. A thought came to her. There was one way that she could register a protest against her boss's view of her friends. She switched on her phone and called George.

This time she had some time to chat but George didn't. She was on some wild goose chase. But she was pleased enough to be invited for a meal that evening. Frances didn't want to attract attention by eating on her own; but nor did she want to risk being asked to share her table with someone else staying there, who was also on their own.

She was, after all, supposed to be alert and on guard.

Harry wouldn't be here for half an hour. Frances suddenly remembered: she'd planned to scan through the list of current guests. She slipped back to reception, there was a guest list lying on the desk but no-one else around. She seized it and sat down in the corner.

Not too many guests at the moment. Just a minute, she couldn't see Harry's name either. Then she spotted a "Henry Tudor". Maybe Harry was into hiding his own name too. Stewart certainly seemed to have demanded a high level of secrecy. If Harry was forced to use any more historical names he might become "Henry Hanover".

Frances smiled to herself. That could easily be mistyped and misconstrued.

The officer glanced through the rest of the list but did not see any name that she recognised. Of course she didn't know every criminal on the Lizard but it was some sort of reassurance. She put the guest list back on the desk and retreated to the foyer. Harry shouldn't be long now.

A few minutes later a taxi turned up and Harry stepped out. He gave her a wink as he passed in the foyer. She gave him twenty minutes to settle in and then she too headed for room 17.

At her knock Harry peered cautiously round the door. Frances could see a chain that prevented it opening any wider. He gave a big grin when he saw who was there and invited her in.

'All this cloak and dagger stuff is a bit of a strain,' he remarked as she settled into one of the easy chairs.

'It could be a lot worse,' she retorted. 'The safe houses which we use for witness protection are humdrum. I'm looking forward to the stay.'

Harry looked suitably abashed. It could indeed have been a great deal worse.

'Would you like some tea?' he asked, 'there's all the kit here.'

'That's very kind of you. Then we can begin.'

A few minutes later the interview restarted. Frances realised that this was the time to push the boundaries. It was now or never.

'I realise that it's all confidential, Harry. I promise that what you tell me won't go any further if it doesn't need to. But it seems to me almost certain that the assault was linked in some way to your current research.'

Harry nodded. He had thought so too.

'So what I'd really like to understand is where your research had got to by Saturday night. And where you think it might have been going next.'

Harry sipped his tea and gave a sigh. His long practice was to tell the police no more than he had to. That was how he had operated for years. But in this case he could see he had no choice.

'When I started this search I couldn't see how it could possibly be that serious. It was a bee in someone's bonnet. But then, by a series of coincidences, I found what seemed to be a valid history.'

In ten minutes he sketched out how the unnamed gravestone linked in turn to the Schiedam at Dollar Cove, the search of the vicarage loft in Gunwalloe and finally the search in Trelowarren Chapel.

'It was at that point I realised that some document really did exist, probably written in Tangiers in 1684. The trouble was that someone had got hold of it before me.'

'So you were stuck,' observed Frances.

Harry paused. 'I would have been, Frances, except that I

happen to be an expert on that period of British history. I wrote my PhD, you see, on a chap called Samuel Pepys. He recorded the Great Fire of London in 1666. It was an outstanding social account: Pepys could relate to anyone, high or low, he cared about people. And he became a friend of royalty for many years, especially King Charles the Second. But Pepys was also a visitor to Tangiers in 1683.'

Frances tried to remind herself that she was not sitting here in this comfortable Inn to learn history. Her primary concern was Harry's assault. But she couldn't help it, she was gripped.

'So what happened next?'

'It was Joy's suggestion. She asked if Samuel Pepys the great diarist continued to keep a diary in his later years.'

'Did he?'

'I had no idea. My PhD was about his early life. But I knew how to find out. There's a Pepys Library at Magdalene College in Cambridge. I spent ages there when I was doing my PhD. It has everything the man ever wrote – which is quite a lot. He was very prolific.'

Suddenly, for Frances, the penny dropped. 'Ah. Is that why you went to Cambridge on Friday morning?'

Harry nodded. 'It was my last throw of the dice. It was just possible, you see, that Pepys had met the man who drowned and was buried in Church Cove, while he was in Tangiers; and also knew what he was trying to say. It would be one more item in the great man's diary – especially if it linked in some way with King Charles.'

Frances put up her hand. 'Can we pause there for a minute,

Harry? You're covering a huge tranche of history and I'm no historian. I think you've blown my mind. I need some space to take it in.'

Harry laughed. 'Of course. You sit and ponder, Frances. Why don't I make us some more tea?'

Ten minute later, mugs in hand, they resumed.

'So tell me, Harry, did you find anything of value in Cambridge?' Frances didn't understand every detail that she'd been told but this seemed the crucial question. It was what had preceded the assault, anyway.

He gave a rueful smile. 'I did. I made two finds, both intriguing and either of which might be what Stewart was really after. D'you want me to describe them first, or simply to tell you how they got lost?'

Frances felt a huge sense of irritation. Finally they'd reached new information. But why on earth had it taken him so long?

Then she reflected that he might never have told her at all if she hadn't first won his confidence. He must care passionately about client confidentiality.

'Tell me briefly about the finds, Harry. Then tell me how you lost them.'

'Right. Well one of them was hand-written comments by Pepys on a Government Paper on Gibraltar.'

Frances tried to hide her disappointment. It sounded dire. 'And the second?'

'That was twenty odd pages I copied from Pepys' handwritten diary that he scribbled while he was living in Tangiers.'

266

That sounded more exciting. 'OK. And where are these items now?'

Harry paused. 'Well, there was a photo of the comments on Gibraltar that I took on my phone.'

'Mm. That's the phone that you've since lost.'

'Yes. But I did make some sense of what he wrote on the train home. I can give you the gist if you like.'

'In a moment, perhaps, Harry. But where are the diary entries? They sound a lot more exciting.'

'I had those in a folder the Library gave me. I kept that inside my rucksack. I was travelling light, you see. I hadn't even realised I'd lost that until I was packing my few belongings after lunch. Those were mostly scrawls. I couldn't make much sense of them as I bounced along in the train. I doubt we'll see them again, either.'

CHAPTER 44

It was half an hour later. Frances had suggested a break while she went for a stroll and tried to make sense of what she had just been told.

That was the official reason. She could also sense that Harry had been tired by the interview and could do with a short rest.

By the time Frances got back to the Inn it was half past four, almost dark. As she passed reception she remembered to book a dinner table for herself and George for seven o'clock.

She must encourage Harry to eat around that time too. He might like to eat with the women but he couldn't without revealing his "guard". It would be good, though, to have him in her line of sight.

Harry was the epitome of caution as he opened the door for Frances while keeping it on a tight chain. She commended him for his prudence. They sat down and the interview continued.

'Right, Harry, I'd like us to imagine. What might Stewart do with your Cambridge finds? Why on earth might original seventeenth century documents be of any value today?'

Harry nodded. 'I've been wondering much the same thing myself, of course. Since I've not had a chance to read them I can't say anything about Pepys' later diaries. Probably just gossip about life in Tangiers, though it might be scandalous. It might

268

even be shocking. But I can say one or two things about Gibraltar.'

'Go on then.'

'Well, in 1684 Gibraltar belonged to Spain. It wasn't a British colony at all. But it wasn't a million miles away. You'd be able to see the Rock from Tangiers, across the straits of Gibraltar.'

'OK.' Frances had no idea where this was going but she trusted that Harry did.

'Pepys was commenting on an official Paper about the relative value to Britain of Tangiers and Gibraltar. He was the Civil Servant in charge of the Navy, could judge them strategically from a Royal Naval viewpoint. He was keen on Britain manoeuvring to swap one for the other. Which was what happened. In 1684 the Crown gave up Tangiers and in 1714 we acquired Gibraltar. We've hung on to it ever since.'

All very interesting but . . . Frances insisted on dragging the conversation back to the present day. That was the nub of her interest. 'Intriguing, Harry, but so what? Does that affect anything today?'

'It might. You see, Gibraltar is a negotiating issue within Brexit. The European Union is one place where Spain can challenge Britain, could make the deal very difficult. So one side or the other here might be able to use it as part of the current argument.'

'I still don't see . . .'

'Well, Pepys' comments make it clear that Gibraltar being a British territory is not just a historic fact, it's a cunning choice. A document which proved that, written by someone as famous and upstanding as Pepys, might have commercial value in Brexit days.'

Harry could see Frances wasn't convinced. He hadn't fully convinced himself. 'I'm only sketching out the possibilities, Frances. I've no idea if any of it would really work.'

There was a meditative silence.

Frances thought again about the Pepys diaries. To her these unguarded scribbles sounded a great deal more promising than his words on Gibraltar. Then she had an idea.

'Did you say, Harry, that the diary extracts in your rucksack were copies?'

'Yes.'

'They're not the originals?'

'No.' He looked puzzled.

'In other words, the originals are still in the Pepys Library?'

One more time Harry nodded.

'Well, why couldn't you ring up Cambridge, ask for them to be copied once again, then scanned and emailed down here?'

Harry's face broke into a smile. 'Frances, you're a genius. Or rather, I'm an idiot. That must be possible.' The historian glanced at his watch. 'Let me ring them now. It's only just after five. They might still be open.'

Twenty minutes later their conversation could resume.

The phone call had gone well. The librarian that Harry had talked to less than a week ago was still on duty. It turned out that she was the girl he had known and once dated twenty years ago. For some reason or other – maybe simply residual emotion? - she had been inspired to help him.

All the diary extracts Harry had assembled the previous Saturday had been found bundled together. They would be scanned first thing next morning and sent down to Cornwall. They already had details of Harry's account. He should have them by midday. The historian would be able to start straight away, assessing their present-day significance.

Frances felt she had better explain her line of reasoning.

'The reason I'm so concerned, Harry, is that it seems to me Stewart is one of the few people who was in a position both (a) to know what you were trying to do and (b) to take advantage of that.'

'But he was going to get all this information anyway, Frances,' Harry protested. 'That was what my project was designed to give him.'

'But he might not have wanted to pay for it. Or else . . . he wanted to see if what you brought back from Cambridge was what he'd expected. If Pepys' scurrilous gossip wasn't anything like he'd hoped for, for example, he might have found it embarrassing. His goal might have been to do away with everything that you'd found.'

Harry considered. There were gaps in Frances' logic: there was no way, surely, that Stewart would know what he'd found until he had examined it carefully? Harry hadn't even known himself.

He recalled that Stewart had behaved a little strangely on the only time the two had met. But many of his clients were slightly odd. You needed to be to spend money on an academic historian.

Harry turned to the police officer. 'Is there any hard evidence you can show me?'

Frances opened her handbag and took out an envelope. 'Take a look at these.'

She pulled out a set of photos taken by the CCTV camera outside the station and handed them over. 'We've had these enhanced, mind. The originals are pretty fuzzy.'

Harry leafed through them. 'Hm. That's certainly me on Saturday evening. You know, I did look a bit wobbly.' He thought for a moment. 'That's right, I'd just woken up and gulped down my coffee. Hey, could that have been spiked?'

He peered at the corner of the photo. 'Is that telling us the time?'

'Yes. As you can see, the camera takes a picture every twenty seconds. And over there, see, that's your taxi in the background. It's started to move by the next frame, that's within twenty seconds of you putting away your phone.'

Harry peered at the last picture closely. 'You can't make out who the driver is, though. But I don't think that's Stewart. He's got no beard for a start.'

'Alright. But the crucial thing is, Harry, they already knew where you were staying. That's why I have to talk to Stewart. If it wasn't him in person then was it someone he'd instructed?'

Harry sighed. It was all very complicated.

'So assuming that Stewart contacts me and suggests coming here to see me, Frances, what should I do?'

Frances hesitated. 'How about this for a plan? Presumably Stewart will phone you or something, to give you warning. He'll want to make sure you're here, for a start. When he does I want you to slip me a note or else call me, say on the internal phone, to tell me that he's coming.'

'What'll you do next?'

'Once he's here you can tell him some of what happened to you and assess his reactions. The question is: is he completely shocked or does he know some of it already? That'll be a big indicator.'

Harry nodded. 'Right.'

'Then I want you to find out his address, or at least a phone number to get hold of him. You can't go on like this, waiting for him to contact you.'

'I've wanted to do that. It's been bothering me as well.'

But Frances hadn't finished. 'Finally, you need to make him aware that I'm going to be dropping in while he's here, and examine his reaction. Is he shocked or is he pleased to help? I mean, I am the Officer in charge of the case. And he's the victim's client if nothing else. It's perfectly reasonable that I should want to talk to him.'

It wasn't certain what Harry would make of this. But at that moment the internal phone on Harry's bedside table started to ring.

CHAPTER 45

Seven o'clock, Wednesday evening. Frances had put on her best outfit for the occasion. She'd be putting the whole meal on her room expenses. It would be bundled in with the overall bill and sent on to Truro. Luxury. Cornwall Police had scarcely ever bought her a decent meal before. Nothing more than burger and chips on a stake-out, anyway.

George turned up almost exactly on time, wearing a dark purple velour dress under a thick coat. She had researched the reputation of Trengilly Wartha and knew what was expected. But she wanted to make sure she would stay warm. It was almost freezing and the forecast said it was going to get a lot colder.

The two women found they'd been assigned a corner table at the far end of the pleasantly-warm restaurant, well away from the main door and draughts. Frances made sure that she claimed the chair which faced across the room. She'd agreed with Harry that he would eat at the opposite end.

'This is all very posh,' observed George contentedly as she glanced around the room, with its dark wooden beams and dancing candles.

'I can explain if you like or you can just eat and enjoy.'

George looked puzzled so Frances explained her deal with her boss. She was here to guard Harry, she said, her boss would cover

274

the expenses incurred. 'They won't know whether I'm eating on my own or with a friend. And they won't much care.'

This was establishment largesse on a grand scale. George was surprised. 'Have the police force been given a fresh subsidy then?'

'No. But we're racking up a huge overtime bill keeping the Brexit bust-up in Cornwall under some sort of control. Unless you come here every day for a fortnight our expenses will be minor by comparison.'

The waitress turned up at that moment and they took a few minutes to make their choices. A bottle of wine was also ordered.

When the waitress had gone George smiled. 'Right. I'll make the most of this evening then. So Harry is staying here too, is he? He's recovered from whatever ailed him?'

Frances had forgotten that George had missed out on all the events associated with Harry since Sunday; she'd been too busy to keep her fully up to date. Briefly she sketched out what had happened.

'But I'd rather you didn't make contact with him for a day or two, George. Till I'm a little further on with my investigation.'

George was surprised but didn't feel that she could complain. Frances was allowed to keep police business under wraps if she wanted. Perhaps she didn't want to get cases tangled. The analyst was getting a good meal out of it all anyway.

'So what have you been doing for the last couple of days, George? Have you made any headway over Anna? And what's this wild goose chase you've been following?'

Her questions made George realise that their professional lives did not overlap. They might be friends but they did work for different organisations, with distinct goals.

But there was no harm, surely, in her outlining the recent alarms at Goonhilly? As a police officer Frances might be one of the people that would get called in if there was any drone trouble.

'Oh, Anna turned up yesterday,' she reported. 'She said she'd been away for most of the weekend, staying with a friend. Her car just had a flat battery. So it was all a false alarm.'

'Thank goodness for that. With two swimmers, then Anna and then Harry, it was starting to feel a bit like "Then There Were None".'

George could see what she meant. 'My wild goose chase, though, might be more serious. D'you know much about drones?'

Frances gave a roguish smile. 'Well, my boss is one. He talks at great length without saying or doing much of value.'

George sighed. 'Not that sort of drone, Frances. I mean those things that fly under remote control. Like the one that appeared at Gatwick just before Christmas.'

Frances could see concern etched on her friend's face. Clearly this wasn't a joking matter.

'Not much, I'm afraid, George. No talk about drones in these parts. But . . . if it happened, wouldn't it be a military matter?'

'Eventually, I guess.' Her friend looked bemused; George could see that she couldn't stop there. 'Alright, what I'm about to tell you, Frances, is totally confidential.'

She outlined the discovery of the new padlock on the old radar hut and the subsequent discovery of recharging batteries inside.

'We think they might be linked to a drone. And it could do as much harm to Goonhilly, with all its satellite dishes, as it did to Gatwick. It could dent our reputation for years.'

Frances pondered for a moment.

'But why on earth did that lead to a wild goose chase round the Lizard?'

'The Security Man – he's called Jim Harvey – knows that big drones are usually fitted with a transponder. We thought it was worth trying a trawl round the Lizard with a matching detector. I've been from one village to another. But to be honest the search was a dead loss.'

Frances sympathised. 'Bad luck. But I'm not surprised. If I had a secret drone I wouldn't keep it in my garage. It'd be too easy to find.'

'Go on, then. Where would you hide it?'

Frances mused for a moment. 'I reckon I'd put it in some sort of bunker or somewhere that was never visited.'

'Ah. You mean, like a cave? I've already thought of that. You see . . .'

'No. It would need to be secure and fairly secret. The sort of thing built by the military in the not-too-distant past.'

George wasn't sure what she meant. 'Can you give me an example?'

'Can't think of one, off-hand. But I know someone whose family has lived in these parts for a long time who might.' Frances took out her phone. 'Would you mind very much if I gave him a quick ring?'

The meals were brought to them at that point and took all their attention. Both women had ordered sirloin steak and vegetables: chips, mushrooms, onions and fried tomato, with a jug of brandy and peppercorn sauce. It looked delicious.

They'd also ordered a bottle of Merlot. 'Just a small glass for me,' said George to the waitress. 'I've got to drive after this, I'm afraid.' Frances felt smug: she was not driving anywhere.

'So who was that?' asked George, once they were into their meal. 'And had he any ideas about bunkers?'

'Someone we had to interview earlier: C.T. Wicks. He runs the antiquarian bookshop in Helston. He asked me if I'd heard of the Python Plan.'

George shook her head. 'Unless he's thinking of Monty?'

Frances smiled. 'That's what I thought. But it turns out there was a secret plan under that name in the 1960s, linked to keeping the government safe after a nuclear war. It was a massive bunker, built at an airfield in Cornwall. It sounded fine for your drone. Trouble is, he couldn't remember where it was. But he said it was described in a modern history book by Peter Hennessey.'

George had a feeling that she'd come across the name Python before. Somewhere round the Lizard; and quite recently. But for now she couldn't remember where.

It was a different angle on hiding a drone, though. She'd give it more thought tomorrow.

In the meantime she tucked into her steak.

It was as they got towards the end of the meal, finishing with Eton Messes, that she sensed Frances stiffen.

George observed a subtle change in her posture. 'What's up,

Frances?'

'Don't turn round, George. Harry has sat down for a meal at the far end. And he's got someone with him.'

Her comment made it particularly hard not to turn round. George did her best to focus on her Mess. But that didn't stop her asking questions. 'How does he look?'

'He's doing well, I would say. He's got a decent appetite, anyway. No doubt a bit tired. But you'd expect that after all he's been through.'

George was finding this very frustrating. She recalled that Harry had once been a special friend. 'Who is he with? Why can't we join them?'

'It must be his client. That's why Harry came back to Trengilly Wartha, you see. He felt it was the only way he'd been given to get in touch.'

There was silence as they continued eating.

Then Frances spoke. 'I'm afraid I'm going to have to leave you for a few minutes, George. I'd like to meet the client myself and book a time to go and see him. I'll be back soon.'

Left on her own, her Eton eaten, George found the temptation to take a quick glance at her old friend, conscious once more, was too strong.

Harry was looking around the room as Frances talked to his client but he didn't seem to recognise her. George guessed that she was looking a lot smarter than she had back in Cambridge, twenty five years before. And somewhat older, she thought sadly.

Had Frances deliberately kept George's name out of her interviews? Did she want to avoid any emotional complications?

Perhaps the poor man hadn't been told how she'd helped rescue him from Kynance Cove? No wonder he didn't recognise her.

Better not look at him too hard, thought George. Who was his client?

George glanced randomly around the room again and then, casually, let her gaze fall on the client. He had a magnificent beard. But it was too grand: surely it was fake?

As an exercise she tried to imagine what the man would look like without it. Then it came to her. She had met this man before.

She'd certainly got something to bounce off Frances when she came back from her chat.

CHAPTER 46

On Thursday morning George Gilbert, still replete from her scrumptious meal the night before, headed towards Dr Jim Harvey's office as soon as she arrived at Goonhilly.

The Chief Security Officer was looking harassed. Next day's visit from the CEO at Newquay Airport was weighing heavily on him, especially given the newly-emerging threat of assault by drone.

'I'm afraid that driving round the Lizard trying to pick one up is a lost cause,' said George. 'But I have a different idea to run past you.'

Harvey looked grateful. 'Go on, George. At this stage I'll try anything.'

'Well. Someone suggested I should skim a book by Professor Peter Hennessey. He's an eminent political historian, top of the league. Last night I managed to find a copy on Kindle.'

'Yes, I've heard of Hennessey.'

'The crucial passage is about political life in the 1960s. He says that back then, when the Cold War was at its height, they made plans for coping with nuclear attack. It was called "Python". One part of that plan was moving all the key parts of government out of Whitehall and into the Regions. And one element of that was to build a massive bunker somewhere on the Lizard.'

281

Harvey was staring at her attentively. 'Go on.'

'If you could find that bunker and access it today, it would make a great place to hide a drone. It must be deep underground for a start. You'd never detect it with a sensor. And you wouldn't get people wandering in by chance. It must have a security fence of some sort.'

'It certainly sounds interesting. A lot better than a domestic garage. Does Hennessey say where it was built?'

George's enthusiasm faltered. 'I'm afraid he doesn't, Jim. Obviously, in its day, the location would be an Official Secret. No point in telling the Russians exactly where to drop their bombs. But I've an idea for how I might find out.'

'Oh yes?'

'There's an exhibition on, you see, in Constantine: secrets children have found about the Lizard since the early sixties.'

Harvey was sceptical. 'That's scraping the barrel, isn't it?'

'I was there on Monday searching for Anna. It had plenty of exhibits, they must have been collecting them for years. One was called something like Python. I gather the curator is on duty on Thursdays. If it's alright with you I could drive over and have a chat with him. It's a chance, anyway.'

Harvey sighed. 'We certainly need to be doing something. It's some excuse for security failure, I suppose, if it all goes pear shaped.'

It was a wild idea but it seemed that was all they had. 'Please have a go, George,' he pleaded, 'give it your best shot. It's better than trawling all the local garages, anyway.'

George knew from her last visit that the Constantine Museum curator was not there till the afternoon. She used the morning to read Hennessey's account more carefully. It was a fascinating read.

He seemed to imply that the Python "cell" (whatever it was) was linked to Culdrose Airfield. That wouldn't be accessible to outsiders, surely? But the account did give her an authentic reason for her questions, especially if there were exhibits with names relating to the topic.

After lunch George headed off for the village, taking the minor road through Gweek. She parked once more outside the Constantine Museum and headed for the door.

As on Monday, there was no one collecting entrance money and the place was deserted. Not many tourists around in January. George wandered round the various displays. Was there anything else that could hint at a future hideaway for a drone?

The youngsters had certainly found lots of peculiarities, many of them underground. Virtually all of them, though, would be insecure. If kids could find their way in then so could anyone else.

She came back again to the article describing the plane spotter – or to be more exact the helicopter spotter – with his binoculars on the airfield: "Exhibit X". This was certainly the most promising item for her enquiry.

Just in case, the analyst took out her camera, photographed all four pages and sent a copy on to Jim Harvey. It was a good job that handwriting was taught more carefully in those days, she thought. Mind, it had probably been rewritten by the teacher. She wondered when the incident had taken place. Could she deduce that from the text?

But before she could start this, George spotted a fellow visitor: a woman in her twenties. She was dressed for the winter, had a full rucksack and was browsing the various entries. After a moment their paths crossed.

'Hi,' said George. She gestured at the display. 'The kids were adventurous in those days, weren't they?'

'They certainly were. Not much scope for Health and Safety. My name is Sam, by the way. I'm camping near here. I'm doing some research for a PhD at a settlement near Scott's Quay. I only came in to Constantine to do my shopping. This is relaxation before I head back. '

'I'm George. I'm usually at the Goonhilly Earth Station.' A question occurred to her. 'So you're here all on your own?'

But before Sam could answer George noticed there was someone else here as well. A red-haired man in his thirties. A second later she realised that she recognised him: she had last seen him paddling, icy water up to his knees, off Mullion Island.

'Hello,' she began. 'Aren't you one of the Constantine Players?'

'That's right,' he replied. 'And you were the camera woman. For the last night, anyway.' He laughed. 'I hope you don't want to film me wading again. That was a one-off. My feet have hardly recovered.'

Sam could see she didn't fit into this conversation and sidled quietly away. The man looked at George more carefully.

'I'm afraid I've forgotten your name. I'm Nathan.'

'And I'm George, George Gilbert. I work at Goonhilly. Are

you the curator?'

'For my sins.' He glanced around. 'As you can see, we're hardly overrun.'

'No. Have you time to help me?'

'I'll do what I can. What's the question?'

'I've been reading a history book, Nathan, by Peter Hennessey. He describes a bizarre event that happened down here. I wondered if you could add any detail.'

Nathan pulled a wry face. 'I'm no great historian but I can have a go. What was the event?'

George outlined what she had read earlier. 'For some reason it was called the Python Plan. I guess it must have preceded Monty Python. It ended up with an emergency cabinet office being built on the Lizard in the 1960s. For use by the Prime Minister, if the Russians ever attacked.'

Nathan looked hesitant so George ploughed on. 'This article here seems to relate to it.' She pointed to Exhibit X.

There was a pause. Nathan seemed to be weighing up options.

'I know the background to that story. In fact I know it rather well. My uncle was the author, you see. But what exactly do you want to know?'

This was better than George had dared to expect. Of course, the man who had reported seeing the special helicopter could be in his seventies by now. This was the nearest she could expect to come to an eyewitness. And in a way she already knew him!

George tapped on the article. 'Great. First of all, can you tell me when this happened?'

Nathan smiled. 'That's easy, George. Remember, the place was built for use by Prime Ministers. So who d'you think was the one seen by my uncle?'

George read the article again and it clicked. 'Hey. It must be Harold Wilson. So this visit happened . . . in the late 1960s?'

Nathan nodded. 'And where did Mr Wilson always go for his summer holidays?'

'That was years before my time,' protested George. It occurred to her that this must be true of Nathan as well. Then a pub-quiz fact came to mind. 'Wasn't he the politician that went to the Scilly Isles every year? He must have dropped in on his way there.'

At last there was some clarity in the fog. But the biggest question of all remained.

'Finally, Nathan, can you tell me. Where exactly was this hideaway?'

'That's an Official Secret, George.'

'I bet your uncle knew, though.'

Nathan laughed. 'He made it his life's work to find out. Course, his problem was the other way round. He knew exactly where the location was that he was spying on. He had to work out what it was.'

George realised suddenly what was going on. 'You're teasing me, Nathan. Come on, you know, don't you? It's half a century ago now. It can't be much of a secret any more. I beg you, please tell me.'

George gave him her most enticing smile. It felt like guile was all she had left. She'd run out of logical appeals, anyway.

Nathan responded with another laugh, almost roguish. Maybe

he was beyond the realm of cold logic as well?

'I could tell you, of course. I guess that then you'd want to know about keys and access and passwords and all the rest.'

He paused. 'So would you prefer me to show you in person? I could take you there later this afternoon if you really wanted.'

CHAPTER 47

The deal done, George and Nathan set out later that day in his rather battered estate, heading away from Constantine. Her own car remained outside the Museum. She would collect it later.

George had wondered whether it was wise to go on her own, with a younger man, to a remote and obscure destination. The trouble was, she felt she had little choice if she was ever to see inside the Python hideaway.

In any case Nathan was not only the curator, he was a Constantine Player, a respected member of the local community. She had seen him perform a week earlier and filmed him twice. That surely gave her some sort of relationship. It would be wise, though, to expand on that.

'So what's your job, Nathan?' asked George, as they headed for the Lizard.

'I'm a farmer. I've got a smallholding just outside Gweek. Hence the big car, I need it to collect fodder for my pigs. What about you?'

'I'm doing a piece of work on performance reliability at Goonhilly Earth Station. I normally live in London.'

'So the quest for the Python hideaway is part of your remit?'

'Not really.' This was potentially awkward. George struggled for a way out.

'Some of my work is with the Security Officer. He put me on to Hennessey. He just didn't like the idea of a massive bunker located close to Goonhilly. We've an important visitor coming tomorrow. So I offered to chase it down.' It was an approximation to the wider truth but it seemed it would do for now.

They drove through Gweek and headed up the minor road that ran past Culdrose Airfield. George knew there was a "lookout point" here; a popular place for tourists to bring their fish and chips on a summer evening. Often they might see helicopters in action.

Ah, so this was where Nathan was heading. If so how was he planning to get in?

But to her surprise they passed the airport and continued driving.

'Aren't we heading for Culdrose?' she asked.

He glanced across and smiled. 'What makes you think that?'

'I thought this Python place was supposed to be built at an airfield.'

'Oh it is, George, it is. But don't for a moment think that Culdrose is the only one round here. We're going on to Predannack Airfield. That's a few miles away, down towards Kynance Cove.'

George remembered that many former RAF airfields had now been abandoned. Davidstow Airfield near Camelford, for example, was now just a straight road through a series of meadows. 'Is that a live airfield?'

'It was. It's a training adjunct to Culdrose. A few of their exercises involve both sites. Apart from that, it was where the Air-Sea Rescue helicopters were based. But all that changed a couple of years ago. That's nothing to do with the Royal Navy any more; it's a separate organisation altogether.'

They continued on, down the main road that led across the Lizard. George was silent, wondering where they would end up. She felt guilty that she'd caused Nathan to travel this far, simply to show her Python.

Suddenly her companion jammed on the brakes and turned sharp right. It was a cul-de-sac but George could see a tall, military style fence at the far end. Was there a military guard as well? Or did Nathan have some other means of access?

There wasn't a guard on the gate. George couldn't see anyone at all. Predannack might still be used for training but not that often.

Nathan parked directly in front of the gate. There was a twenty second pause and then slowly the gate opened. Looking round, George spotted a camera peering down on them as they drove through.

'That's connected to Culdrose, and they know the car number,' explained Nathan. 'I do occasional maintenance work here.'

George saw that Nathan was enjoying showing off his gadgets. Was this part of him demonstrating the hideaway? She shut her mind to any other motivation that might run alongside.

Predannack Airfield was vast, a mile across. But they couldn't be far from the sea – or from Mullion Island.

Nathan drove slowly, quietly along the main runway of the airfield. George couldn't see what he was aiming for. There were no buildings on the other side, just a distant fence.

But he wasn't after a building. There was a patch of gravel near the far end, just beyond the runway. They drove onto this and halted. Then Nathan pulled out his phone and texted a message. Was this a link to Culdrose, or to somewhere else? It couldn't have worked like this in the 1960s.

For a minute nothing happened.

Then there was a gentle shudder. George looked out: something was moving. In fact the moving item was their car, slowly sinking.

Lower and lower they sank. Her eyes were level with the airfield now but they were still dropping. Down and down. Ten feet, they went . . . twenty feet . . . thirty feet . . . forty feet. The light faded.

There was another shudder and the car came to a halt. Another creaking noise and the covering over their heads slowly closed.

Now they were sitting in pitch darkness. This was not what she'd expected. George felt a smidgeon of fear.

But Nathan was beside her. He exuded confidence and still had hold of his phone. He peered at it, sent another message. A pause and then various lights started to come on.

'Right, George,' said Nathan. 'We've arrived. If you want to see the Python Cabinet Room for yourself then we'd better get out.'

The whole sequence was mind-blowing. Later, when she looked back, George realised it was one of the most stunning places she had ever visited. There were no windows and the views were non-existent. But somehow that had allowed the vision of the architect, and now the imagination of the viewers, to expand to fill the vacuum.

Certainly the place, when it was built over half a century ago, hadn't been handicapped by any lack of funds. The stance seemed to have been, "if the bombs have come and the country has been destroyed, if this is all we have left, then let's make it as good as we possibly can".

When she got out George had expected to be treading on a hewn-out rocky floor, at best it might be slate. She'd consoled herself, it was a good job she was wearing flat heels. But the floor here was nothing like that.

Best quality oak planks had been laid everywhere. There must be some sort of ventilation down here, she mused, or the wood would have warped over the years. But it hadn't. There was even a high-quality varnish, gleaming in the subdued glow.

Where did the light come from? George looked up and saw bulbs squirreled away, half concealed, in the ceilings.

George had expected the walls of such a place, created from scratch fifty foot below ground, to be crude: plain and simple. But they weren't. Instead they held a sequence of fine art paintings that would have done justice to the Tate Gallery – no, she told herself, these weren't Old Masters, these ones would have graced the Tate Modern. Except that that wasn't there in the 1960s. Maybe they came from the Courtauld Gallery?

George guessed this must be the source. If she had known more about art she might even have recognised one or two. Of course, if they had all disappeared from public collections during the sixties, any publicity (or notoriety) would be long before her time.

'Come on,' said Nathan. 'The Cabinet Room is along here.'

It was like a dream, like stepping through the wardrobe into Narnia. George gave herself a pinch to make sure she wasn't hallucinating. Ouch, she could feel that anyway. She shrugged and fell in behind her host.

There weren't paintings all the way along the corridor. Probably that had just been to create an opening effect. The walls now were smooth and cream, though there were occasional dark wood doors.

But before George could ask what lay behind these, they came to a grander opening. This had a security lock but Nathan knew the code. Now the doorway opened and they stepped inside.

There must be some sort of electric gadget to make the lights respond to the opening. For George found she was looking into a replica of the Cabinet Room in Downing Street. There was a long oval table down the middle, mahogany probably, with a dozen swish chairs on either side. George had never been inside Number Ten, but she had seen it often enough on the news: the heroic start of every new government.

Then, at last, reality broke in.

'This is crazy, Nathan. If there was a nuclear war and the country had been smashed to smithereens, the Cabinet couldn't just sit here and carry on as usual. They couldn't just keep playing their clever mind games.'

He frowned. 'If you were deluded enough you might. Look at

the present lot. Several members of today's Cabinet are fairly mad. The calm wouldn't last for long, though.'

George tried to get her brain round what she had come to. Someone had designed this: how would she have organised it?

'Surely it'd be more important to have the intelligence capability? And the communication links? I mean, you'd be desperate to keep in touch with survivors round the world, wouldn't you?'

Nathan nodded. 'They have these as well. Would you like to see them?'

He led her back to the corridor and along to another door. 'This one's the Library. No fiction, but plenty of confidential documents about countries around the world in 1968.'

There was some sense here anyway. George was eager to see. She hastened inside and moved forward. There were plenty of bookcases on the far side. What topics were covered?

The folders were all colour-coded. She stepped forward, grabbed a pink one at random and plonked herself on the nearest chair. This was fascinating.

Nathan smiled. 'I'll go and see if I can make us some coffee.' Then he slipped back into the corridor and closed the Library door.

CHAPTER 48

Frances Cober had slept well at Trengilly Wartha. The Inn was located in the back of beyond; it was a relief to be away from all noise of traffic.

The police officer had knocked at Harry's door as she went past on Thursday morning and was reassured by an answering call. Even so caution prevailed. She decided to eat her meal – a full English breakfast – at a table on her own.

She was pleased to see the historian arrive in the breakfast room a few minutes later. Judging by the items on his plate there was nothing wrong with his appetite. She ate slowly so they both finished at roughly the same time. Then she followed him back to his room.

'Harry, as you know, I'm seeing Stewart later this morning. That means leaving you here on your own. Can I trust you to stay in your room, with your door on the chain?'

It was an unusual request but Harry was willing to comply. He'd had enough of drug attacks for the time being.

Under pressure Stewart had revealed where he lived to Frances, when she had accosted him during his meal with Harry the previous evening. It turned out to be a small farmhouse not far from Constantine.

There was a possibility, she reminded herself, that this man had instigated the attack on Harry. So Frances spent some time on the phone before she set out, reporting her latest news and intended destination to her colleagues.

'I'll ring you again, Tim, when I'm back to Trengilly Wartha. If you don't hear from me by lunchtime, I'm ordering you to come and investigate.'

Stewart's farmhouse, when Frances got there, was certainly well hidden. Off the road at the far end of a long track. If he hadn't given her precise details it would have been hard to find.

But the man was friendly enough when she finally got there.

'Sergeant Cober, do come in.'

It seemed there was no-one else at home. He made her a coffee and the two sat down in his drawing room. 'Now how can I help you?'

'I'm here about the assault last weekend on Harry Jennings,' she began. 'I assume he told you about it?'

'Yes, a dreadful business,' he responded.

'The thing that bothers me, sir, is that the taxi driver already knew where Harry was staying when he picked him up.'

Stewart frowned. 'Yes?'

'Harry tells me that he hadn't told anyone where he was staying. So it must have come from someone that knew already.'

'Go on.'

'Harry tells me that you knew. In fact you'd more or less told him to go and stay in Trengilly Wartha while he was doing the project.'

Stewart reflected. 'That's certainly true. I have a long-standing financial interest in the place, you see. So I always encourage people to go there. Once they've been they usually want to go again. It's top of the range for the Lizard.'

'Right. So then, here's the crucial question. Had you told anyone else that Harry was acting as your consultant and also staying there?'

Stewart didn't answer at once, seemed to be running through options. 'You know, I'm almost certain I didn't. I mean, I was keeping the whole project secret. I'd even asked Harry to use a false name. He'd registered at the Inn under the name Henry Tudor. Good name for a historian.'

Frances, though, was not going to be diverted. 'Why was the project so secret, sir?'

'I'm not sure I can tell you that, Sergeant.'

'My only goal is to find Harry's attacker, sir. What you tell me won't go any further unless it leads to something specific.'

There was an edgy silence. Frances wasn't sure that Stewart was going to say anything. Then she recalled George's observation. Was this the time for extra pressure?

'Is this anything to do with your double life, sir?'

Stewart blinked. 'What on earth do you mean, Sergeant?'

'Didn't I see you the other night at Trelowarren Manor?'

This time Stewart looked uneasy.

'I believe that when you take off your beard, which seen close up is obviously false, you're the Director of Constantine Players. You're Charles.'

Stewart shook and gave a huge harrumph. Then his face broke into a guilty smile.

'I guess I should commend the police on observational skills, Sergeant. Well done, it's true. The beard is an extra when dealing with my project.'

He sat back as though this had finished the whole topic. But of course it didn't.

'The thing is, sir, you'd got yourself one extra role for dealing with Harry's project. So did you have any more sidelines?'

Stewart looked like he wanted to dismiss the idea. But he had misled Frances once. It would be a risk to do so again.

'I'm a farmer, Sergeant. These days I have just a small herd of cattle. Not many workers so I have to do most of it myself. I don't have time for another role, as you put it.'

It sounded plausible. No doubt it was true as far as it went. Frances had seen as she drove in that Stewart lived on a farm.

The police officer had almost accepted his tale, was ready to move onto a different topic altogether, when she recalled a comment by her boss. Hadn't he complained only yesterday that one of the local political leaders had proved very elusive? It was worth a punt anyway.

'You know, Mr Stewart, there are one of two Lizard locals that the police are finding very hard to pin down. Maybe they, too, are masters of disguise.'

'Who are you thinking of?'

Frances sensed uncertainty. The confrontation on the false beard had come to Stewart out of the blue; perhaps he feared another revelation? It was time for another challenge.

'Well sir, my boss and I are trying to meet all the local leaders of parties associated with the debate on Brexit. Just polite conversations, you understand. There are marches every weekend, it's getting very fraught. You wouldn't have any stake in Brexit politics, would you?'

It would have been easy enough for Stewart to respond with a lie. No doubt it would have worked for the time being. Frances had no evidence at all. But he'd been caught once. A direct lie to a police officer, once revealed, could have damaging consequences.

Stewart gave a wry smile. 'You're doing very well today, Sergeant. Actually, I do have a role in local politics. It's been low profile so far but I'm hoping that's going to change.'

Frances smiled back. By some miracle her shot in the dark had scored a direct hit. Now she needed time to think about it: was there any connection between the politician and the historical project that Harry had been involved in?

'Thank you, sir. Maybe this aspect of the interview would be better conducted with my boss. I might have a few more questions relating to Harry, though. Would you be around to talk to both of us, say, late tomorrow morning?'

Frances didn't want to be away from guard duty at Trengilly Wartha for longer than necessary. She hadn't exhausted the questions for Stewart that related to Harry but she judged it best to quit while she was ahead. She looked forward to having a fellow officer present when the interview resumed.

Half an hour later she was back at the Inn.

Harry was still in his room. He hadn't been disturbed. But he had just received the copies of the section of Samuel Pepys' diary written while he was in Tangiers. Transcribing and analysing these would keep him busy for the next couple of days.

'How did you get on?' Harry asked.

Frances wondered how much to tell him. But he was an intelligent man and there was danger in ignorance.

'I've learned one thing that might link to your project. Stewart is a small-scale farmer. But he also has a second role. He leads one of the Cornish Brexit factions. My boss and I are going to see him again tomorrow, find out what he's pushing for.'

Frances sighed. 'I'll let you know what we glean. Does that give you any incentive to make sense of these diaries?'

'It certainly does.' Harry turned to his desk and started transcribing.

CHAPTER 49

As Friday morning arrived, everyone was on tenterhooks at Goonhilly Earth Station. Kelly Symonds of Newquay, who was expected later, was not the highest profile business leader on the planet. On the other hand she had several strongly overlapping business interests with the Station. There'd be lots to talk about and plenty of systems to demonstrate.

The possibility that commercial space flights taking off from Newquay Airport might be tracked into space from Goonhilly was still a long way in the future. It might never happen. Even so, there were plenty of collaborative ventures already taking place between the two organisations. Goonhilly's Chief Executive knew that this visit, like many before and many still to come, was important. In today's world scientific excellence was not enough; marketing the Station was essential.

Dr Jim Harvey was expecting to see George Gilbert as an early arrival. What, if anything, had she discovered about the Python Plan hideaway? What actions was she going to recommend? In the meantime he double-checked other arrangements. As far as he could see everything was running smoothly – so far, anyway.

Today was another that would be dogged by mid-winter fog. It was a good job the Newquay leader was coming by car. It would have made things a lot trickier if she had been arriving by air.

The fog was patchy. For a few minutes it was dense, then came a period when it lifted. Harvey was thankful Kelly Symonds wasn't coming to the Lizard for the coastal views – not this time, anyway.

Harvey was surprised that George was not yet present. Since her project was directly connected with Newquay Airport, he had assumed she would be a key player, maybe showing the CEO round the site in person. He hoped that she would turn up soon.

In fact George Gilbert would not be coming to Goonhilly today. She would not be going anywhere. For the analyst was still trapped in the underground site, the Python Pad, beneath Predannack Airfield.

She was feeling angry, frightened and hugely stupid.

What on earth had she been thinking of, to come here, alone, with a relative stranger like Nathan? And worst of all, without leaving a note outlining her plan with anyone. How gullible had she been?

Once she realised she was locked in, and given the door many abortive kicks, George had calmed herself. Then she'd reconstructed the events of the previous afternoon as carefully as she could. At what point had it all gone wrong?

Exhibit X, like all the rest, had been on display for ages. It was her question which had linked it to here. And it was reasonable enough to ask the curator about it.

But if it was something he'd wanted to hide, why hadn't he just brushed the topic aside? Or claimed ignorance?

What else had she said that had given her away?

George thought through her patter on the way. She'd learned that he farmed pigs. Then Nathan had asked about her job and she had mentioned Goonhilly. And possibly the Security Officer.

So why might that matter?

Then the penny dropped: the idea of a drone to meddle with the Station wasn't just theoretical. It was really planned to happen. Today was the critical Friday. Hence Nathan hadn't dared to put her off the scent, he had decided it would be best to keep her a prisoner, offline, while it all happened.

Presumably he had taken away the drone in the back of his vehicle, after he had left her locked inside the library? And was intending to use the remote control craft this Friday, during the Kelly Symonds visit?

George tried to find an upside: at least Nathan had made no move to attack her.

Indeed, the opposite was the case. She had found an annexe to the library. Inside was a table with a supply of bread, cheese and apples. And a large bottle of water. He wasn't starving her to death, anyway.

Maybe, once the drone attack was over and the surprise element had dissipated, he would come back and let her out. There was a huge difference, she supposed, between bother from an inanimate drone and direct, personal attack.

Whatever happened with the drone, there was no reason to link Nathan with what had happened to Harry. His goal, to tarnish the reputation of Goonhilly, was altogether different. She could still hope to come out of this alive.

George had gone for a walk around the library to take stock. She completed two dozen circuits and gradually her anger faded. Her aim was to keep her mind and her body active. Then she sat down.

What should her tactics be if, when, she next met Nathan? Might this be the time for negotiation?

It was eerily quiet in the library and she had plenty of time to think. Why was Nathan opposed to Goonhilly in the first place? Could she offer to keep quiet, provided she was allowed to leave uninjured?

For the first time George wondered why she had been locked in the library rather than anywhere else. It was practical, anyway. There was a toilet; and a long couch that would give her somewhere to sleep. She'd even found a duvet and pillow stuffed beneath it.

But was it more than that? Did Nathan sometimes stay in here himself? Had he intended her to discover something to make sense of his actions? Was there something in here that she was intended to find?

George halted her circuits and looked more carefully at the bookcases in front of her. Every document was an Official Secret in 1968. One of them, perhaps, had made Nathan so angry that he had conceived of a drone attack. It would certainly help the conversation, when he did return, if she had managed to find it.

Anything that could help make sense of her captor's perspective must be a huge advance.

George gave a big sigh. Then she started on a systematic review of the library contents.

Over at Goonhilly the visit was going well. Kelly Symonds had been given the usual high-level briefing and asked a few intelligent questions. They had been asked before and received equally intelligent answers from the senior staff present.

Now she was being given a tour of the site. It was a pity that today the fog restricted the view. Arthur, the huge satellite dish dating from the 1960s was almost too big to be appreciated. Its top faded into the mist.

After hearing various old stories the CEO was escorted back to the Control Room. Here she was shown a vast array of panels.

'These are signals, ma'am, from all over the world.' She was led to a second room. 'And these are the satellites currently in our range of view.'

Of course they weren't visual images, simply signal traces. Symonds couldn't distinguish one from another. Occasionally the signals flickered.

'Why do they wobble?' she asked.

Dr Harvey was ready to smooth things over. 'It's due to minor variations in the upper atmosphere, ma'am. But we never lose any signal for long.' Symonds kept watching, could see that this was the case.

She turned to her host. 'Right, very impressive. So what else have you got to show me?'

Half a mile away, on a track out on the Lizard heath, confidence was similarly high.

Earlier the saboteur had been pleased that the thick fog had hidden his efforts as he assembled the sections of the drone and slotted in the batteries. He'd also inserted a large collection of foil pieces into the container fastened underneath.

The four lifting propellers, one at each corner, had been started and the craft had taken off fine. There was a whine but he couldn't do anything about that. With a bit of luck the fog would mask it. He couldn't see the Station through the murk but he knew exactly where it was. His control gave him the drone's exact GPS position and detailed maps had given him the coordinates of each large dish.

The timing of the CEO's tour had been given to all staff at the Station earlier. There was a standard schedule for these visits. He knew what time the visitor was due to see the dishes and a few minutes later to be shown the satellite traces.

Swiftly the drone rose out of sight and positioned itself over the Station.

He waited half a minute: now it was time. He pressed the button on his control panel to release the foil on the drone. If his briefing was correct that should severely affect the signals received at the Station.

The saboteur kept his finger on the button for five long minutes. He gave a satisfied sigh. That should do the trick.

Finally, he called the drone back to its starting point. The saboteur looked forward to hearing reports of the disruption later that morning.

CHAPTER 50

Inspector Marsh had been happy enough to come with Frances Cober to talk to Stewart on Friday morning.

'You've done very well to identify him and to find out where he lives,' said Marsh. 'He'd hidden away pretty well. His political rivals couldn't help me either. To be honest I'd more or less given up.'

Frances decided that it would be wise to let her boss take the lead in the interview, though she warned him she had some questions relating to the assault on Harry Jennings that still needed answers.

'The Long Arm of the Law, here once more,' murmured Stewart as he came to the farm door. 'Do come in. I'll go and put the coffee on, shall I?' He sounded friendly enough, anyway.

The police officers followed him into the drawing room. Marsh claimed the sofa and sat down but Frances took the chance to see what kinds of books were on the bookshelf. They were mostly political volumes, many written a long time ago. A narrative on the Civil War in Cornwall attracted her attention. She was skimming the back cover when Stewart returned with a tray of coffees and biscuits.

Frances felt a sliver of indignation. He hadn't done as much for her yesterday. Was this respect for Marsh's higher rank or affinity with his gender? She did her best to mask her feelings.

'So how can I help?' Stewart asked. He sounded benevolent.

'The Chief Constable is very concerned about the recent tenor of the political debate here in Cornwall,' began Marsh. 'He's asked me to have conversations with the leaders of the factions on every side of Brexit. He's very concerned, you see, that political differences between us, however strongly felt, don't boil over into violence on the streets.'

'I don't think there's been any evidence of that so far on the marches I've led,' responded Stewart.

'Mm. Let's go back a step. Can you explain, please, Mr Stewart what your campaign is all about? I've seen your posters but to be honest I found them rather confusing.'

Stewart seemed pleased to be asked and skipped the implied criticism.

'My starting point is that Cornwall, despite its rich heritage, is one of the poorest parts of the UK. So any changes arising from Brexit, if they are to help Cornish people, need to make a difference to our whole economic structure.'

It was a fair point. Marsh nodded. 'So what policies does that mean for your party?'

'Well. It's clear to me that Cornwall's existing position within the UK is disastrous. We're hundreds of miles from Westminster, lacking in industry, taken for granted and largely ignored.'

It was a familiar tale of rejection. 'So you're in support of Brexit?'

Stewart shook his head. 'That'd be even worse, Inspector. In the current world we all need friends. The Brexit campaign will choke off the few we already have.'

Marsh looked confused. 'So where do you stand?'

Stewart took a deep breath. 'I want Cornwall to be independent of the rest of the UK but to remain part of the European Union. It's basically the same stance as they take in Scotland.'

Frances found her head spinning. Marsh, slightly less muddled, wanted to move from ideas into practical policy. 'So what's your first demand?'

'I think that in the current state of Parliament we will end up with a second referendum vote. When we do, I'd like the idea that I've just expressed to appear as a third option, alongside Remain or Leave, on the Cornish ballot paper.'

Marsh took a sip of his coffee and considered. He wasn't here to rate the policies or judge if they'd work, simply to make sure they didn't lead to violence. But what he'd just been told sounded like it would alienate Remainers and Leavers almost equally.

'There's plenty of logic in favour of your position, sir,' he began. 'But could it lead to mass violence?' A thought occurred to him. 'Have you had any attacks so far?'

'One or two skirmishes, Inspector. But we've had pretty small numbers and kept out of the way. I'm hoping that from tomorrow we'll do much better.'

Frances wasn't sure exactly what "better" meant. Stewart looked belligerent. Did he mean larger and peaceful; or more antagonistic? Then she recalled what Harry had told her about Gibraltar.

'Is Gibraltar part of your argument, sir?'

Stewart beamed. 'It is indeed. Gibraltar wants to remain in Europe, even if Britain leaves. What I'm after is that Cornwall should have a similar status. We were promised that once by Charles the Second.'

Marsh wasn't here to discuss history. 'Whatever your manifesto, sir, as the leader of a public march you have a responsibility to maintain the peace. One way of doing that is to make sure there are no big surprises in your speeches. Could I have your assurance on that?'

Stewart looked doubtful. 'But Inspector, surprise is an important way that things get changed. Generally the bigger the surprise the bigger the change. But I'll do my best to make my announcements peacefully.' They argued the point for some time but it seemed that this was the best Marsh was likely to achieve.

Finally it was Frances' turn. She helped herself to a chocolate biscuit and glanced down her notebook.

'I've a couple more questions from our conversation yesterday, sir.'

'Go on.'

'Can you tell me where you were at eleven o'clock last Saturday evening?'

Stewart pondered for a moment. Then he remembered. 'That's right. I'd been invited out for the evening by my daughter. And her husband, of course. It was a splendid meal: they fed me well, even brought me home. I wasn't back till after midnight.'

'Right sir. Would you mind giving me your daughter's name?'

'She's called Miriam, that's Miriam Harrison. They don't live far from here, down towards Gweek.' He told her the location.

Frances would check it out but it sounded like a solid alibi. Despite all her efforts, Harry's assault was still shrouded in mystery.

Not far away in Trengilly Wartha, the victim of that attack was fully engrossed in historical research.

Harry now had copies of all the handwritten diary entries made by Samuel Pepys during his stay in Tangiers in 1683. There were twenty pages.

The historian had enlarged and printed them all, then spent several hours transcribing them. He'd had to do this in several stages.

Stage one had been to transfer Pepys' entries as accurately as he could onto his tablet. It wasn't that the great diarist had bad hand writing, simply that writing styles had changed over the last three centuries.

Stage two had been to paraphrase each day's entry into modern English. That was quite an effort. There were plenty of allusions from the time that could only be guessed at today.

Pepys had also omitted the names of most people he was describing, or else used initials. Harry thought it would be almost impossible to work out who these all were. He could make some sense, though, of what they had done and could guess why they might have caught the diarist's imagination.

Finally he went through the pages once again. Was there anything hinting at something untoward, something that might have made its way to the Lizard on the Schiedam a few months later?

By this point Harry was tired and he needed a nap. He was still recuperating from the drug attack a week before, gradually recovering his strength. When he awoke he was eager once more to make progress.

Pepys had been staying in the Palace. Many people there caught his attention. Most of the time, though, the antics described might have sounded funny at the time but had no long-term appeal.

Then Pepys depicted a worker at the Palace. Hassan, the King's personal assistant in Tangiers. Further checks revealed that Charles the Second had been in Tangiers himself just a month before the diarist.

Pepys had had plenty of contact with Hassan. He'd also had indirect dealings with Hassan's wife.

It was clear to Pepys that Hassan had been unaware of his wife's role. He must have known, presumably, that the King found her attractive. But he had not found out – maybe not wanted to find out – what the exact relationship had been.

King Charles was well-known to historians as a philanderer. He had produced several illegitimate children during his reign. It wouldn't be surprising if he continued this proclivity while out of the public gaze in the depths of North Africa.

No surprise, too, if the frenzied activity had the same result. By 1684 the King was back to Britain, probably unaware of the complications left behind.

But Pepys was aware and the events made his diary.

He noted "H"s comments at length, rejoicing in his innocence.

312

For example, H had complained to Pepys that his wife had been sick regularly. And was starting to look plump. But a possible cause for all this never seemed to occur to him.

Harry could find nothing else in the diary that was half as interesting.

Even so, he found it hard to discern a long-term effect. One more illegitimate Royal offspring, tucked away in the depths of Morocco, was not a big deal in the scheme of things.

Then he had a thought. There was one way that it might matter a great deal.

The ever-watchful eye of Samuel Pepys

CHAPTER 51

'You'll have to quit special guard duty after today, Frances,' instructed Inspector Marsh as they walked out of Stewart's farm. 'We've more Brexit marches happening tomorrow. I'm calling in everyone to make sure we keep them under control. That will include you.'

Frances had learned not to argue with her boss's direct orders. In any case, pleasant as it would have been, she couldn't stay in Trengilly Wartha forever. There had been no problems for Harry there so far, anyway.

'Right sir. I'll go back and give Harry some final advice on keeping an eye out for trouble. I'll also check Stewart's alibi for last Saturday evening.'

Marsh nodded and drove away. Frances got into her car and checked her SatNav. It wasn't far to where Stewart's daughter lived. Maybe a visit out of the blue would be fruitful?

Twenty minutes later the police officer turned down the side road just before Gweek and headed for Miriam's farm. Another out of the way location. The Stewart family certainly kept themselves out of the public gaze. It was an odd contrast with the man's desire to lead political marches.

The farmyard was tidy enough. Frances parked on the far side

314

and headed for the front door, gave it a hearty knock. Was anyone at home?

Silence for a moment, then she heard noises. Someone was in. Finally, after a rattle of bolts, the door opened. A woman peered out, she was probably in her thirties. She looked cheerful enough, perhaps glad for an excuse to stop her chores. She had the sort of face you would see in a shop anywhere: pleasant enough but not a riveting beauty.

Frances held up her warrant card. 'Good morning, ma'm. I'm Sergeant Frances Cober from Helston Police. Could I ask you a few questions, please?'

The woman nodded. 'Right, you'd better come in.' She led Frances down the hall and into the lounge.

'I'm conducting inquiries about Charles Stewart,' the police officer began. 'I'm after his daughter, Miriam.'

'That's my Dad alright,' the woman replied. She gave a sigh. 'What's he done now?'

'Probably nothing, ma'm. Why, has he been in trouble in the past?'

'He's always ranting on about the status quo and how it needs to change. "Cornwall needs a new start." The poor man would be a revolutionary if he wasn't so old. Trouble is, he's left it far too late.'

It was an epilogue of sorts, but maybe not the sort you'd want. 'When was the last time you saw him?'

The woman racked her brains. 'He doesn't live far away. We make sure we see him every few weeks. Hey, that's right, he was here last Saturday. It was Nat's birthday, you see. We invited him to join us for supper.'

'Who is Nat?'

'He's my husband. Nat King Cole, I call him, on a good day. Right now he's somewhere outside with his pigs.'

'How late did this meal go on? What time did your dad go home?'

'It was pretty late, actually. Dad doesn't like driving at night so Nat fetched him over. The old man drank plenty while he was here, mind. We didn't get rid of 'im till gone midnight.'

'Nat took him home, I presume?'

'It was me, actually. Nat had had plenty to drink by that stage. When that happens, he and Dad usually fall into an argument.' She sighed. 'It's a narrow road but I know it well enough. My sisters and I were brought up there, see. Dad's lived there for years.'

Frances couldn't think of anything else to ask. There didn't seem much point in hanging around to see her husband. No doubt he would tell much the same tale.

In Trengilly Wartha, Harry was wrestling with a problem. He could see why Stewart might, possibly, have initiated the research which the historian had been conducting for the past two weeks. But knowing where it might go did not mean that he needed to go there.

As he pondered, his internal phone rang. Was this Stewart, wanting to access more of his findings? Harry lifted the receiver gingerly.

'Hello?'

A female voice, clear as a bell, came through. 'Harry! I've got you at last.'

He recognised the voice. 'Joy. Am I glad to hear from you. I've rung that Gunwalloe vicarage so many times over last few days but you were never there. Are you alright? Where on earth are you ringing from?'

'Some policewoman came to see me on Monday, Harry, and told me about you. I was devastated. She warned me that I might have been seen with you and to keep my door locked. I wasn't going to do that. I decided I'd take a few days off and go back to my Mum and Dad in Marazion. I was due some leave anyway. But because of what had happened to you I decided it would be safer not to tell anyone where I'd gone.'

Harry felt guilty at the trouble he'd caused. 'Joy, I'm so sorry.'

'I tried to phone you, of course. But something odd has happened to your phone. It doesn't get through to you anymore.'

That was no surprise. 'No, I don't suppose it would.'

'The police officer told me that you'd been taken to Truro Hospital. I tried to call but you weren't there – under the name of Harry Jennings, anyway. I kept trying but I couldn't get hold of you. I've been ever so worried.'

'Joy, I've missed you so much. They let me out on Wednesday afternoon. There's been a police guard here ever since. I have to keep my door on a chain when they're not around. But I'm more or less fit again.'

'Did they know what had happened?'

'They found a huge dose of some drug in my system. I don't remember much until I woke up in hospital on Tuesday.'

'You poor old thing. Could I come and see you?'

'That's the most wonderful thing I could imagine. How soon could you get here?'

Joy laughed. 'If you're safe, Harry, then I suppose I must be too. I might as well leave my family and come back to the Lizard. I'll have to pack but I can be with you in, say, an hour and a half.'

'Great. I'm in room 17. Tell reception you've been invited to come up. I'll still have the door on a chain so call me when you get here.' A further thought struck him. 'Hey, could I possibly treat you to another meal? It's been a week, you know, since our last date.'

By mid-afternoon in Goonhilly Earth Station the excitement was dying down. Kelly Symonds had declared herself impressed and excited by everything she had seen and gone back to Newquay. The Goonhilly staff could relax: it would soon be another week-end.

Jim Harvey was increasingly worried about George Gilbert. She had still not appeared and did not answer her phone.

George had set out for Constantine the afternoon before. As a last resort he looked at the analyst's last call: a set of images showing the key article on display in the exhibition: Exhibit X. He had received it yesterday.

Harvey hadn't had any spare time until the CEO visit was over but now he could give it some attention. It didn't take him long to print the images out at a readable size. Then he got a cup of coffee and settled down to browse.

He recalled George's excitement at the notion of a massive

bunker somewhere on the Lizard, the final escape for government in the event of a nuclear attack. She'd been going to ask the curator about it. What if she had been told; and then had gone to see for herself?

Harvey had two advantages over George in making sense of the article. Firstly her disappearance meant it was important, not just a vague idea. In addition Harvey had a better appreciation of the details of the Lizard: he had lived here for many years.

So what did the article tell him?

It was entitled Python's Pad, for a start. That chimed in with the reference from Peter Hennessey, which wouldn't have been known at the time the article was written. It must have been added by a recent reader.

The article was based on a Lizard airfield. Harvey assumed at first that this must be Culdrose. But if it was, there would be substantial problems with gaining access. Was there any alternative?

Then, as he read the article for perhaps the tenth time, he noticed the word near the start: "windmill". Where could that be, exactly?

He got a copy of the Lizard Explorer map and opened it up across his desk. Then browsed it carefully, kilometre square by square.

Finally he spotted it. There was a Windmill Farm just south of Predannack Airfield. The map also said "windmill (remains of)". This must be where the Exhibit X lad had been watching from. Presumably the windmill itself had been standing fifty years ago.

So the Python Airfield wasn't Culdrose at all.

But Predannack was still a plausible place to build a backup base. The two airfields were connected. Maybe, in the 1960s, they were even more closely paired. In any case it might be easier to build a top secret base at a backup airfield than at the main site, with its myriad of visitors from all over the world.

Harvey considered the problem for some time.

He could get as far as Predannack but would find access difficult. It would take time, anyway, to get clearance from Culdrose, even for a Security Officer like himself.

Then it occurred to him that Goonhilly was also a post war, government-owned development, built at around the same time. And the two sites were not far apart. He checked his map. Yes, they were barely four miles away as the linear crow might fly.

Expense had been no object in those days. But wasn't there a good argument for making sure the two sites were linked? In the event of a war Goonhilly might still have connections to the outside world; surely the "Python Pad" would want to maintain access?

Harvey looked at his map again. Predannack and Goonhilly were the same elevation with no drop in between. If he'd been the designer, he'd have put cables between the two places; and a tunnel to contain them.

Excited now, he headed for Goonhilly Library. All the latest documents were on line but the ones relating to the original design were archived in a back room cupboard.

As he went through the security staff open plan office he noticed Anna was still at her desk; and remembered that she and

George were friends.

'Are you doing anything this evening?' he asked.

'Not much, Dr Harvey, the drama is over now.' It wasn't clear whether she was thinking of the visit by Kelly Symonds or the Agatha Christie revival.

'Your friend George seems to have disappeared. Are you interested in a bit of out-of-hours work to try and find her?'

Anna looked a little surprised at this odd request and then gave a nod. 'I'd be glad to help. What did you have in mind?'

Harvey didn't answer. Instead he unlocked the archive and peered at the dust-laden folders stacked inside. There was nothing that matched his ideas.

Then he saw one near the back: 'Links from Goonhilly to nearby Government bases.'

'Let's have a look at this,' he said, a hopeful smile on his face.

CHAPTER 52

By mid-evening on Friday dinner at Trengilly Wartha was in full swing.

At one table, in a quiet alcove, Henry Jennings sat with Joy Tregorran. They'd both ordered lamb shanks and were engrossed with one another, oblivious to anyone else in the restaurant.

They had swapped experiences since their last meal here a week ago in some detail. Joy had described the few days of calm on her parents' farm. Then Harry had told Joy about his visit to Cambridge; and how her suggestion that he examined the later Pepys diaries had born a mixture of fruit, good and bad. Ending with him being drugged and lying in Truro Hospital.

There followed a few minutes of medical details, sympathetically received, about his treatment and eventual discharge.

Then the historian had told Joy how he'd ordered fresh copies of the lost entries from Cambridge and what he had gleaned from these today.

'From Pepys' own writings it seems that King Charles had a dalliance with the wife of his servant Hassan, while he was in Tangiers in 1683. An affair which had the effect of making the woman pregnant.'

'Poor woman,' said Joy. She tried to imagine the emotional ramifications. 'When that baby was born, it would be of mixed race. She couldn't even pretend that Hassan was the father.'

Harry nodded. 'Hassan came to Britain on the Schiedam in spring 1684, was shipwrecked in Dollar Cove and later buried in Church Cove: I've seen his gravestone. You and I spent the last week chasing documents that he brought with him.'

'Right, Harry. That's the history. Why does it matter today?'

'If his wife had been left behind in Tangiers I doubt it would matter much. But what if Hassan brought his wife – his real treasure – with him on the Schiedam?'

Joy ate some more lamb. It was an interesting question.

'Would that be possible, Harry? Were boats willing to carry female passengers in those days?'

'Well, remember that the Schiedam was part of the withdrawal from Tangiers. They might have had to leave in a hurry. Hassan might not have wanted to leave his wife there after the British left. He might have feared reprisals for someone like her, who'd consorted with the English King.'

'OK. But what if she'd come with him all the way; and had survived the shipwreck – not just for a few days but for years?'

'Joy, she'd be completely on her own. She'd have had to merge into the local population. I mean, she couldn't go back home, could she? She'd have her child in due course. The infant might have been baptised in the church in Church Cove.'

Joy mused again. These were big ideas to get her head around.

'So that would mean that descendants of the old Royal family – the Stuarts – could have lived unrecognised in Cornwall for the last three hundred years. Wow.'

For a few minutes they both concentrated on their meals.

Harry finished first and continued his discourse.

'It would be fine as long as they were completely unrecognised, didn't even "recognise" themselves. But suppose that a present day Cornishman constructed a family tree which led back to this child and knew the wider story. He might conclude that he was the legitimate heir to the British throne.'

Joy seemed to choke and grabbed a glass of water. Once she'd recovered she explained. 'Harry, I've just had a thought. There was someone who came to see me last year. He was trying to construct a family tree. He asked to see the church records for Church Cove. Of course I said yes. He came back later to say thank you, he must have found something. Until just now I didn't think anything of it.'

Just at that moment the waitress came along. 'Would you two like to see the dessert menu?'

'Yes, please,' said Harry. He felt able to speak for Joy. A menu was produced and after some debate treacle sponges were ordered. It was a very cold night.

As the waitress went off, Joy observed, 'You know, that was the same waitress as we had last week.' For some reason Harry didn't say more until she'd brought their desserts and gone away again. He sensed Joy's observation might matter, though he had no idea how.

Harry shrugged and moved onto the question that had bothered him earlier.

'All these ideas may be way over the top,' he said. 'The immediate question for me is, do I pass them on to Stewart when I next see him? Or should I pretend to forget what I've just told you?'

'Won't you lose your fee if you don't say anything?'

'But I don't want my research to threaten the British Crown.'

Joy considered for a moment. 'That's very noble of you, Harry. But what you've found is neutral, isn't it? I mean, it would only matter if someone started to act on it and used it to challenge the Crown.'

She paused and then continued, 'Why don't you tell Stewart, but also tip off the police. They can keep an eye on his speeches, arrest him if he sounds like he's lapsing into treasonous heresy.'

It was wise advice. Harry tucked into his treacle pudding gratefully.

Frances Cober had been sitting alone at the far end of the dining room. Her final guard duty. She couldn't sit with Harry, but she'd been pleased to see Joy was with him. The two looked very happy together. Frances was on duty. She could see no reason why she shouldn't have a chargeable meal at police expense.

Then she noticed a woman in her mid-twenties wander in, looking slightly lost. She had looked eagerly across at Harry, noticed he had a female companion and turned sadly away.

Something jogged Frances' memory. Harry had talked about a younger woman that he'd met at Trengilly Wartha: could this be her?

The woman passed near to her table. 'I'm eating on my own,' said Frances. 'You can join me if you like.'

'Well, if you don't mind that'd be great. My name is Sam. I'm doing an archaeology dig, just down the road.'

Frances silently applauded herself. Exactly what Harry had

said, wasn't it?

'I'm Frances,' she replied. 'I'm with the police in Helston.'

Sam seemed eager to talk. 'D'you come here often? This is rather special, isn't it?'

'I live just down the road in Gweek; this is my favourite place to eat out. But I can't afford to come here very often.'

'I've only been once. I came in for breakfast on my first day and met Harry – that man over there. He's some sort of historian.'

Frances didn't want to admit that she knew Harry. 'There are a lot of clever people around here. There's Goonhilly Earth Station, for a start. You know, the place with the satellite dishes.'

'I've met one of them, too. Yesterday afternoon, in Constantine. I was over there shopping when I met her at an exhibition on "Secrets of the Lizard".'

Keeping the conversation going, Frances asked, 'Did you find out her name?'

Sam struggled, she'd only heard it once. 'Yes, that's it. She was a woman of about your age: she was called George.'

'How very odd. I know her. Even odder, we ate here a couple of night ago. What on earth was George doing at an exhibition?'

'I can tell you. There was an article she was interested in: Exhibit X. I read it afterwards: a lad's trip to a helicopter base. Must have been a long time ago: it also mentioned steam trains.'

At this point a waitress came and took their orders. It dawned on Frances that she'd met this woman earlier. It was Miriam. Frances had been in uniform then, she must look very different now with her hair down, in her going-out gear.

Odd. She didn't think any more about it at the time.

So what could they talk about? Frances was aware that she couldn't say much about her work. She couldn't make much of archaeology either. Best to stick with the Constantine Exhibition.

'So what did George do once she'd read the article?'

'Oh, she asked the curator about it: where it had happened and so on. I wasn't eavesdropping but I couldn't help overhearing.'

'Did you find out where the place was?'

'The curator didn't say. But he seemed to know. He offered to take her over there himself. Your friend was keen to take up the offer.'

Frances frowned. That sounded a little reckless. 'Perhaps she already knew him?'

'I think she did. He'd been in a play that she'd filmed.'

'Hey, I saw that play too. George and I went to see it a week ago. What did this chap look like?'

'The only thing I can remember is that he had red hair.'

Frances could only recall one male actor in the Agatha Christie drama with red hair. She'd kept the programme, would look up his name when she was back home.

The meal continued. Sam told Frances about her morning with Harry and their visit to Scott's Quay. 'It's a popular place. I've seen the red-head down there more than once of an evening.'

Towards the end of the evening Frances' phone rang. She glanced down, saw it was Tim Barwell. She knew he wouldn't be bothering her unless it was important.

'I'm sorry, Sam. I need to take this, I'm afraid.'

'I need the toilet anyway.' Sam slipped away. Frances grabbed the few minutes on her own.

She turned towards the wall and spoke quietly. 'Tim. What's up?'

'Boss, I thought you'd like to know. You remember the CCTV pictures from the railway station?'

'Yes.'

'Well, Forensics had another go at enhancing them. They identified the make and colour of the vehicle, also got part of its registration.'

'Go on.'

'I've spent this afternoon in contact with staff at the DVLA. Looking for vehicles from around here that might fit the photo.'

'Well done. So –'

It's quite an old car, you see. There aren't many like it. Not round here anyway. In fact I could only find one.'

This sounded promising. 'Should I know the name of the owner?'

There was a pause as Tim consulted his notes. 'It's some chap called Stewart. He owns a small farm near Constantine. I can give you the address if you like. It's – '

It gave Frances great satisfaction to turn him down. 'That's alright Tim. I've been there twice this week already. But you've given me a good excuse to go back one more time. Well done. Thank you very much indeed.'

Frances thought hard about what she had just heard. More investigation was certainly needed on the Stewart family. Stewart's alibi needed rechecking, for a start. Maybe she could start that right here . . .

Sam returned a minute later and Frances leaned over the table. 'Arising from that phone call, Sam, there's some data I need. Could you help me?'

Sam looked intrigued. 'I'd be glad to. What should I do?'

Frances explained.

A few minutes later, as Miriam headed past their table, the police officer contrived to knock over her glass of Merlot. It went all over Sam's half of the table.

'Damn,' she exclaimed. 'I'm so sorry, Sam.'

The waitress was used to spills. 'The trick with red wine is salt,' she commented. She seized the salt cellar and shook the contents liberally over the stained area. Sam made sure that nothing was missed.

After the waitress had gone, Frances produced a plastic bag and, making sure she didn't touch it, took charge of the cellar and slipped it into her handbag.

It wasn't the best DNA sample she had ever taken but it was worth a try. She would take it back to the Police Station later.

Their meal finished a few minutes later. Frances insisted on paying their combined bills. 'My treat, Sam,' she said. 'It's my way of saying thank you for your contribution.'

CHAPTER 53

O ver in Goonhilly, despite all their hopes, Jim Harvey and Anna Campbell were making little progress.

Between them they had devoured the original Goonhilly Station Security Book from cover to cover but without success. They'd found no mention of anything that could possibly relate to Python.

Then Anna had peered once more into the back of the library file cupboard. She was younger and more athletic, could wriggle further.

'There's this file here, Dr Harvey. It's dropped down behind the rest.' She produced another file which looked even more neglected.

'Give me that.' Harvey grabbed it and started sifting through. He was desperate now. Then he gave a sigh. 'Well done, Anna. I think this is what we're after.'

She peered at the page he had reached, it would have been easy to ignore. It talked in elliptical terms about "other government facilities", gave no clue to location but did mention "links from one to the other". Then it spoke cryptically of "access from the lower floor".

'Goonhilly doesn't have a lower floor does it?' she asked.

'Not now,' he replied. 'But it used to.'

330

Harvey was determined now. 'Go off and get your coat,' he instructed. The Security Officer did the same. He grabbed each of them a safety helmet. A few minutes later he led his colleague out of the main building towards one of the huts at the rear. 'We never use this one these days. But I seem to recall, it does have a cellar.'

'Shouldn't we tell someone where we're going?'

'The less people that know about any of this the better,' he muttered. She saw that from somewhere or other he had collected a large torch and a bunch of keys. Then he led her over to the hut and wrestled with the door.

Five minute later they were inside the building and down into the cellar.

'There's nothing here,' Anna said as she looked around. She was disappointed but also relieved.

'But there is a hatch. Here.' Harvey pointed to a large chest standing over by the far wall. He gave it a shove and revealed something else below: a board set in the floor. He selected another key and grabbed the padlock that fastened it down. It was stiff from years of non-use but the security man had strong wrists.

'Done it,' he exclaimed exultantly after a minute's effort. He lifted the board and the two peered down into the darkness. They couldn't see far but there were some steep stairs leading down.

'I think, you know, that this will lead us to the Airfield,' he said. 'And, I believe, also to George. But it'll take us some time. Are you game?'

331

Once they had struggled down the steps, the passage ahead of them was fairly level: one and a quarter metres high, oval in outline but fairly straight. Harvey assumed it had been drilled though the rock in the 1960s. He had an engineering background and knew the technology for such work existed in those days. It wasn't that long ago.

'This passage will run for about four miles,' he predicted. 'Let's hope there've been no rock falls over the years.'

The height of the tunnel meant they were continuously bending. It was a strain for Harvey, who was over six foot tall. Anna was glad that she wasn't much more than five foot. She wished, though, that she'd brought her own torch. Without one she had to trail behind Harvey but making sure she didn't fall too far behind.

The floor, though, was fairly clear. There were plenty of puddles and every so often the odd rock had come down from the roof, but mostly it was firm under foot. There was a dank smell but it wasn't too odorous: presumably there must be some form of primitive ventilation. Anna had no idea what that might be.

Harvey kept going relentlessly. They had been walking for almost an hour when he proposed a five minute breather. The ground was dry at this point and the pair sat themselves down, thankful to stretch out their aching backs.

'Where on earth are we heading?' asked Anna.

'If I'm right, we'll end up under Predannack Airfield.'

'You think George might be there?' She couldn't take the

shock out of her voice.

'I believe so, Anna. But I have no idea what state she'll be in. We need to be prepared for anything. Come on.' Unable to contain himself any longer, Harvey rose to his feet and seized his torch once again.

They were tired now and moving more slowly. If Harvey was right about the distance, they would soon be under the Airfield. But it was not until nearly an hour later that they came to another strong-looking door.

There was a metal handle. But of course it wouldn't open.

Harvey shone his torch all around the doorway. There was no padlock, anyway. Then, high up on the left, he noticed a keypad.

'All we need now is the security code,' sighed Harvey. Why hadn't he thought of this earlier?

'There was a page of numbers at the back of the file,' said Anna.

'Great, Anna. If you wouldn't mind just nipping back to fetch it . . .'

'It's here, sir. I brought it with us just in case.'

Harvey made a noise of obscure emotion. 'Well done, Anna. One of us is thinking straight anyway. Right, let's have a look.'

He shone his torch. There was a list of office rooms, each followed by a code. Right at the bottom a line declared, "Emergency Access: 583924".

'OK. Let's give it a go.' Steadily, digit by digit, Harvey entered the number. Then he reached for the handle.

There was a creak and then, slowly, the door opened towards them.

'I've no idea if there's anyone in here or if they're armed,' Harvey whispered. 'Keep as quiet as you can, Anna. We'd better not talk.'

The Security Officer put one foot over the doorway and stepped inside.

Suddenly lights came on ahead of him. For a second he thought he'd been spotted. Then, when nothing else happened, he realised that a detection device had been triggered, possibly responding to the weight of his foot. After all this was an emergency government HQ. You'd expect decent security.

Silently, slowly, they stole along the corridor. They passed an occasional doorway, labelled, with a security pad beside it. Harvey tried one or two but they wouldn't open.

After fifteen minutes they could find no door unlocked and no-one else roaming about.

'There's no-one here,' whispered Harvey. 'Unless George is inside a room. We'll give each door a knock in turn.'

They could be more systematic now, they knew the overall layout. The corridor had around thirty doors in total. They gave each one a heavy knock and waited for a response. For a while they found nothing.

Then they came to a door marked "library". Harvey knocked.

Suddenly they heard a voice from inside. 'Help. Help, I'm locked in.'

Anna turned to Harvey, her eyes shining. 'That's George,' she said. 'Can I see the security code list again?'

Harvey took it out of his pocket and handed it over. Anna

glanced down.

'Look at these office names. There's a code for the library.' Harvey reached up for the key pad and slowly entered the code.

Now the library door would open. He pushed it carefully.

There was someone behind it. It was George Gilbert, nervously waiting to see who was going to come in. Her face lit up when she saw that it was friends from Goonhilly.

'Jim! And Anna! Wow, am I glad to see you.' She gave a sigh of relief, then gave them both a big hug.

'Are you alright?' asked Anna.

'As well as you'd expect, for someone facing a slow, lingering death.' George replied.

'We need to get you to somewhere more comfortable, George. You can tell your tale once we're out of here,' said Jim Harvey. A thought struck him. 'I assume we don't need to look for anyone else?'

George frowned. 'A chap called Nathan brought me. He's the curator from Constantine. He slipped out to make us a coffee and never came back. That was twenty four hours ago, mind.'

'Right. We'll knock on all the other doors on the way out. Check he's not still here.' Privately Harvey thought this was a complete waste of time.

But as they knocked on the dining room door they heard another shout. 'Help! Help me please.'

'That sounds like Nathan,' said George.

And when they opened the door it was.

'Oh, thank goodness,' the man exclaimed. 'I only came in to make coffee for George and the door slammed behind me. I didn't know the number to get out. I've been stuck here ever since.'

It sounded like he had suffered equally badly. But Harvey didn't want to spend any time now hearing a long account. After a brief reunion they headed through the corridor with the paintings and then to Nathan's car, which was still standing in the well.

'I'd better drive,' said Harvey. 'You'll need a check up if you've been locked in here for twenty four hours. And a decent meal.'

Nathan handed over the car key and slowly, laboriously, they all got in, Harvey and Anna in the front and the two recently released captives in the rear.

Harvey twisted round to face them. 'Relax, you two. You're safe now. All you need to do right now, Nathan, is to tell me how to unlock the various doors and gates.'

CHAPTER 54

Saturday in Truro was going to be a busy day for politicians and police officers alike. Frances was there early and briefed Inspector Marsh on her latest findings and theories. She also told him about Harry's latest discoveries and how that might impact on today's march.

'Right, Frances, I want you to take the lead on covering Stewart's march: "Detached Remainers", or whatever they call themselves. Thanks to Harry you've got advance warning on what he's planning to say. Don't hesitate to haul him in if it's treasonous. Arrest first and argue later. I'm happy to throw the book at anyone today that might incite violence – whichever angle they're coming from.'

Frances felt encouraged that her boss was giving her such a key role. Perhaps, at last, his confidence in her was rising.

Inspector Marsh had insisted that the marches today, for and against Brexit in all its forms, would happen in sequence and not in parallel. The leaders had drawn lots two days ago on which one would go first and Stewart's Detached Remainers had won the opening slot.

Their march would start in the space outside Truro Cathedral at ten o'clock and move steadily round the main streets towards

Market Square. No stalls would be allowed in there today. Marsh was doing everything he could to minimise trouble.

The television companies had been given the running order. They had arranged their cameras to cover the procession starts and also the main speeches in the Market Square. Everyone would have a due share of attention. The policeman assumed they would show wisdom on which messages ended up with the most air time in the evening bulletins.

There were a couple of hundred folk milling about behind him when Stewart led his band of followers slowly away from the Cathedral. Police Sergeant Frances Cober, back in full uniform, stood to one side. She was unobtrusive but she was sure that Stewart had clocked her; he had even smiled once in her direction.

The marchers carried a variety of banners with a selection of headlines. They were mostly grammatically sound and correctly spelt. None of them were incendiary, to Frances' mind anyway.

Eventually, just after eleven o'clock, Stewart's march reached the Square. Numbers had grown as they had processed and there were perhaps five hundred present by now to hear the speeches. The television camera crews nodded to one another. This was where the real work began.

Charles Stewart was looking smart today, authoritative, almost presidential. His hair was for once smoothed and tidy; he was clean shaven and wearing an elegant cream suit. This was his moment. He seized the lectern microphone; a hush fell across the crowd.

'Ladies and gentlemen, we live today in turbulent times. 'Tis not our choice, but maybe it is our destiny.'

Frances noticed his Cornish accent was becoming more pronounced under the stress of public speaking. But he was still easy to understand.

'I have no doubt that every one of us – every citizen in this land – is sick to the back teeth of the word Brexit. The notion dominates every press release and every news bulletin. The Westminster bubble, like a nightmare soap opera, has taken on a life of its own, a million miles from the people it claims to represent. The minutiae of alleged behind-the-scenes briefings and counter briefings also have a life of their own. No doubt the next stage of the drama will be for the parties themselves to splinter and divide. I don't think anyone could honestly claim that where we are now is "strong and stable".

'There have been many stories told to us of what a Brexit nation might do at some ill-defined point in the future. Hopes and dreams, perhaps true, if only we could live that long. We just need to wait, they say, for the elixir of youth to be re-discovered.'

A ripple of laughter went round the crowd. Some were not here today as Stewart supporters but simply to enjoy the political knockabout. It was Saturday after all.

'But the Brexiteers do not have a monopoly on wishful thinking,' Stewart went on. 'Oh no. There have been matching tales told for the opposite position too.' He went on to list some of the latest controversies and messages of "Project Fear".

'What I want to say to you is that all this is an opportunity for those of us that love Cornwall to fashion a different future.'

The speaker paused for dramatic effect and took a sip of water.

'It was not so long ago,' he went on, 'that Cornwall was a leading part of the British nation. In Roman times, Cornwall was the only bit of Britain that was worth visiting. But I'm not looking back that far. In the days when our Cathedral here was being built, our mines were the world's leading producers of tin and copper. Our mines and steam trains, with Trevithick and Davy and all the rest, made us pillars of the industrial revolution. And now. . . now our mining expertise is spread round the world because it has no chance to flourish here.'

Plenty of locals agreed with that, anyway. He could see heads nodding.

'Some of you will say that Cornwall is far too small to be independent. But take Gibraltar – a place far smaller, even, than most of our headlands. It desperately wants to remain a part of the European Union. Europe can be a home for small nations as well as large ones. Malta, for example, is given respect. Ireland matters. Luxemburg provides the current European Commission President. Size is not the only thing that counts.'

He paused once again for effect.

'That is why our march today – our movement – has just one request for our political leaders. Sooner or later the vote in Parliament will mean that there will be a second referendum on these issues. When that happens, our demand is simple. For the referendum conducted in Cornwall, we want a third option to be put on the ballot. We should be allowed to remain inside the European Union but to gain independence from the rest of England.'

That last sentence – the hub of his message – caused commotion. But Stewart had expected to be challenged, even banked on questions to drive forward his address. He invited comments and they came thick and fast.

Frances watched from the sidelines. If Harry's research was to have any bearing it would surely happen here.

Eventually there came the key question. 'If Cornwall did become independent how would we be governed? Would we still have a Royal family?'

Stewart seemed to puff himself up. 'It would be up to the people. We could do as we liked, become a Republic if we wanted.'

He paused and then continued. 'But I have been doing research on this question. There is a royal line in Cornwall that can be traced back directly to King Charles the Second. His child, conceived in Morocco, came to Cornwall in 1684 and was shipwrecked on the Lizard. That line still persists today. It could be rededicated, if required, by public demand.'

Frances tensed. The claim had been made. If no-one claimed to notice it might be forgotten. But it was such a striking item that it quickly became the hub of the whole address. No more boring statistics on trade, instead someone offering to be a replacement King. It sounded like that anyway. Question after question demanded answers and Stewart, armed with the lessons from Harry's findings, from the Schiedam to Samuel Pepys, was more than happy to supply them.

Frances could see that the television crews were ecstatic. At last: something fresh and new within the Brexit saga. No doubt personal interviews would follow. There was absolutely no question that this would be the headline of the day.

The police officer became more and more convinced. The consequences were unavoidable. When this was over Stewart would need to be taken to the Police Station for more formal questioning.

The Cathedral overlooking the streets of Truro

CHAPTER 55

Frances Cober made sure she kept Stewart in view as the speeches ended and the interviews took over, fierce and incisive. Michael Crick from Channel Four was particularly insistent. She waited until Stewart looked like he'd had enough and was starting to wilt.

Then she approached him, smiling, aware there were still television cameras operating. Image mattered, even for junior police officers. 'I have some more questions for you, sir. Would you mind coming with me?'

Suddenly he looked deflated. 'Am I under arrest, then?'

'No sir, but we need to interview you again; under caution if necessary.'

Still appearing to smile (after all he was a politician) he walked with her up the road.

'Wait here for a few minutes, please,' Frances asked as she ushered him into one of the smarter interview rooms.

She slipped upstairs to the officers' open plan to check up on her other queries. Tim Barwell was grinning as she came in.

'You've got something then?' She'd asked him to put weight behind top-speed processing of the DNA sample she'd taken from the waitress in Trengilly Wartha the evening before.

Tim grinned widely. 'All done, boss.'

He was a good lad. 'And?'

'You're right. They've checked her DNA with the others and it implies another familial match. In fact Miriam is the sister of both our swimsuit sisters. So – at last –we've got a name to work with.'

Frances felt excited. There was some sort of connection between all the incidents she'd been dealing with over the past fortnight.

She made a decision. 'We need to have Miriam in here for interview. She might not have done anything. But she must know something about what's been going on. More than she's said so far, anyway. Could you go and bring her in, please, Tim. But when you get back, make sure you keep her away from Stewart. Remember, she's also his daughter.'

Frances was just wondering how much longer Tim would be when her phone rang. She saw that it was George.

'Hi George.'

'I guess you're on march duty, Frances? Have you got ten minutes, there's something bothering me?'

'You've caught me in the gap between bringing someone in for questioning and making a charge. So you're in luck. What's the problem?'

George realised that Frances knew nothing about her incarceration in the Python Pad, nothing even about the Pad itself. But for now she needed to be succinct.

'Frances, I'm sorry I didn't ring earlier. But I couldn't. I was locked in, you see, held in that underground bunker thing you put me on to.'

'George, you poor thing.'

'If you'd like to come for supper this evening I'll tell you all about it. It was very dramatic, especially the final rescue.'

'Hey, I look forward to hearing. I'll certainly be ready for a decent meal by the end of today. Thank you very much.'

Frances paused. Surely she'd not been rung up at work just to be invited for supper? 'Is there something else?'

'Yes. I was shown into the Python Pad by someone. He was in that Christie play you and I saw, actually. It was Nathan.'

Frances wasn't sure where her friend was going but she knew there would be some point to all this.

She thought back to the drama. There'd been so many disappearing bodies over this last two weeks, real and dramatic, that they started to merge together. Then it came to her. 'A red-haired chap, was he?'

'Well done. He's also part-time curator at an exhibition in Constantine. That's where I met him on Thursday.'

'Right. So why might he matter?'

'As I say, he took me into the Pad. When I was rescued, twenty four hours later, he claimed he'd been locked in there as well. He was certainly locked in another room when they found him. Said there'd been some sort of system failure.'

It sounded suspicious. Frances always doubted people who blamed systems. Bad systems usually started with bad people. 'Right.'

'But I've been thinking it all through, Frances. It seems far-fetched. So I'd like to challenge his alibi. What I wondered was

345

whether anyone had seen Nathan outside the Pad, in the twenty four hours starting Thursday afternoon?'

Frances smiled. 'We can ask around. Can you give me any clues on where this Nathan might be found?'

'We chatted on the way over from Constantine. He told me that he was a pig farmer, had a smallholding somewhere near Constantine.'

'That should narrow it down. Do you have his full name?'

'He never told me, actually. But I looked him up in the drama programme this morning. He's called Nathan Harrison: Nat for short.'

"Harrison", eh . . . Pennies were starting to drop.

'Thanks, George. I've got his wife coming in now, as a matter of fact. On something else altogether. Leave it with me. I'll see you this evening.'

So now she had even more questions for Miriam Harrison. She hoped Tim would not be long.

Stewart was looking very bored when Frances and Tim got to him half an hour later. His day had certainly been one of highs and lows.

Frances introduced Tim, Stewart and herself for the recorder and noted that it was half past two.

'I'm sorry you've had to wait, Mr Stewart. We've been assembling the evidence, you see.'

Stewart looked puzzled. 'What evidence?'

'For a start there's a great deal of television footage. With your speech and the interviews that followed. One of our experts is working through them. There may be questions on some of the things you said but I haven't got to those yet.'

He didn't look too worried. He was an intelligent man, must have expected repercussions, especially for his comments on the continuing royal line within Cornwall.

'I'd like to start, Mr Stewart, with the railway station here in Truro, last Saturday night. We've got a picture of the taxi, you see.'

Frances unfastened a large envelope and drew out the enlarged photos of Harry outside the station. She eased them towards him.

Stewart put on his glasses and peered at them one by one. 'That's Harry Jennings, isn't it?'

'It is. Is there anything else there that you recognise?'

He studied them again. 'I don't think so.'

'How about the vehicle?'

He shrugged. 'It's hard to say. You can't even see the complete number.'

'But does it look familiar?'

He looked again. 'It could be the same make as mine. I suppose you're going to tell me that it is mine?'

'Well sir. Our Forensics specialise in CCTV pictures. They tell me that this vehicle is a dark green.'

'That's the same as mine, certainly.'

'And it's an old Jowett.'

'That's the same too.' He sounded almost surprised.

'The five middle letters of the number that are visible are "JC 158".

'Well, well, well. Another coincidence, eh.'

Tim Barwell leaned forward. 'I spent yesterday afternoon on the phone to DVLA staff in Swansea. Between us we established that this is the only dark green Jowett with those middle registration letters based in Western Cornwall. So d'you think, sir, that it might be yours?'

Stewart didn't answer for a minute. He was considering the options.

'I'd be inclined to think so. Except that last Saturday evening, as I told you yesterday, I was out for dinner with my daughter.'

Frances took over. 'And you were there for the whole evening?'

'I was.'

'Where was your car at this time?'

He looked puzzled. 'Nat used it to fetch me. I don't much like driving at night, you see, so they fetched me and later took me home.'

'And have you any spare keys?'

Stewart considered. 'I keep 'em at home, by the front door. They were still there when I got back.'

'So your explanation for this photograph is that someone broke into your farm, borrowed your keys, came to your daughter's, took your car to the station and picked up Harry. And later brought it back and restored the keys.'

Stewart pondered for some time. He scratched his head. 'I suppose so, Sergeant. It's a bit odd, isn't it? Why ever would they do that?'

'I don't know sir. Especially when the person who was nobbled, Harry Jennings, had been hired by you. I think we need to examine this theory more carefully. You also need to think how it might sound in court.'

Twenty minutes later, with no further progress made, Stewart was left to ponder. The two police officers went down the corridor to see Miriam Harrison. Unlike her dad she was looking agitated.

'Good afternoon, Mrs Harrison.' Frances once again did the introductions for the recorder. Then she gave her a tight smile.

'A host of queries have come up about your family. I'll start with more questions about your Dad.'

Miriam sighed. 'I was watching him this morning on the News Channel. He's blown it, hasn't he? Boasting about his link to Charles the Second. Nat and I knew that would get him into big trouble.'

So she was in a mood to talk. Good. Frances pressed on.

'We'll come to all that shortly. I'd like to start with a few questions about your husband, Nat. Where is he now, by the way?'

'I left him at home with his pigs. They're his pride and joy.'

Frances paused. She needed to phrase the next question carefully. 'A week ago, you had your Dad over for supper. Was Nat with you?'

'Oh yes.'

Frances pressed her. 'For the entire evening?'

'More or less.' Miriam paused. 'He went out at one point, "to make a phone call". I was telling Dad all about the kids, see, showing him photos of them over Christmas, when Nat disappeared. He'd already seen the pictures. But he was there most of the time, certainly. I mean, he had to be. He was Dad's driver.'

Frances was far from convinced. She could see now that Stewart might have been telling the truth. She'd leave that for a while.

'When I came to see you yesterday, Miriam, Nat wasn't in the house. But he was around somewhere?'

'Oh yes. We'd just had lunch together. He'd been out for the morning. He was in a good mood for once.' She laughed. 'It made a nice change.'

Frances decided to change tack again.

'Do you have any close family, Miriam?'

Miriam looked uncomfortable. 'I have two older sisters, Louise and Carrie. Neither of 'em are married. They've moved out of Constantine. Louise has a small flat in Helston: she's a hairdresser in St Ives.'

'And Carrie?'

'Carrie lives around Penzance, she only moved there recently. We don't see much of either of 'em, to be honest.'

'But you'll have their phone numbers?'

Miriam sounded reluctant. 'They're at home, I suppose.'

This sounded odd. 'So I could phone Nat and he'd get them for me?'

Miriam sniffed. 'I'd much rather you didn't, Sergeant. Nat and I have disputes over my sisters. I try to keep them apart these days.'

'Right. So when was the last time you all met?'

'Carrie has been busy with her house move. I haven't seen her since just before Christmas.'

'And Louise?'

'Louise invited Nat and I over for a New Year drink. But she and Nat had another row; I had to drive us home before it turned violent. That's why I'm hiding their phone numbers from him, to be honest.'

Dimly Frances started to see a pattern but she needed time to think it out. 'Let's take a break for a few minutes, Miriam.'

Outside the door Frances turned to Tim. 'Phew. We've got two members of this dysfunctional family in here, Tim. You'd better go back to Constantine and fetch the one that really matters.'

Cottages at Porthoustock, Eastern Lizard

351

CHAPTER 56

It was half an hour later.

The short break had given Frances an idea. Miriam hadn't told any lies but had she been completely truthful? Was there a gap in what the police woman had been told?

When she went back in she challenged Miriam. 'Do you have your phone with you?' It turned out that she did.

'So despite all that guff about not telling Nathan, you can look up your sisters' numbers and tell me them right away?'

Miriam nodded, more compliant now. She took her phone out of her handbag, fiddled around and then read out the numbers.

Frances mused. Had she been misled in another way? 'And do you have any record, a diary or something, with Carrie's new address?'

Deep in her handbag it turned out this was available as well.

'Thank you very much. Mrs Harrison. That's more helpful this time. But to investigate what you've just told us I'm afraid I'll need to keep you in here for a while longer.'

Tim was still away, bringing in Nathan. Frances took the number she had just been given and tried to ring Carrie. But there was no answer.

A few minutes later she had a call from Tim. He was at the

Harrison's farm but he could find no sign of Nat.

Disturbing. Had the man done a runner? If so, where had he gone?

'Stay there for the moment, Tim. Have a good look around. Make sure he's not outside, communing with his pigs.'

Frances thought hard. She knew Carrie was the sister of Louise and that something dreadful had happened to Louise. Miriam had admitted Nathan had rowed with Louise just before she'd disappeared. But if Nat was brother-in-law to one sister, he was to both. So might he have an unhealthy link to Carrie as well?

Was this why she had disappeared off the radar? Had Nathan's wife's forced journey to Truro given him a rare chance to search the house more thoroughly for Carrie's address?

More anxious now, Frances rang Carrie again but there was still no reply. Then she rang the Police Station in Penzance. Her opposite number, Sergeant Percy Popper, answered. He was a notorious pedant but he would pull his weight in a crisis.

'Percy, I urgently need someone to check an address in Penzance.' She read out Carrie's details. 'She's not answering her phone. I know she's been the victim of one attack. I'm very much afraid her attacker may be going after her again.'

Frances sat back. For the moment there was nothing else she could do.

A few minutes later her phone rang again. This time it was George.

'Hi Frances. Have you got a minute?'

'I've not got long. I'm waiting for other calls. By the way, I've checked on Nathan Harrison. His wife says he was out and about yesterday. Not locked away in the Python Pad, anyway.'

'Thank you. In that case, Frances, you need to find him. I can testify that he tried to keep me prisoner down there.'

'We're trying to do just that, George, on two other issues. It seems Nat has been a bad boy. Trouble is, he's just done a runner. We think he might be heading for an address in Penzance.'

There was a short pause then George responded. 'No, he won't be going that way, Frances. He's going to end up at the far end of the Lizard, in Porthoustock.'

Frances recalled the comments from her policeman friend, Peter Travers. He'd said George was very insightful. Did she know something or was this simply a wild guess?

'Have you got a specific address, George? You and I went to Porthoustock, remember, two weeks ago.'

'Yes.' George cited an address and France jotted it into her notebook. 'I hope you've got some reasoning behind that.'

'I do. But it'd take a while to explain. I'd better get off your phone. See you this evening.'

Frances Cober thought for a moment.

Whatever happened she wasn't doing much good sitting in Truro. Stewart and Miriam could await further interviews. At the very least they were material witnesses. If there was going to be action, it would be either in Penzance or, obscurely, in Porthoustock.

Helston was en route to either. She would drive that far, anyway; and hope that by the time she got there she would hear something from Penzance that would finalise her choice.

Before she set off she called her Constable. 'Still no joy with Nat, Tim? Well, can you get to Helston Police Station? I'll meet you in the car park. I've an idea on where he might be going.'

She had reached Helston and just parked behind the Station when her phone rang. It was Sergeant Popper.

'I'm at the place you said, Frances. There's no-one here. But I've peered through the window. It looks like there's been a fight.'

'Right. Thanks, Percy. I think I know where they've gone. Maybe you could ask the neighbours if they heard anything.'

So, if George was correct, Frances needed to get to Porthoustock. A moment later she had collected Tim from his car and the two set off across the Lizard. Tim found the target address using his Google map as they drove. It was one of a row of cottages overlooking the cobbled bay.

Frances had never driven across the Lizard faster. They raced past Goonhilly and reached St Keverne ten minutes later.

'More slowly now,' said Tim. She noticed he was gripping his seat, pale and tight-lipped; maybe she'd been overdoing it? They were only a mile away. She dropped a gear and drove sedately down to the coast.

'Surprise is our key weapon,' said Frances. 'There's no reason why Nat should expect us. We mustn't let him see my car. We'll park outside the village and walk the rest.'

They strode steadily down the hill.

The address they'd been given was the third thatched cottage along the road leading out the other side. Frances studied them as they approached.

'There's a path round the back, Tim. I'll knock at the front door while you keep guard at the rear.'

The police officer waited a minute to let her partner get into position. Then she strode forwards, stood firm and knocked on the door.

Silence.

Had this been a complete waste of time, she wondered? Had George's logic failed or been misdirected? Was she off-track altogether?

A minute went by. Then she heard someone coming to the door. A rattle of keys and it swung open. A red-haired man stood there. It took her a second to recognise him: she'd last seen him at Trelowarren Manor.

'Nat Harrison?' she asked.

'That's me. Can I help you?'

Frances pulled out her warrant. 'I'm Sergeant Cober, Helston Police. Can I come in, please?'

He was obviously surprised. She saw him weigh up options, then, reluctantly, he invited her in.

It was a small cottage. She could see straight out to the back garden. 'Could we let my colleague in as well, please? He's out the back.'

Nat hadn't expected that either. Stony faced, he went to the back door and unlocked it. Tim was standing there, saw his boss and stepped inside to join her. His face had a look of triumph.

'I think we need Mr Harrison in handcuffs, please, Tim.'

Unusual at this early stage. But Harrison was still coping with the shock of discovery and did not rush to disagree.

Tim was surprised as well but he wasn't going to admit it. The handcuffs went on. Now they'd escort the man back to their car.

But not yet. For, as Harrison had turned to open the back door, Frances had noticed a cellar door half-hidden in the corner. And recalled that Carrie had disappeared from her home in Penzance after a fight. So might she be here too?

She nodded towards the doorway. 'Can you check there's no-one down there please, Tim.'

Trust his boss to dot all the i's. The door wasn't locked. Cheerfully he opened it and peered down. Then he saw a light switch on the wall.

As he turned it on he saw that his boss had been right. There was someone here.

In fact there were two women. One was tied up and gagged. The other looked resigned and defeated.

Tim was into the swing of it now. 'More handcuffs, boss?'

'Yes please, Tim. After that we can untie the prisoner.'

Frances wasn't certain who the prisoner was. Had she seen her before, wearing a lot less? She was a victim of this crime, anyway. Then it clicked.

As Tim produced more cuffs, Frances stepped into the cellar and turned towards the tied up woman.

'Carrie Stewart, I believe? We've already met, I think. I helped save your life on Coverack beach, two weeks ago.'

CHAPTER 57

George had splashed out on her Saturday evening dinner with Frances. There was much to celebrate, not least that she was out of the Python Pad and a free woman. A convenience meal seemed inadequate. So she'd scoured Sainsbury's and brought back their best Chinese banquet and a rather expensive Sauvignon. This meal might take some time.

Frances turned up just after seven. Both women were tired from the week just gone but also exultant. There was a lot to share as they sat down and started on the aromatic duck in pancakes, accompanied by spring onions and hoisin sauce.

'Go on, George. Tell me how you found the address in Porthoustock. It made all the difference. We found Nathan there and, down in the cellar, your friend Anna Campbell. Inspector Marsh was mightily impressed.'

George smiled. 'It was all really due to Nathan being so prolific. I got onto him via the Python Pad and the way he locked me in there. I'm not sure I was ever supposed to get out.'

Frances chewed some of her duck. 'So how did you escape?'

'The whole scheme hinged on a drone set up to sabotage Goonhilly. It was kept at the Python Pad. I threw a spanner in the works when I asked about it, the day before it was going to be used. Nathan didn't know how much I knew, decided the safest thing was to take me prisoner.

'The first thing that went wrong, from Nathan's point of view, was that Friday was foggy. That didn't affect the drone – it could still fly – but there was no dramatic view of it from inside Goonhilly. He'd banked on that to trigger widespread panic.

'Later on my boss, Jim Harvey, started worrying about me. He knew what I was trying to do and worked out, somehow, that the Python Pad must be under Predannack Airfield.'

'Clever chap,' murmured Frances.

'Then – stroke of genius – it occurred to him that two semi-secret government buildings in the back of beyond, four miles apart and both developed in the 1960s, might have a connecting link. He consulted the Station archive and found out where the Goonhilly end began.'

Frances nodded. 'Right. So your escape was primarily down to him.'

'Yes. But the great piece of luck for me was that he brought Anna with him. He'd remembered, you see, that she and I were friends.'

George took a sip of Sauvignon. This story was not to be hurried. Then she resumed.

'Nathan knew he'd be in big trouble if I ever escaped, so he had a fall-back plan. He would claim that he'd been locked in too: blame it all on a systems failure. So he had to creep back to Python, put his car exactly where he'd left it the day before and shut himself into the canteen. Then claim that he'd been locked in too.'

Frances was stunned. 'That's outrageous. But you'd never

believe him? And could he do that, all on his own?'

'Well, crucially, he'd need to know that there was a rescue party on the way, so he could get back there in time. I went round and round. There were only two people that could be: one was Jim Harvey, the other was Anna Campbell. The rescue was all Jim's idea; so that meant Nathan's ally had to be Anna.'

Frances pondered. It was indirect logic, but it did all make sense.

'So how did you get from that to the address in Porthoustock?'

'Oh, that was easy. Jim Harvey came round this morning, to check I was OK. He was ever so kind and we talked it all through. Jim also pointed out that if Anna was involved, she'd have moved the suspicious items away from the hut outside Goonhilly, once I'd started to raise questions about it.'

'Hey, would that explain why she disappeared last weekend?'

George shrugged. 'Maybe. So I asked him for Anna's address. He's a senior manager, has access to personnel files at Goonhilly. Once you told me that Nathan was lying – he wasn't in the Pad for at least some of Friday – that meant my friend had to be guilty.'

There was silence. George realised that she had been talking for too long. 'Shall we go onto the next course?'

George went to the oven and came back with two dishes, beef with black bean sauce and sweet and sour chicken. 'We'll use the same plates, I think.'

She poured each of them another glass of wine, served the banquet and they started to eat.

'Frances, please tell me about Nathan and the "swimmin' women".'

'We've got names for them now. The one who drowned was Louise, the one we rescued in Coverack was her sister Carrie.'

'What told you they were sisters?'

'I'd got Carrie's thermal blanket from the ambulance. That gave me her DNA. Forensics checked and found the match.'

George was struggling. 'Remember, Frances, I'm starting from some way back. What was the link to Nathan?'

'Well, I had Miriam in to ask her about her dad – she's Stewart's daughter and also Nathan's wife. She mentioned she had two sisters so, for completeness, I compared her DNA with that of Louise and Carrie. And that linked them all together. But I'm afraid that didn't make them all a big happy family.'

Frances took another spoonful of bean sauce and rice before she continued.

'This afternoon, in separate interviews, I talked to Stewart, Miriam, Carrie and Nathan. And Anna. I managed to piece quite a lot of it together.

'It seems Louise had invited Miriam and Nathan for a drink just after New Year but they had a big row and left early. Nathan was livid. He went back, let himself in, found Louise in the bath and pushed her head underwater. I'm not sure if he'd planned to kill her but that's what happened: she drowned. He was horrified and panic-stricken.'

'Well, he wouldn't want her found in her own bath, Frances. It would soon emerge that he'd been one of the last to visit.'

'No. So he decides to make it look like a drowning in the Loe

Pool. That's local to Helston and lots of accidents happen there. He goes to Tesco and buys a couple of costumes, maybe one's a reserve. Then he calls his friend Anna Campbell. She helps him put the costume onto Louise and together they drive her out to the Loe.'

'Right,' said George cautiously. She wasn't sure how much of this could be proved; and was a row enough motive for murder?

'So how does Carrie get caught up in this?'

'She was also invited for the drink with Louise but turned up late. She finds her sister missing and Nathan and Anna mopping the bathroom. She suspects something awful has happened and starts asking questions. Nathan sits her down, gives her a glass of water and a moment later she keels over. I guess he's spiked it with the same drug that he'll later use on Harry.'

George was following closely. 'So now that's a second person they've got to get out of the flat.'

'Right. They can't put both of 'em into the Loe, not if it's to play as an accident: they've got to keep 'em apart. Anna offers to hide Carrie in the cellar of her cottage in Porthoustock, to give 'em time to make another plan. Where three days later, as we know, she manages to escape, steals the windsurf board and later is capsized off Coverack.'

George ate some of her sweet and sour chicken and pondered.

'But how did she manage to disappear so quickly, so completely, from the hospital?'

'Oh, for Carrie, that was easy: she spent the night in Louise's flat. There was a spare key under the mat. Borrowed her sister's clothes. Next day she crept back to her new home in Penzance.

Nathan had never visited it; she thought she'd be safe there. She rang Miriam, made her promise that she'd never, ever, tell Nathan where it was.'

'But why on earth didn't she go to the police?'

'Well, she didn't know what had happened to Louise. All she knew was that she'd lost consciousness and ended up in a cellar. Not sure where and she hadn't a clue who Anna was. All she had was a deep mistrust of Nathan.'

'But Frances, what about your press release?'

'Carrie saw that a few days later but how could she respond? Why had she delayed in coming forward? She feared she might collect the blame. In any case she had no confidence she'd be safe once Nathan knew where she was. She was right on that: it's lucky that we got to Porthoustock when we did.'

By now they had finished their main course. George piled the plates and headed for the kitchen. She'd bought a range of fresh fruit to round off the meal.

As they enjoyed desserts Frances outlined Harry's research and how it affected Stewart. George had watched the latter live on television that morning, been amazed by his royal claims.

'There's another mystery,' said George as they settled down with coffee and After Eight mints.

'What's that?'

'Why ever did Nathan go for Harry? Why did his research matter to anyone except Stewart?'

'Not yet sure. Perhaps he didn't want Stewart to complicate his political campaign with an assault on the Crown.' She laughed. 'Maybe he didn't want to become part of the new Cornish Royal Family.'

'But wasn't his assault on Harry way over the top?'

'It's not that simple, George. Nathan and Stewart never got on. Did he intend to kill Harry? He certainly intended to drug him, so he could destroy the results of his research. I'm struggling to prove anything beyond that.'

'How did he know about Harry's research trip to Cambridge?'

'Miriam told him. She's a waitress at Trengilly Wartha. She'd overheard Harry discussing it at his meal with Joy. Nathan's a tell-me-everything kind of husband. No doubt he'd wrung it out of her when she got home.'

Frances gave a sigh. 'Trouble is, it all went wrong. GHB is a powerful drug and Harry was overdosed. Nathan feared he would never come round; decided he had to finish him off.'

'All on his own?'

'Oh no. Remember, there was someone else in that taxi. She hasn't admitted it yet but I believe it was Nathan's friend Anna in the back seat who applied the drug. And helped move Harry to Kynance Cove, early on Sunday morning.'

It was plausible but George could see a flaw. 'So you're saying that Harry Jennings didn't even notice that the person sharing his taxi was an attractive woman?'

But Frances was aware of a higher chemistry. 'Well, her face was hidden. Anyway, George, there's only one woman that Harry has got an eye for these days: his new friend Joy. They're full of one another. Let's hope it all works out.'

CHAPTER 58

It was late evening as the two women wrestled on with this surfeit of crime. By now Frances had accepted George's invitation to stay the night. Her police conscience was muted as she helped to finish the Sauvignon.

'So George, we've got three distinct crimes. There's the drowning of Louise and imprisonment of Carrie; then Harry's drugging and attempted murder; and finally, late this week, there's Python Pad and your kidnap.

She paused. 'But how strong are the links? Are they just a series of impromptu actions? What's really behind them?'

George smiled. 'You've interviewed Nathan and Anna this afternoon, Frances. How does it appear to you?'

'Anna hasn't said much. I'm not sure how big a part she played. The main thing we've got on her so far is that her cellar was used to hold Carrie.

'Meanwhile Nathan's done plenty of talking. His story is that it's a series of desperate acts that went wrong. But it must be more than that. I just can't see how.'

Frances filled her glass and glanced at her friend. She recalled Peter Travers had said she was incisive. 'Go on then, tell me.'

George smiled again. 'I've not been doing the interviews so I've had plenty of time to ponder. I also made a phone call this afternoon to Tim Barwell. We'd met, of course, at Truro hospital. What if it went something like this?'

She took another After Eight and made herself comfortable.

'Nathan married Miriam years ago but he and father-in-law Charles never really got on. Last year Charles put together a family tree and discovered he was descended from King Charles the Second. He started to dream of Cornish independence. When the Brexit shambles led to talk of a second referendum, he saw a way it might be achieved. So, secretly, he approached Harry to collect the evidence to back his cause.'

'Hm. It was a stroke of luck that Harry had done a PhD on Pepys.'

'I don't think so, Francis. I bet that's why he was picked. Charles Stewart is very manipulative. But he's powerful, let's say, rather than popular.'

George took another sip of her wine. 'Charles was Director of the Constantine Players when Anna joined them. Somewhere along the way he shared with her his royal dreams. She responded by telling him about the Newquay space link. "Even if your dreams don't make you wealthy, Charles, the space link could make Cornwall rich." At some point she and Nathan started an affair. Nathan's marriage to Miriam had long been flaky; he was always keen to sample the field.'

Frances nodded. 'So the core threads of the crimes were laid down.'

'There was one more. As he contemplated independence, Charles Stewart became passionate about Goonhilly and the planned link to Newquay. He enthused over the Space Station. It was the most promising way he could see that an independent Cornwall might one day gain status. It could be very profitable. And that was when Nathan and Anna started to look for ways to ruin it.'

'But George, I don't understand. Were Nathan and Anna for Charles' dream to be king of Cornwall, or against it?'

'Ah. At first they were both for it. Later Anna realised that kingly connections would make it harder to win Nathan from Miriam, so she changed her mind, moved to sabotage it.'

Frances was unsure but George continued. 'Anna already had a job at Goonhilly. Maybe the impact of last month's drones on Gatwick gave her the idea of a series of drone attacks. Through the exhibition they already knew about the Python base at Predannack. They ordered a drone, smuggled it in at Scott's Quay and kept it there, waiting for the chance to use it.'

'Waiting. Huh.' Frances looked doubtful.

'The thing is, Frances, Nathan wasn't the prime mover. Anna was always the planner. She was behind the New Year attacks on Miriam's sisters. She wanted him to leave Miriam altogether.'

George stopped. That wasn't a good answer, there must be something more. The question was, what? She wished Harry was here: he might have unravelled the vital detail.

Frances responded. 'Wait a minute, George. You're saying the attack on Louise wasn't just Nathan losing control? It's down to Anna? What on earth makes you say that?'

'Two items. Firstly, Anna misled me about where she lived. She told me early on that it was near Constantine but, as you've found out, it was past St Keverne. Secondly, I've had lunch with

Anna in the Nature Reserve outside Goonhilly several times. To keep out the cold she always wears a thick scarf and a bobble hat.'

'And . . .?'

George smiled. 'That's why I had to get hold of Tim. You need to look again at those pictures from Tesco. It wasn't a man buying those swimming costumes, Frances, it was Anna. I got Tim to check the other items on the swimsuit receipt. One was a set of hair clips, the other was a female-friendly DVD, "The Guernsey Literary and Potato Peel Pie Society". I bet it's still in Anna's cottage.'

'If it is, George, it'll also have her fingerprints. Hey, that could prove the link to those Tesco purchases.'

'If you find it hard to believe me, Frances, check the dates. The purchase wasn't the night of the drinks with Louise. That was Wednesday: this was the night before. Anna had it all planned. Nathan was just following her orders.'

There would be further interviews next day. Frances now had plenty more issues to probe. She was grateful that George had helped her to think them through more clearly.

EPILOGUE

In the Ship Inn at Mawgan I was having a last meal with Joy Tregorran. It was Sunday lunchtime and my project was over. I'd just had the privilege of listening to Joy preach in Church Cove. I'd be back to Exeter tomorrow for the new term, so I had to make the most of the opportunity.

But I hoped – intended – it would not be my last chance for ever. There was talk of Exeter starting a historical research hub in Truro. Maybe I could be in the vanguard to lead it forwards?

This was the first time I'd left my "safe house" at Trengilly Wartha. Frances had called me this morning. I'd been told that my assailants were now both under arrest. That was another cause for celebration.

Joy and I took some time to greet one another before ordering our meals. Then my friend smiled. 'I've got some news, Harry.'

'What's that?'

'You know I told you about that family-tree hugger in Church Cove?'

It had been a small but significant piece in the overall patchwork. 'Yes.'

'Well, I've found out the man's name. He'd given it to me before he consulted the church records.'

'Ah. So who was he?'

'Charles Stewart, Director of "Then There Were None". You know, I thought I'd seen him before, when he popped out at the interval, but at the time I couldn't place him.' Joy mused for a moment. 'Isn't he your client? Does that help make sense of your research?'

I grinned. Collaboration was good. 'It adds to the picture, Joy. I had a long phone chat with Stewart yesterday, as a matter of fact. He'd been leading a Brexit march in Truro, ended up in the Police Station. I'm afraid he'd got over excited by my findings. He thought I'd proved he had an alternative line to the throne from Charles the Second – that I'd found him a "Crown Dual".'

Joy looked disappointed. 'I thought that, with the help of Samuel Pepys' diary, you had.' She paused. 'That's a pity, it would be good to have a King that was born and bred in Cornwall. Hey, would that be the start of a new Royal Family?'

Harry nodded. 'That's what Stewart was hoping. I was talking to him about it on the phone yesterday. But it's all gone wrong. At the start of the year he had three daughters. He's just learned from the police that one drowned two weeks ago in the Loe. Another's been forced into hiding. While the youngest, Miriam, our waitress at Trengilly Wartha, is having troubles in her marriage.'

'Harry, what a shame. Is any of that related to your research?'

'Charles wanted me to find documentary proof for his royal dream. He was hoping that, if that led to him becoming King of Cornwall, he would also inherit great wealth – all the land currently owned by the Duke of Cornwall, for a start.'

'There's plenty of that,' observed Joy.

'Yes. And in due time that vast wealth would be handed on to his children. That might have caused conflict over succession: there often is. D'you remember Police Sergeant Frances Cober?'

'Oh yes. She came to see me when you disappeared.'

'Well, she rang me this morning. She tells me that Miriam's husband, who was the man that went for me, also went for both her older sisters. I told Frances that was all motivated by long-term succession planning: he wanted her to be the sole heir. William Shakespeare dabbled with similar ideas.'

Joy frowned. She had a science background, was still trying to make sense of the research. 'So is Charles Stewart not descended from King Charles the Second?'

'I spent last night checking it out. The old King Charles has dozens of descendants. Every one is illegitimate, so by law none can claim the throne. There's only one that has a chance.'

Joy did not follow historical niceties. 'Who on earth is that?'

'Prince William, the current Duke of Cambridge.'

'You mean, through his father?'

'Oh no. Through his mother, Princess Diana. It turns out that she was descended from the old Charles in two distinct ways. So all being well, King Charles the Second will one day have a descendant on the English throne. But I'm afraid that it won't be Charles Stewart of Cornwall.'

AUTHOR'S NOTES

Britain once had a colony in Tangiers; the Schiedam, helping with the exit, was shipwrecked in Dollar Cove in 1684. Samuel Pepys, overseeing the British Navy, had visited Tangiers the year before.

Conan Doyle once stayed at Poldhu. BBC's version of Christie's "Then There Were None" was filmed on Mullion Island in 2016.

The 1960s Python Plan, to safeguard government after nuclear attack, did include a new unit on the Lizard. Despite Peter Hennessey's efforts, its exact location is still an Official Secret.

Goonhilly Earth Station may one day monitor space flight from Newquay Airport. But the Station has no tunnel link to Predannack Airfield, nor has it been subject to drone attack.

Trengilly Wartha is a delightful Inn just outside Constantine. And Kynance Cove is one of the finest views in Cornwall.

The saga of Brexit is still underway, though the link to Cornish Independence is a fiction of my own.

I met a real C.T. Wicks at a Christmas Gala and agreed to put his name in this book. He'd make a good antiquarian bookseller.

So, as in other Conundrums, the story has a real context but all the characters are entirely made up.

My website includes more pictures of the Lizard. I welcome any comments on the book; or ideas for further Conundrums.

David Burnell   *www.davidburnell.info*
May 2019

DOOM WATCH

Bill Gilbert, a Watcher of the Doom Bar sandbank on the River Camel, asks his niece George to help Padstow plan an upgrade.

A few miles away, a headless body is discovered in the old quarry at Trewarmett but identification proves tricky.

It takes the combined efforts of George and local Police Sergeant Peter Travers to make sense of a crime which seems, simultaneously, to be spontaneous and pre-planned.

"Cornwall and its richly storied coast has a new writer to celebrate in David Burnell. His crafty plotting and engaging characters are sure to please crime fiction fans." Peter Lovesey

"A well-written novel, cleverly structured, with a nicely-handled sub-plot..." Rebecca Tope, crime novelist

SLATE EXPECTATIONS

George Gilbert buys a cottage overlooking Trebarwith Strand.

The analyst is drawn into an outdoor drama based on 19th century events in Delabole Slate Quarry – a drama heightened when an actor is found dead during the opening performance.

The combined resources of George and Police Sergeant Peter Travers are needed to disentangle the past and find out precisely how it relates to the present.

"Slate Expectations combines an interesting view of an often overlooked side of Cornish history with an engaging pair of sleuths who follow the trail from past misdeeds to present murder."
Carola Dunn, crime author

LOOE'S CONNECTIONS

Business analyst George Gilbert is on a project to study floods in Looe when her colleague vanishes.

George is drawn into a web of suspense and foul play. But when her personal and professional lives begin to overlap, is she the unwitting suspect or the next victim?

The trail roams over flooding in the town and events over many centuries. Even the Romans have a part to play.

"History, legend and myth mixed with a modern technical conundrum makes this an intriguing mystery." Carola Dunn, crime author

TUNNEL VISION

Can the old North Cornwall Railway be turned into a cycle trail?

Journalist Robbie Glendenning, exploring the only tunnel on the line, finds first a hidden chamber and then a skeleton.

Making sense of a death half a century ago is not easy. Who were they? When and why did they die? Who had reason to intend them mischief? And who intends more now?

It takes George Gilbert's late arrival to rescue Robbie and move the case to a dramatic conclusion.

"Enjoyable reading for all who love Cornwall and its dramatic history." Ann Granger, crime author

TWISTED LIMELIGHT

George Gilbert is in Bude to acclaim Goldsworthy Gurney, the pioneer of the limelight which lit Parliament for fifty years.

Meanwhile Sergeant Peter Travers takes over Bude Police Station. A missing chimney sweep and an escaped convict are only the latest cases to attract his team's attention.

But it not till coding expert Maxine Tavistock tells George her tale of abduction that the various strands start to weave together.

"The plot twists will keep you guessing up to the last page. This is a thrilling Cornish mystery." Kim Fleet, crime author
"A clever, exciting story of modern-day skullduggery and romance on the beautiful north Cornish coast around Bude." Roger Higgs, Bude geologist

FOREVER MINE

Policeman Peter Travers could have done without the discovery of a dead body found down an old mineshaft, one week before his wedding in St Just, close to Cape Cornwall.

Local police are unconcerned; but he is convinced it's not just an accident. What to do? He can't leave a murderer on the loose.

Key members of the wedding party, including George Gilbert, are enlisted to help find the killer. But in the end it is Peter's new wife that unravels the crucial detail.

"An intriguing mystery set against the backdrop of a wedding in sleepy Cornwall, where all is not as it appears on the surface – or even far below." Sarah Flint, crime author

Printed in Great Britain
by Amazon